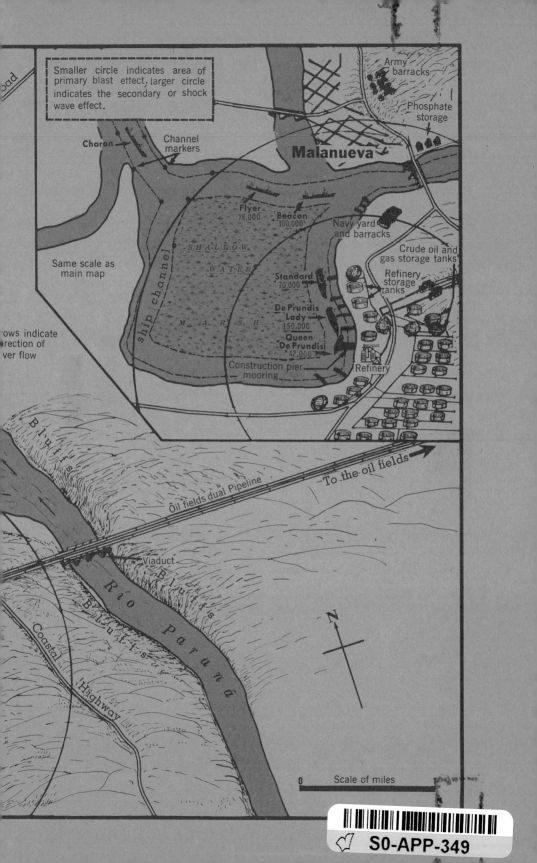

Smaller circle indicates area of primary blast effect, larger circle indicates the secondary or shock wave effect.

Army barracks

Phosphate storage

Charon

Channel markers

Malanueva

Same scale as main map

Flyer 78,000

Beacon 100,000

Navy yard and barracks

Crude oil and gas storage tanks

ship channel

S H A L L O W

W A T E R

Standard 70,000

Refinery storage tanks

ows indicate rection of ver flow

M A R S H

De Prundis Lady 150,000

Queen De Prundis 42,000

Construction pier mooring

Refinery

Bluffs

To the oil fields

Oil fields dual Pipeline

Viaduct

Río Paraná

Bluffs

Bluffs

N

Coastal Highway

0   Scale of miles   1

The Black Gold of Malaverde

The Black Gold of Malaverde

RICHARD L. GRAVES

STEIN AND DAY/Publishers/New York

First published in 1973
Copyright © 1973 by Richard L. Graves
Library of Congress Catalog Card No. 73–82144
All rights reserved
Designed by David Miller
Printed in the United States of America
Stein and Day/*Publishers*/Scarborough House, Briarcliff Manor, N.Y. 10510
ISBN 0–8128–1642–0

FOR MY FATHER
RUSSELL BRIGGS GRAVES

Even so will I break this people
And this city as one breaketh a potter's vessel
That cannot be made whole again;
And they shall bury them in Tophet,
Till there be no place to bury.
                    Jeremiah 19:11

PROLOGUE

IT'S THERE.

North of Brazil; east of Venezuela; close to hell. Malaverde. Fifty-one thousand square miles of miasma, tucked like a boil into the coastal folds of the continent.

Near the coast it is gray-green. There the low altitude and the heavy rainfall conspire to make the vegetation grow. Away from the coast it becomes increasingly dry until, a few kilometers inland, the surface is pitted umber rocks and sand and desperate twisted plants.

From the interior, across the arid wastelands, the Rio Paraná slides from the mountains and curls indolently, reaching toward the eastern edge of the Caribbean that everywhere is azure except here, where it is verdigris.

The river reaches languidly for the sea. It loops around and past the tacked-up, fetid, and busy port of Malanueva. There, tankers throb against the embrace of the oozing Paraná, clinging to the deep-dug ship channel. The great hulls move cautiously to strike a mooring in the scooped-out harbor and there, at ease, gulp into their bellies through black coils of rubber and plastic that one redeeming—and redeemable—virtue of an unblessed place.

Oil.

The
Takeover

1

I

THE POWDERY MASS of dust rose and billowed and then hung suspended in the desert sky. The cloud stretched out for a mile behind the compact lead vehicle and hovered over the long line of canvas-top trucks.

From a small turret on the lead vehicle emerged the bulky torso of a man, arms akimbo, elbows resting on the steel sides. *El Coronel* Jaime Mercado y Suarez clung precariously to the turret of the obsolete M–8 armored car, the ghost of American military aid long ago. It had been seized only last night when the armies of Malaverde had succumbed to the People's Liberation Army and then joined in casting aside the corrupt and loathsome running dogs of the capitalist imperialists. Mercado's brain cramped negotiating the contortions of such jargon. But then it was all a necessary part of the revolution. And the revolution was a success, was it not?

A scowl passed across the grimy face. Moments before, Mercado had seen the Bradford Petroleum jet soar across the crystal sky. He regretted that such a beautiful plum would not fall into his hands. But such planes could be acquired in due course. After all, he had seized the Bradford Petroleum helicopter without damage during the fierce battle last night.

Mercado's white tunic was ashen with the powder of the desert, but he felt as if he were riding on parade before cheering throngs. He was exultant. He wore his goggles on his hat, like the pictures he had seen of Erwin Rommel, the Desert Fox. He, Jaime Mercado y Suarez, would also have such a *nom de guerre*, something like *El Jaguar* or *El Condor*, or some other appropriate and respected beast. All would come in due course.

"More speed!" Mercado shouted to the driver. The M–8's wheels churned faster as the old Chrysler engines roared their complaints and the dust-choked transmission whined.

Mercado looked back at his obedient "army." Behind *El Libertador* the convoy of battered trucks was barely visible in the billowing powder of the road. Had there ever been such fine troops? Such discipline? Ready to follow a true leader within minutes after they had surrendered to him in the hour before last midnight.

Now his army would take the oil camp by surprise, a lightning attack befitting *El Jaguar* (or *El Condor*).

Last night, he personally had led the platoon that had seized the palace. There, each member of the ruling junta had given up ceremoniously, without a struggle, in order to save his life. His former colleagues were strong ones, indeed. They had accepted him with an *abrazo* after he had taken everything from them. Graciously they accepted his offer of transportation to the airport, under guard of his own men, for a flight into exile. That they were instead bound and thrown screaming to the sharks in the Rio Paraná channel was immaterial. He, Mercado, was touched, truly, by their faith and trust in their captor.

Mercado sighed. It had been a glorious night.

One of his squads had seized the communications hut of the oil refinery in Malanueva. Not one word of what had transpired escaped to warn the gringo encampment! Surprise would be total.

Mercado's heart was full to bursting. He was certainly *now* the biggest man in all Malaverde and if that was not true in actuality, it certainly was true in accomplishment. Like Napoleon!

The column roared into the middle of the oil encampment. Until dust clouds obscured everything, workers gawked at this change of routine. Some stood holding tools or cables. Others stared from heaps of tubing. One was immobile at the wheel of a truck.

Mercado's M–8 skidded to a halt in the center of a ring of frame buildings and Quonset huts. Behind him his trucks pulled into a ragged rank, and dusty soldiers piled out, coughing and spitting dust. But for all that, they were armed and they looked formidable.

"Round them up!" shouted Mercado from the turret. He rested his elbows on the hot iron, and his chin jutted. "Over there!" He gestured, indicating a wooden shed.

The swarming troops jabbed and prodded the frightened workmen, about thirty of them, into a crowd by the building's wall.

A sergeant scrambled out of the settling dust and handed Mercado an electric bullhorn. *El Libertador* smiled. The bullhorn, such a useful device. It gave him the voice of a hurricane. He flicked the switch.

"You are now war prisoners of the People's Liberation Army! The masses of Malaverde have finally had their call for help answered! We have proclaimed the Malaverdian People's Republic! If you cooperate, you will be well treated. If you cause trouble, you will be shot!"

"Now," the metallic voice continued. "Which of you is the leader?"

Behind Mercado a door flew open and a voice, heavy with anger, shouted in English, "What the hell is going on here?"

It was D. J. Bradford. He held his briar pipe like a pistol.

II

Mercado worked the lever that swung the turret around until its 50-caliber machine gun pointed directly at the tall man standing on the steps of the hut. Mercado itched to pull the trigger.

"Who are you?" the amplified voice inquired.

"D. J. Bradford," the American replied in Spanish. "My father owns this oil company."

"Correction," snapped Mercado. "This oil company is now the possession of the People's Republic of Malaverde." He heaved himself out of the turret and, with some grunting and the assistance of the sergeant, made it to the ground.

Bradford was struck by how incredibly short Mercado really was. The man was scarcely more than five feet tall and his breadth made him seem even shorter. He wore flared riding breeches and a peaked cap a full six inches high in front perched on top of a very large and round head. The hat was emblazoned with an enormous golden eagle clasping a red star. He affected the pencil moustache, the badge of South American military men. His brown eyes flickered with internal energy.

Bradford looked around at the motley soldiers now standing at all points around the perimeter of the area, holding their weapons at a variety of dangerous angles. Amateurs. Bradford's gaze returned to Mercado.

"We have met before, have we not, Señor Bradford?" Mercado inquired unctuously.

"Once. You were taller then." It was true, Bradford recalled suddenly. Mercado must have been wearing special shoes at the reception they both had attended.

Mercado's eyes narrowed. After a moment, his tongue catching on the complex words, he shouted, "You are under arrest as an enemy of the people and an instrument of imperialist aggressors!"

"Horseshit!" snapped Bradford in clear English.

"Seize him!" Mercado waved his arms at the sergeant, who was already moving forward with a squad of troops.

"You can't do this," Bradford heard himself saying. "It's a violation of international law." The sergeant pinned his arms.

"We can do *anything*, Señor Bradford." Mercado unsnapped a pocket of his tunic and removed a folded piece of paper. Ceremoniously he unfolded it. He looked about him to signal silence. Putting the bullhorn to his lips, he read:

"A proclamation:

"To the citizens of the People's Republic of Malaverde!

"Whereas, American imperialism in the guise of the Bradford Petroleum Company, and its running dogs and lackeys, have falsely and criminally expropriated property of the people and,

"Whereas, said American imperialists have repeatedly exploited the toiling workers, making of them veritable wage slaves, and

"Whereas, American imperialism must be attacked and its numerous evil heads chopped off like the tentacles of a sea monster and destroyed,

14

"Therefore, it is proclaimed that all property, capital, plant, equipment, lands, leaseholds, and other assets of Bradford Petroleum Company are herewith claimed as the rightful property of the people for use and/or disposition as the People's Republic might see fit.

"Signed this day, and sealed, by Jaime Mercado y Suarez . . ." His voice rose triumphantly. ". . . *Libertador.*"

Bradford's enraged reply was drowned by cheering from the soldiers. Mercado could not hear what he said, but he saw the venom in Bradford's eyes. "Take him away!" he commanded.

The cheering subsided. "You goddamned midget!" Bradford shouted as the soldiers started to drag him toward a truck.

"Wait!" said Mercado, furious. He hated gringos. He hated their size and their stride and the way they did things. "You see fit to call me names, eh?" He motioned to his sergeant. Mercado whispered something into the sergeant's ear. The man nodded, then scrambled up into the turret of the M–8. "So, soldiers," Mercado bellowed. "Señor Bradford wants to shout insults. We say to him that every insult means a life in Malanueva. And sometimes life—such as the life of an imperialist—means an insult. So, I ask Mr. Bradford: Any more insults?"

"Go to hell, you syphilitic runt!"

Mercado held up two fingers for his troops to see. "So now we have two insults." He sneered. "Only two insults, gringo? Have you nothing more than that?" When he grinned, the gold caps on his teeth shimmered in the sun. Bradford shook his head.

"I have nothing to say."

"No?" grinned Mercado. "Nothing more? I am insulted that you have nothing more to say to me." He held up three fingers, showing them all around to the soldiers.

"All right," said Mercado. "Sergeant, the number is three."

The turret of the M–8 swung toward the prisoners.

The heavy machine gun thudded three times. Three men fell.

"And three more for good measure!" shouted Mercado. His troops roared approval.

The gun thudded three more times.

As Bradford's guards dragged him away, he saw bizarre forms sprawled in the dust, one figure still writhing.

Behind Bradford the bullhorn proclaimed, "There will be no insults to Malaverde. *Viva Malaverde! Viva la revolución!*"

There were loud and prolonged cries of *"Viva! Viva!"*

Bradford was cuffed on the ear and hauled roughly behind a big six-wheeled truck, where his guards produced a belt and some rope. They pulled his arms behind his back, twisting the shoulders, and he let out a gasp of pain. A fist caught him on the mouth. His blood dribbled from split lips onto the sand. Another fist caught him on the temple and he fell to his knees, doubled over, his face in the dirt, his arms wrenched up behind him.

"Gringo swine," a voice snarled and there was a kick to his ribs. He gasped. Another kick.

"Put him in the truck."

There was a whining sound far away and another fist hit him. "In the truck!" said the voice sharply. *"El Libertador* wants him a prisoner."

Bradford was hauled to his feet. Through eyes clouded by sweat, blood, and dirt he could make out a long, low, black limousine, halted fifty yards away in the desert. Like everything else, it was coated by the desert's pale dust, but through the tinted window glass of the air-conditioned vehicle Bradford could make out a pendulous face, wearing dark glasses and topped by a Panama hat. From the dark, cool interior of the mammoth sedan the face, its mouth slightly open, peered out at the desert like a fish in an aquarium.

Bradford's guards bound his feet, then picked him up and hurled him into the back of the truck. In the background the metallic bullhorn still sounded. Cheers and *vivas* responded.

But the image in Bradford's mind was the face watching from the limousine.

DePrundis.

2

I

IN 1575 A SPANISH priest roaming up the Rio Paraná in quest
of savage souls discovered instead a deposit of saltpeter in the
arid and empty wastelands. Because the word of Jesus was prop-
agated largely from the mouths of Spanish cannon, the port of
Malanueva was established as a base to exploit this God-given
resource. Following the custom of the times, the city was
organized around a large central square of nine acres that fronted
on the delta of the Parana to the north. To the east, a handsome
baroque palace, white and touched with gold leaf, was built for
the Spanish governor.

To the west of the square, facing the palace, a hexagonal
fortress was erected of native shale. The fortress, called "The
Castle," was soon transformed into a prison for dissidents and,
later, for victims of the Inquisition.

The demise of Philip II's Armada in 1588 reduced the heavy
demand for explosives, and better sources were found elsewhere.
Malanueva's economic, moral, and physical fortunes declined
steadily over the next three centuries. Through all that time the
crumbling baroque dignity of the palace confronted the slowly
sinking gothic of the castle across the acres of tropical park.

II

D. J. Bradford peered out on the park. Banners, flags, and

17

streamers of crimson, and the sounds of throbbing steel drums and smacking sticks added to the chaotic effect, a teeming picnic of revolution. The thick, humid air and the oppressive delta stench and heat did nothing to dampen the frenzy.

In the park, among the jungle shrubs and palms, old and young snake-danced in and out and around the trees and fountains. Sepia faces shouted. Some guzzled rum until they collapsed, others danced around them.

The side streets that Bradford could see through his window-slit fed hordes of people into the square. Some carried baskets, some carried loot from stores: lamps, chairs, broken fixtures, gadgets they didn't comprehend.

Behind the silhouette of the palace, columns of smoke arose from the foreign quarter.

Perspiration pouring down Bradford's battered face stung. His wrists were lacerated from the rope. He ached, and his chest and back were bruised and swollen. Despite the pain, this all seemed to be some hallucination, a touch of desert sun perhaps.

Behind him the ancient wrought-iron door of his cell creaked open. A tall hat on a huge head appeared past the uniformed arm and belly of his guard, who was holding the door. *Coronel* Mercado had showered and shaved and redecorated himself in a fresh uniform of powder blue, displaying battle ribbons and stars and decorations. He carried a stubby silver baton. Dove-colored suede gloves were peeled halfway down his hands.

Bradford's faint amusement turned to surprise, for behind Mercado, gliding on small, pointed feet, came another figure: DePrundis, dressed entirely in white.

DePrundis was a middle height, his only dimension that was not bizarre. His body was nearly oval, his legs were pencil-thin and his tailored trousers clung to them skin-tight. He walked up on his toes, but since his feet turned sharply outward, he moved from side to side like a man ice-skating. The skin of his face was dark and smooth, but it was a face of shadows, not sun.

DePrundis clutched his Panama hat in white-gloved hands. He wore green glasses.

Mercado waved the guard away from the cell door. "You have met Monsieur DePrundis?"

Bradford wondered why DePrundis warranted a French address. "We have met."

DePrundis skated forward, gloved hand extended. "How are you, D. J.? And how is your father?"

Bradford spoke softly. "I know that, Mercado. But I'm an American citizen. Look—" He gestured at his torn clothes, his bruises and cuts. "What the hell is all this for?"

"I can answer that," said Mercado. "There has been a people's revolution. I am now Premier and also Chairman of the People's Party."

Bradford spoke softly. "I know that, Mercado. But I'm an American citizen. Look—"he gestured at his torn clothes, his bruises and cuts—"What the hell is all this for?"

"My men are impetuous," said Mercado evenly. "And they hate gringos. It could not be helped."

"How many of my work crew did you murder?" asked Bradford.

Mercado smiled. "Traitors in the pay of the enemy must consider the consequences."

"They were workers. They hurt no one."

"They had been warned."

"It was butchery!"

"Please." Mercado held up a gloved palm. "We are here on important business."

"Oh? Business dealings by a People's Army Commander?" Bradford stared past Mercado. "Or is Monsieur DePrundis really the commander? And Jaime Mercado y Suarez, all dressed up in his pretty blue suit, is he the doorman?"

"Enough!" shouted Mercado. He cracked his baton against his palm. The guard scurried into the background wearing an anxious expression. "Get out," Mercado croaked at him. "Stay out." The guard faded back through the door. Mercado turned to Bradford and scowled.

"Perhaps . . ." said DePrundis. "Perhaps . . ." DePrundis repeated, insistently this time.

"Yes, yes," snarled Mercado. "*You* talk to the fool."

DePrundis glided forward and presented a business card. Bradford took it, puzzled. It bore the DePrundis name and his initials—and the Greek symbol for Delta. Discreet type spelled out "Petrol/Malaverde."

"Petrol/Malaverde will be operating the oil properties of the People's Republic of Malaverde on a profit-sharing basis,"

DePrundis explained. "It will be the best thing for the people. To have professional management, I mean. To run their refinery, the pipeline. Pump the crude."

"Professional?" Bradford laughed without humor. "You're a pirate, DePrundis. You've used this toad"—he gestured at Mercado—"to steal for you."

"Come now, Mr. Bradford," DePrundis said. "These *ad hominen* expostulations are not going to accomplish anything. In fact, anything you might have to say about the matter is immaterial. The deed is done."

"A regiment of Marines would change your view," Bradford recited. It was an ancient line, better forgotten. Why couldn't he think?

It was DePrundis' turn to laugh. "You know as well as I do, Mr. Bradford, that the U.S. Government no longer uses the Marines to punish naughty boys. Washington is so terrified of triggering a holocaust by taking any kind of firm action that they all but invite such places as Malaverde—such *exploited* emerging nations—to expropriate American property. Why not? It is the right of any nation to do anything it wants to do. Isn't that so, Mr. Bradford?"

"Anything you say, as long as you're holding the key to this place." He tried to see what kind of eyes were behind DePrundis' green lenses.

DePrundis smiled. "Be that as it may, Mr. Bradford," he said, "that really is not the purpose of my visit here today, you see."

"No?"

DePrundis spoke brusquely. "I have come to speak of the indemnity."

"Indemnity?" He had to rummage for a definition. "Indemnity?"

"Of course." DePrundis carefully extracted his handkerchief, looked at it as if it were a specimen, and then dabbed at the spreading patches of moisture on his brow. "Colonel Mercado happened to mention to me that he would make a demand for indemnity payments from the U.S. Government for the . . ." His lip curled in amusement, but the words rolled smoothly. ". . . the depredations of the aggressor imperialist cat's-paw. The Bradford Petroleum Company."

"Garbage," said Bradford tonelessly.

"No, my dear friend . . . the indemnity will be paid because Washington will have no choice, if it intends to save your life. And, sentimental oafs that they are, they will happily spend the millions and greet you at home as the long-lost prodigal."

"That's not indemnity, that's ransom."

"Call it what you will." DePrundis shrugged. "It seill means money."

"DePrundis, you're a fool. The U.S. Government doesn't make budgets for ransom. If they did, every thief in the world would be raiding the Treasury."

"But," said DePrundis, "in this case they have a special budget. A very special reserve, more than amply funded to cover the five-million-dollar indemnity we will request."

"What special reserve?"

"Bradford Petroleum Company, Houston, Texas. In essence, your father."

"You're mad!" shouted Bradford. "He'll never pay ransom! He will be just as hard as he has to be—and that's just what I want."

DePrundis shrugged. "So be it. However, we have already taken the liberty, without your permission, I regret—" he bowed slightly—"to communicate our demand to the U.S. State Department. And, unofficially, we have told them where to seek the funds. I rely on them completely. I have every confidence that they will do the wrong thing, as far as diplomacy is concerned, and give us the cash."

"And if you are dead wrong?"

Mercado moved forward. "*I* can answer that, gringo. You will die." He moved closer and looked up into Bradford's face, then turned on his heel and strode out.

In his wake DePrundis glanced at Bradford. Without saying anything, he raised one hand, palm upward, and followed the Colonel out. The ancient iron door creaked and clanged shut.

Outside, the drumming and the smacking of sticks continued.

3

I

FORTY-EIGHT HOURS later, the elder Bradford picked his way across the eroding lobby of a bank erected in 1864 in hopes of economic growth in the northeast quarter of the District of Columbia. As it turned out, the northwest quarter prospered.

This slightly concave rhomboid of badly repointed brick was the Grain Exchange & Merchant's Trust, a subsidiary of another organization. To its parent it was known simply as The Bank. The Bank, in turn, referred to its parent—usually with a grimace—as The Company. The Company, in its place, was a subsidiary of the United States through its Federal government, though hardly anyone knew it.

In fact both The Company and The Bank were engaged in collecting, collating, assessing, analyzing, and sometimes acting upon, information otherwise known as intelligence. The Bank's particular forte was fiscal and monetary policy requirements.

For the record, the Grain Exchange & Merchant's Trust existed as an ordinary, if eccentric, commercial bank. It had demand and time deposits. It managed trusts. Occasionally, it lent money to a limited list of clients. It turned a small profit, part of which it grudgingly passed on to The Company.

Federal bank examiners, ignorant of The Bank's peculiar status, appeared from time to time to look at its immaculately kept books. To them, the accounts seemed no more bizarre than those of hundreds of other commercial banks. If anything,

GE&MT's accounts appeared to be more keenly managed than comparable small commercial institutions.

There *were* obscure trusts; payments to a disproportionate number of beneficiaries in foreign places; dim commercial transactions abroad; sustained liaison with certain Swiss institutions; a number of checking accounts in the names of small firms doing business in such places as Tangier and Brunei and Kuala Lampur.

But nothing really odd, except the crusty little building. The examiners wrinkled their noses with distaste at its musty odor, the peeling brown enamel, the threadbare floor covering of post-Civil-War motif, the layer of dust on the dessicated rubber plants, the missing last *T* in Trust on the institution's exterior sign.

Two of the tellers were in their cages, watching Bradford.

"The Chairman is expecting me," he said to one of them.

The teller studied him blandly. "You have an account here, sir?"

Bradford hesitated. "Yes," he said, finally. "Under the name Cosmo Construction Company, Montreal."

"I'll see if The Chairman is in." The teller picked up a telephone. "A gentleman from the Cosmo Construction Company to see The Chairman." There was a pause. The teller put the telephone down and nodded. "You may go in, sir." He pointed toward a grilled gate.

A loud buzzer sounded and Bradford went through the gate. Directly in front of him was a varnished oak door with the caption "Chairman" on it in black type with chipped gold-leaf edging.

On the other side was a modern office without windows, carpeted in a deep pumpkin-colored material. The walls were a clean off-white. It was air-conditioned and there was a hum of electrical equipment somewhere nearby. Men working at desk-top instruments didn't look up as he walked across the room toward still another door, this one smooth metal with black enamel, marked "Chairman" in modern bold-face white letters. Without hesitating, Bradford opened the door and went inside.

"Come in, come in," rasped a voice from a man seated in the large black leather chair behind the desk. "Good to see you again, Bradford." He made no move to shake hands. Bradford didn't expect him to.

"And it's good to see you again, Chairman," Bradford said

insincerely, sitting down in a black leather armchair, a companion piece of the desk chair. Like the outer office, the room had no windows. A portal effect was achieved by drawn drapes made of gold material. The large desk top, covered with gold plastic to match the drapes, was barren.

There was an awkward silence while each man waited for the other to make the first move. Bradford moved first.

"Something has come up, Chairman."

"Something involving The Bank?"

"No. Something involving me."

"But you come to The Bank?"

"I thought The Bank might be able to . . . neutralize my problem." Corporate purr words eased the burden.

"As you know, Bradford," The Chairman replied, "it is not the business of The Bank to work on personal problems."

Bradford frowned. "I know the special nature of The Bank. I was an active correspondent on several occasions, as you'll recall."

The Chairman nodded, but said nothing.

"Chairman," Bradford went on, "I believe you know the general nature of my problem."

"I read the papers."

"Then you know what has happened in Malaverde."

"Of course." He had been looking directly at Bradford. Now he turned slightly to look at a charcoal-gray wall decorated with nothing but a chart showing red, green, blue, and yellow trend lines. "You want to know if The Bank had a hand in what happened, is that it?"

"Partly."

"The answer is no, we did not have a hand in it." He looked back at Bradford. "Frankly, who the hell cares what happens in Malaverde, except you. And your interests are purely financial." He paused. "Besides, you must have gotten your investment out of that cesspool by now."

"I got my investment out in terms of oil shipped. Barely."

"You knew the risks. It's unfortunate that you couldn't have turned a more handsome profit."

Bradford smiled wanly. "Actually, I hedged my bets. There is a foreign company, Petrol/Malaverde, which will operate my investment—my former investment—in Malaverde. I've taken a very heavy position in that company's stock. Naturally, it's soaring." He looked down at his hands, pressed together almost prayerfully. There was a tremor in them. "I have to confess, Chairman. I thought that perhaps The Bank also had taken a position in Petrol/Malaverde."

The Chairman looked at him sharply. "Why would we do that?"

"Because the team managing the company is, in turn, controlled completely by one of The Bank's competitors."

"Competitor?" He spat out the word.

"DePrundis."

The Chairman's eyebrows rose slowly and he leaned back carefully in his chair. "You know this?"

"I suspected it some months ago. It was confirmed several weeks ago."

"How?"

"My sources."

The Chairman punched a button on his desk. One of the outside desk men appeared. "Do we have a file on a company called . . ." He looked at Bradford.

"Petrol/Malaverde."

". . . Petrol/Malaverde? If we do, bring it to me. Also, bring me the file marked DePrundis."

They sat in silence until the assistant returned with a blue-covered folder and a white prospectus in French. It bore the name Petrol/Malaverde and a Greek Pi symbol. When the assistant had left the room, The Chairman turned to Bradford. "Any shares traded in the United States?"

"All common is traded abroad. Principally, Zürich, Paris, and Tokyo, as well as all the South American bourses."

"Any debt?"

"Twenty million in Hong Kong dollars from the Bank of China. Apparently for some capital expenses."

"Bank of China? Any significance?"

Bradford shrugged. "None apparent. It's not an uncommon kind of loan for them to make."

"And so? DePrundis uses the proceeds of his securities' sale to finance . . . what? Bribes? Has he bought someone in the new government?"

"What he bought was the revolution. Cheap. Having bought

the revolution, he is awarded my refinery, my pipeline, my oil fields."

"You have my deepest sympathy," The Chairman said unsympathetically. "But aside from bringing me some interesting information about a competitor, you have given me no hint as to what The Bank's interest in this situation might be."

"They haven't taken just my property, Chairman. They have taken my son."

"What do you mean, taken?"

"He's a prisoner. The new regime is demanding five million U.S. dollars as a ransom. They call it an indemnity."

"I *am* sorry, Bradford." The Chairman was pensive. "I suppose they consider the indemnity approach gives them some kind of international legal command of the situation. Have you or your company responded?"

"The demand for indemnification was made to the State Department. They also have advised our government that my company has ample sources of cash for such things. They use a lot of Communist jargon."

The Chairman shrugged. "Everyone uses Communist jargon these days. That says nothing."

"Does that mean that The Bank does not have Malaverde on its list of clients for competitor encroachment? The Bank sees no competitor in Malaverde?"

"We haven't had to contend with anything in Malaverde," The Chairman said emphatically. "Who cares, Bradford?"

"I thought," Bradford said hesitantly, "that perhaps The Bank could . . ."

". . . intervene, Bradford? Foreclose, as it were?" The Chairman smiled.

Bradford flushed. "I feel The Bank owes me something, Chairman."

"The Bank owes no one, Bradford. In fact, I sometimes feel that almost everyone owes The Bank."

Bradford exhaled slowly.

"But let's assume," The Chairman continued, "that The Bank considers you a good risk. Understand"—he raised a cautioning finger—"we do not concede that we owe you even that. But let's tolerate the assumption. What would you want from The Bank?"

"Some special support."

"Underwrite a loan?"

"No, no, no." Bradford didn't know how to ask for help. "I thought perhaps The Bank could bring some influence to bear on, say, The Company. Extricate my son. I have the funds, you see, but I have no tangible assurance that he will be freed." His voice dropped, as if he did not believe this himself. "I have the money, Chairman, but I have no power in this context."

"You mean you believe they might take the money and then not complete the bargain?"

"The new leader is mad. And DePrundis hates me, just as he hates you."

The Chairman's eyes narrowed.

Bradford continued. "But I doubt they really would do anything if they thought something they couldn't cope with would fall on them."

The Chairman was suddenly impatient. "It's not The Bank's function, Bradford. You know that. Our responsibilities are *economic*: fiscal, monetary. What can we do?"

"Get the goddamned Company to warn this crazy Colonel Mercado to back off or there'll be big trouble! Or say it to DePrundis!"

"And have the State Department kick our teeth out? They've been out to get The Company for years. The Company isn't in the negotiating business, nor are we. The Company barely tolerates us, as it is—if we weren't self-liquidating, I doubt they would."

"I know all that!" snapped Bradford. "But this wouldn't be a negotiation. It would be a covert threat of violence. It would be the only thing that Mercado could understand."

"Out of the question," said The Chairman. "My advice to you is to raise the money and hope for the best."

"And DePrundis? If you let him alone, he'll move into Venezuela next. He'll grow."

The Chairman stared at the wall chart for a long time. Then he conceded, "I *would* like to scratch him."

Bradford pursued. "He's always been in The Bank's path. And now he has a strong base. He *competes*."

The Chairman spoke softly. "Your properties in Malaverde, the producing properties."

"Yes?"

"How good are they?"

"Superb. And getting better. We had just completed some successful test wells at the time of the change. DePrundis is sitting on hundreds of millions of dollars."

"The Bank could not involve itself with stimulating a counter-revolution," said The Chairman.

"Certainly not directly," Bradford agreed.

"But if you had, say, some instruments, you might accomplish something *economic*."

"I want to save my son."

"Certainly, certainly," The Chairman said impatiently. "But could you use an economic instrument? Something The Bank might provide?"

"I don't know. I just don't know."

"Anyhow," said The Chairman blandly, "why not reactivate your account? What was it?"

"The Cosmo Construction Company, Montreal."

"Yes, yes. Cosmo Construction has done a lot of good work." He scribbled a note on a small white pad. "Now then, the Cosmo Construction Company offices will be in full operation by . . ." He looked obliquely at his wristwatch. ". . . Wednesday. And when can we expect your proposal?"

Bradford stared at him for a long time. "My first objective is to extricate my son. I may or may not avail myself of the Cosmo Construction Company."

"The Bank would like you to feel free to avail yourself in any event, Bradford. We all have a general interest in this. Now I have a *special* interest."

Bradford nodded slowly. The Chairman scribbled another note on his pad, tore it off, and slid it across the desk to Bradford. "Here's a note to a friend of mine. An Undersecretary of State. Perhaps he can help you."

Bradford took the paper. He felt like a doorman accepting a tip.

The Chairman pressed the desk button. A nondescript face appeared at the door. "Please show this client out. The other entrance, of course."

It was nothing personal. Security.

II

The New State Department Building was not at all like The Bank. The building was modern, white, and plumb. Not one clerk wore a black alpaca jacket. In fact, the most common uniform was a blue cord washable suit and a striped necktie.

Bradford threaded his way through the assured bureaucracy of socially oriented receptionists and second-echelon secretaries. It was the ultimate insult to the owner/manager of an oil empire to have to cope personally with his government. His already low opinion of government plummeted further when it took him thirty minutes to determine that the Undersecretary to whom The Chairman had referred him was in Mozambique. However, the Undersecretary's secretary assured that a Mr. Guy would be happy to discuss the problem. Bradford regretted that it was the only straw visible for grasping.

Mr. Guy glanced quickly at Bradford's business card. "You are here," Mr. Guy said, "to get up-to-the-minute on what we are doing about the expropriation of your properties in Malaverde?"

"No. My company's legal department is in communication about that. My personal appearance relates only to the kidnapping of my son."

"Surely not *kidnapping*, Mr. Bradford. Detention." He raised a cautioning finger. "We do not condone this improper detention one bit."

"My son is being held for five million dollars' ransom. I want to know what is being done."

"As of now"—there was a lengthy pause as Mr. Guy rummaged through what appeared to be newspaper clippings—"our intelligence is not clear on your son's precise status. However," he smiled, "we're confident that he is safe."

"Why?"

Mr. Guy inhaled deeply and frowned. "Well, our information," he glanced at a news clipping, "indicates that he is in the central penal institution in Malanueva. It's called the Castle," he said authoritatively. "So we *do* know that."

"Tell me, Mr. Guy," Bradford said slowly. "Is this department incapable of demanding the release of my son?"

"It is not a matter of what we *can* do, Mr. Bradford, it is a matter of what we *will* do."

"Or won't."

"We are in a very, very delicate situation there right now. We can't send in the Marines to rescue one's family. We cannot risk a confrontation with the new government. It is touch-and-go whether we will even be able to maintain diplomatic relations with Malaverde. And if relations are completely severed, then we are almost totally proscribed from assisting your son. You see the problem."

"They may kill him." Bradford hadn't really considered the prospect before.

"Mr. Bradford, I don't want to minimize your situation. I do want you to appreciate the problem *we* have."

"What about the indemnity? Are you going to pay it?"

"It is fundamental in international relationships to recognize the sovereignty of each nation within its borders. *We* emphatically recognize this concept. For example, during the Suez situation in 1956, we recognized the inherent right of Egypt to take over the Suez Canal, and we brought pressure to bear on Great Britain, France and Israel to end their expedition into Egypt."

Mr. Guy enjoyed lecturing. "Even more to the point, the U.S. Supreme Court in its 1964 decision, *Banco Nacional de Cuba* v *Sabbatino*, refused to question the legality of Castro's expropriation of American property. We refer to the right of such expropriation as the Act of State Doctrine." He smiled triumphantly

"And, furthermore, the Act of State Doctrine is available to third parties who have purchased property from expropriating governments. It gives them a defense against claims by the original owners. As I understand it, that is the case with your properties in Malaverde. Our intelligence advises us that a foreign company will manage the former Bradford properties taken over by the new government. Now then . . ."

"Wait!"

"What is it?"

"All of what you say is most interesting and probably pertinent to the seizure of my properties," Bradford said, patiently.

"However, the seizure of my son is another matter. He is not real estate or a pipeline."

"I only meant to put you in the picture."

"I am in the picture, Mr. Guy," snapped Bradford. "I want to get out of the picture. I want my son out."

Mr. Guy slowly took a tobacco pouch out of a side pocket and filled a long-stemmed pipe. "It's a serious problem," he muttered. "Legally, Malaverde has jurisdiction over your son just as it would have over anything else in the country. All that we in State can insist upon is equal application of the law, and our hands are tied even there."

"Are you telling me that my son can be destroyed at the whim of some foreign agency and this department can do nothing?"

"That kind of situation is recurrent, Mr. Bradford. I am sure you have read about such cases as the Peruvian seizure of our fishing boats and crews."

"And the United States happily turns the other cheek," Bradford said morosely. "I remember when we threatened war when one of our ships was attacked by Japan in Chinese waters, back in the 1930s."

"Things change, Mr. Bradford. We have enormous responsibilities now." A smile lit his face. "You know the old vaudeville skit about the man and his lawyer on a subway? The man bites off the end of his cigar and spits, whereupon he is arrested. The lawyer, of course, insists on a court test. It keeps getting more and more out of hand until finally the poor man is in the electric chair with the lawyer in the background promising appeals." Mr. Guy chuckled. "All through this thing, the poor chap keeps wailing at the lawyer, 'Pay the man the two dollars. Pay the man the two dollars.' It was the *fine*, you see. A two-dollar fine for spitting on the subway."

Bradford was clearly not enjoying the story.

"And there's truth in that, Mr. Bradford," Mr. Guy concluded soberly. "In this case I think that's the only choice."

"Thank you, Mr. Guy," said Bradford wearily, rising from his chair. "You have helped me chart a course."

"Yes, that's my advice," Mr. Guy called as Bradford made his way out of the office. "Pay the man the two dollars."

4

I

BERNARD SIMON, EMBARKED from Houston in the Learjet at 8:00 A.M., now sat holding a Scotch, gazing through the window. Five miles below, the Caribbean sparkled, punctuated here and there with islands. Except for the steady rush of wind around the fuselage, it was silent in the air-conditioned atmosphere of the plane.

The vinyl-covered attaché case beside him contained five million dollars' worth of U.S. Treasury bills.

Simon finished his Scotch. The financial—versus human—permutations and combinations that could be worked out of five million dollars were limitless. This five million was to purchase out of bondage one D. J. Bradford, forty-four, oil engineer. From his jacket pocket Simon withdrew a notebook to review once again the instructions given him by his boss, G. B. Bradford, early that morning.

Item: The State Department had authorized the transfer of funds. It refused to participate in the negotiations. It would not pay "indemnity."

Item: Simon could not in any way represent himself as an agent of the United States Government. He was to avoid signing any kind of receipt, statement, transfer paper, legal release, or other document unless the Malaverdian authorities refused to release their prisoner without such signature. In that case, he was to announce that his signature signified nothing.

Item: He was not to make any verbal statement.

Item: He was not to relinquish control of the case containing the Treasury bills until D. J. Bradford was released into his custody.

The exchange was to take place at Aeropuerto Malanueva, the American-built, American-financed terminal fronting on the delta a few miles west of Malanueva City. Arrangements had been made for the arrival of the corporate jet. It was to touch down precisely at noon. It then was to taxi to a point directly in front of the control tower. There, one person—himself—could debark with the Treasury bills. He would be met by Malaverdian authorities.

It sounded simple enough.

Simon closed the notebook and put it back in his pocket.

The white wing dropped abruptly. The yellow-green Malaverdian coast, basking under a sun-streaked layer of tropical haze, came into view. As the plane moved eastward along the coast, Simon could make out the glittering delta of the Rio Paraná. The indolent river seeped into the Caribbean, staining the sea the color of bile for miles offshore.

The descending plane banked again. Beyond the white streaks of airport concrete, Simon could see horizontal smears of yellow smoke over what had been the Bradford refinery. A black streak from the refinery—the pipeline—went underground for a distance south of its terminus, passing inside a shallow ridge, and then reemerged, crossed a loop of the Paraná, and faded away over the southern horizon into the arid wastes of the Gran Matto. Simon looked at his watch. It was one minute before noon.

The Bradford Petroleum Company jet touched down with a screech of tires.

II

As Simon stepped down from the aircraft, he looked around warily at the ring of infantry surrounding him. Each man held an American M-3 submachine gun at the ready. An officer stepped up to him and said sharply in English, "You will accompany me, señor."

Gripping the attaché case in his right hand, Simon stepped into the familiar chill of the airport lobby. A mob of people behind some flimsy barricades and a handful of soldiers shook their fists and shouted obscenities at him.

"This way." Simon's escort led the way into a room that ordinarily served as the building's restaurant. Its decor reminded Simon of an American motel: fake-brick facades, tin shields on the walls, chandeliers with glass chimneys on each tiny lamp bulb, a carpet of maroon flowers. Captains' chairs were arranged in rows.

At one end of the room, large tripods supporting tiers of unlit photofloods stood around a raised platform dominated by a table covered in green cloth. Chrome microphones studded the table. Facing the platform on each side were batteries of movie cameras. Simon recognized the initials and insignia on some of them as extensions of the American television industry. Groups of men stood apart in separate pools of language. The Spanish-speaking huddles were subdivided into uniformed and nonuniformed men.

Simon was led to the front of the room.

"Wait here," snapped his escort, pointing to a spot by the table. The escort stepped back and arranged himself at a stiff parade rest. Looking down, Simon noticed that at one place on the floor by the table there was a raised section about four inches high.

A brace of klieg lights went on, temporarily blinding him. An American voice called, "Care to make a statement?"

Simon ignored the voice.

Another voice, speaking English with a Spanish inflection, asked, "Is it true you are an agent of the State Department?"

Simon heard some scuffling, but he couldn't see what was going on beyond the lights. The kliegs went off suddenly, leaving him staring at pink dots dancing before his eyes. Gradually, the dots faded and images of people and chairs began to reappear. The sounds in the room settled into a buzz. From time to time, members of the various groups turned to stare at him. Simon picked a blank tin shield above the vinyl-padded bar at the other end of the room and watched it.

As the moments passed, he felt a growing ache in his locked knees, but he didn't move.

Outside in the lobby the noise level rose, and Simon could hear shouts of *"Libertador! Libertador! Libertador!"*

The double doors from the lobby burst open and a trio of uniformed submachine gunners strode through. Two positioned themselves to hold each door open with their backs; they faced the room, guns at the ready.

The third member of the trio moved quickly through the room, head turning left and right, looking for suspicious characters. He was followed into the restaurant by another trio of submachine gunners, who lined themselves up in appropriate places to stand guard and make a path for what came next.

El Libertador wore a tailor-cut powder-blue uniform and a peaked cap. With him were four men, almost as short as Mercado, dressed in striped pants and swallowtail coats. The group moved en masse to the platform as klieg lights flared and cameras ground into action.

Mercado moved quickly behind the green-covered table and stepped onto the raised box. A swallowtail injected himself between Simon and Mercado and tapped microphones with his forefinger. The piercing squeal of electronic feedback was slowly tuned out until only the background buzzing of a half-dozen correspondents whispering into tape recorders remained. The swallowtail bowed respectfully to Mercado, who drew himself a fraction of an inch taller and spoke passionately in rapid Spanish that Simon could barely follow.

Then Mercado switched to English. "For benefit of worldwide TV viewers, we will conduct these proceedings into English."

He turned to Simon.

"I will ask question and you will answer."

Simon's grip tightened on the attaché case.

"Question one: Have you brought the indemnity payment for the peoples of all Malaverde?"

"I have the ransom in this case," Simon replied, laying the bag on the table.

"Señor, as an agent and representative of the United States Department of State, you know that these monies is the indemnity paid by the United States to the peoples of Malaverde for the criminal exploitation and oppressions of same."

"I am not an agent of the U.S. Government, and I will not give up the ransom until D. J. Bradford is delivered to my custody."

Mercado laughed and said something in Spanish into the microphones. His audience dutifully roared with laughter. "You may call these monies anything you want to, señor." He gestured to the swallowtails. "Take it! It is ours rightfully!"

As the swallowtails moved forward, Simon grabbed the case. "Not on your life!"

"No?" said Mercado. Again he gestured, this time to the submachine gunners. They came forward, their weapons aimed at Simon. "Give my men our rightful indemnity, señor, or my guards will shoot you right here."

After what seemed an incredibly long time, Simon, quivering with rage, thrust the case at the nearest swallowtail.

"Thank you, señor," Mercado said unctuously. "We are so grateful that you cooperate with us. Now, *por favor*, to stand as you are. I have one important announcement to make here."

He turned toward the cameras and hooked his thumbs in his military belt. Arms akimbo, he cast a liberating eye on each camera before beginning.

"As *libertador*," he said, "it is my primary concern that the laws of Malaverde be enforced. But more important is that we have *justice*! Justice for all!"

He paused. "Therefore, we must make very, very clear that this payment today is for indemnity. Not for the purchase of the life of one man, as has been implied in some quarters.

"Therefore, the criminal D. J. Bradford must—I repeat *must*—be brought to trial for his crimes against the people. The trial will begin as soon as arrangements have been made."

Simon heard this as if through a closed door. The whole scene had to be unreal.

Then reality struck him.

"You double-crossing swine!" he screamed. To hell with the M–3s! He made a move toward Mercado, but was immediately intercepted by swallowtails. The armed guards held him.

Mercado looked at him with contempt. "As for you," he said, "you will be on your plane and on your way out of Malaverde in five minutes or my guards will open fire on you and your pilot and your white jet plane."

As the guards began to pull Simon across the room, the cameras droned on, the lights illuminating his contorted face all the way to the door. Behind him *El Libertador* stood, two thousand feet tall, on a box.

III

Simon knew Bradford would be waiting when the corporate plane touched down again at the company field outside Houston.

As the aircraft rolled up to the hangars, Simon could see Bradford standing alone beside a limousine. The plane stopped and the whine of the engines faded. Simon climbed out and approached Bradford in the gathering dusk. "I'm sorry," he said.

Bradford stretched out a hand. "Thank you," he said. "It was on the newscasts over an hour ago."

"I'm sorry," Simon murmured again. "I mean about having to hear it that way."

"Actually, I had official word earlier in the day from the State Department." His voice was uncharacteristically listless. "They were full of regrets, one of their specialties."

Both men fell silent. They got into the limousine, and the chauffeur moved out smoothly.

"It was quite bad at the airport," Simon began.

"Regrets, regrets."

"I think they mean to kill him, G.B."

"Maybe if I'd known the handshake . . ." Bradford's voice trailed off.

"I doubt that there was anything that could be done. Mercado is a madman."

After a time Simon asked, "Did you try some of your other friends in Washington?" He knew nothing of The Bank. He never would.

"They tried to be encouraging, but there's very little they can do. They keep referring me to this or that cord suit at State."

"Is there nothing that can be done by government in some clandestine approach? Didn't you do some work for some kind of government agency during the war?"

Bradford said, shortly, "It was all *economic*—fiscal, monetary warfare."

"I didn't know there was such a thing."

"Oh yes, there is always something economic that can be done. It's just that people keep getting in the way, Simon."

It was dark now. The day had left Houston to itself.

5

I

DARKNESS HAD CLOSED on Malanueva, and with the demise of the sun a tropical deluge fell. Huge raindrops struck the edges of D. J. Bradford's cell window and splashed into his face.

At least, thought Bradford, the torrent had washed away the clouds of dust and driven away the revolutionary masses. Now he could see nothing in the park. Except for flashes of sheet lightning and some far-off feeble bulbs bringing shadows into relief, there was utter darkness.

Bradford struggled down from his perch, his face and torn shirt wet from the splashing rain. At the peak of the vaulted ceiling of his cell, a twenty-five watt bulb flickered inside a heavy wire cage.

Suddenly there was a commotion in the corridor. His cell door creaked open and a white suit came gliding in. DePrundis carried a small package. "A few things to help you battle time," he said. Despite the dimness of the chamber, DePrundis retained his dark glasses.

Bradford opened the package: a tin of tobacco, a pipe, paper matches, a paperback novel. "I'm touched by your generosity," said Bradford.

"My dear Bradford, I see no profit in your continuing antagonism. Actually, I have come to *help* you."

Bradford sat down on the cell cot, opened the tin of tobacco, and carefully filled the pipe. "You've bought my undivided attention."

"First, I want to assure you that it was not I who suggested that our friend, Colonel Mercado, fail to set you free on receipt of the indemnity."

Bradford puffed thoughtfully at the new pipe. "Mercado's insane. You must know that by now."

DePrundis raised a cautioning hand. "Please, he will be here shortly. We have some things we would like to review."

"Review?"

DePrundis smiled. "Some legalities. We would like your cooperation—about the oil properties. We have papers we want you to endorse."

"You're as mad as Mercado."

DePrundis ignored the comment. "Most of the papers concern the various oil properties. As a member of the Board of Directors and a Senior Vice President of Bradford Oil, your signature will prevent injunctions." He paused to mop his forehead.

"You see, the thought occurred to me that your father's attorneys might try to enjoin our oil shipments at ports of entry."

Bradford seemed unperturbed.

DePrundis' smile was ingratiating. "I need a legal document —a release, as it were, or a receipt, from you. Then we could go into the courts of this or that country—if your father's attorneys attempt injunction—and we tell them, 'Look, your lordship, we have these legal documents signed, sealed, and delivered, by the Vice President in charge of the very operations in question.' "

"Nuts!"

"And then," DePrundis said jubilantly, "the burden of proof is on the Bradford corporation."

"But you will need my signature, won't you?" Bradford smiled grimly. "And a signature by coercion is not legally valid, of course."

"By whose laws?"

Bradford said nothing. Once again there was the sound of heels in the corridor and the rumble of voices, and Colonel Jaime Mercado y Suarez stumped into the room, slapping his baton against his thigh. Three guards armed with M–3s wedged in with him.

Bradford sighed. "Colonel, it's too damn hot in here for this crowd. Why don't the gunmen leave?"

On Mercado's order, the guards backed out. Mercado glared at Bradford for a moment, then drew a scrap of paper from his breast pocket. "Tomorrow morning at 11:00 A.M., you, Señor Bradford, will go on trial in the Theater on charges of crimes against the People's Republic of Malaverde; said crimes including, but not limited to, exploitation of the masses, economic imperialism, economic and industrial espionage on behalf of a foreign power, theft of natural resources, and mismanagement."

Bradford chuckled hollowly.

"Do not mock me, Señor Bradford. I am the only man in all Malaverde who can save your life."

Bradford relit his pipe. "I thought I already was saved by five million dollars. Why should I pay any attention to what you tell me now?"

"If you cooperate with us, all will go easy for you," said Mercado.

"Cooperate?"

Mercado reached inside his jacket and produced some papers. "Some documents," he said. "Formalities."

"Give him the release statement first," DePrundis advised.

Mercado handed it to Bradford. He read it slowly and nodded. "What else?" Mercado passed him another document bearing an official seal. Bradford glanced at it, then looked sharply at Mercado. "It's a confession!"

"It will speed up your trial and remove the necessity for—many problems."

"If I had committed any of these crimes, I would shoot myself and save you the trouble, Mercado."

"Here is a pen, señor. You have the papers. Perhaps you would like something firm to write on."

Slowly, Bradford put the documents beside him on the cot and lit a match for his pipe. But instead of lighting the pipe, he picked up the documents by their corners and held the flame to them. "I hate to poison the atmosphere with this kind of smoke," he said. "But in lieu of shoving them down your throat, this seems to be the best approach."

"Guards!" shouted Mercado.

The machine gunners caromed into the cell. "Put out that fire!" Mercado ordered. The guards knocked the half-consumed papers from Bradford's hands and extinguished the fire.

"So!" said Mercado. "You show your contempt!"

"Get the hell out," Bradford said listlessly.

"I will tell you something, Señor Bradford," said Mercado. "You *will* sign those documents. Fresh copies will be brought to you by my assistants. And I guarantee, señor, by the end of this night you will beg to have the honor of signing."

Mercado spun on his heel and left. His gunmen tripped and stumbled to make room for him. DePrundis followed. The cell door creaked and clanged shut.

Outside the rain had stopped. A few stars glittered through the remaining wisps of cloud.

II

Midnight came and went.

Mercado watched the darkened plaza from the upper window of the Palace.

Behind him DePrundis cleared his throat. "How much longer will this be?"

"Not long now," said Mercado, not turning around. "My men have had much practice."

"Both documents are extremely important to our cause, Colonel."

"What's the difference? We have the man."

"It's a matter of international law. You see, Colonel, courts in many of the nations where we—where Malaverde—hopes to sell its oil may have . . . upsetting attitudes on the right of this nation to abrogate prior commitments."

Mercado frowned. "This could cause trouble?"

"In some countries, perhaps. You see, suppose we ship oil to X country. BRAPCO files suit in that country's court to seize the shipment on grounds that we—that is, Malaverde—are marketing products that were acquired illegally."

"But *I* am the law," Mercado protested.

"Here, yes. There, no," DePrundis said smoothly. "But, with the proper documents, signed by Mr. Bradford, we would immediately counter the claim with a document transferring the properties to us and relinquishing the concessions."

Mercado smiled. "And then *our* law prevails in this other place, too, no?"

"Probably." DePrundis knew it would be a tricky business.

The Bradford document should at least prevent an injunction against marketing the products. It would, of course, be challenged. But without the living signatory, without proof of coercion, the document would stand on its own.

Heels echoed on the shale paving below. Minutes later the sounds came to a halt outside their chamber. The tall double doors opened and the guard announced, "The officers have come from the Castle, *Coronel.*"

"Send them in," said Mercado.

Two men in fatigue uniforms, wearing heavy pistols, marched into the room, snapped to attention and saluted.

"Have you brought the documents?"

"We have obtained a signature on the last page of each document and his initials on all other pages, *Coronel.*"

"Excellent." Mercado riffled through the proffered papers.

"I regret, *Coronel,*" one of the officers volunteered, "that the subject was most difficult and in our anxiety to obtain this signature for you we had to be most harsh."

"His condition will not prevent him from standing trial tomorrow, will it?"

"No, sir. We have him well preserved now, *Coronel.* The doctor has been to him and they were speaking well when we left."

Mercado stared at them coldly for a moment. "Speak of this to no one or you will hang on Saturday instead of him."

The double doors slammed behind the officers and their footsteps faded rapidly in the direction from which they had come.

Mercado looked at DePrundis. "Now, my friend, Mercado's law can stretch into the foreign courts and foreign commerce."

DePrundis picked up his brandy glass and silently toasted the blocky figure standing before him. Also in silence, DePrundis saluted himself, king of all that Mercado could not see.

6

I

MALANUEVA'S JOHN F. KENNEDY Memorial Theater, previously the Grand Opera, had not been host to an opera since 1889. Built at enormous expense by the then-current *Libertador* to celebrate the cultural growth of Malanueva, financed from a crusade for precious minerals in the Gran Matto, the opera house, like the treasure hunt, lost its glory suddenly and, apparently, irrevocably.

Now the moldering opera house, renamed after the assassination of President Kennedy, was tinseled over with the banners of revolution.

ONE PEOPLE—ONE REVOLUTION!
DEATH TO IMPERIALISTIC TRANSGRESSIONS!

Gaspar Villareal looked upon these banners with anger. Why had he, of all attorneys in Malanueva, been called away from his small but relatively lucrative practice to defend D. J. Bradford? It was absurd!

Worse, it could be fatal. His future would be inextricably bound up with the fate of the gringo.

Villareal was a slight, dark man with suspicious eyes hidden behind amber-tinted spectacles. He wore a dark suit of wrinkled material. His shoes, very small with pointed toes, were concealed behind a red-draped table that would serve the defense.

43

Five guards armed with submachine guns stood at attention near him. Others were in front of the stage.

Villareal was worried; he, of all the participants, was told to be early. He alone would already be on stage, like a piece of prop furniture. The others would enter later, like stars, to the acclaim of the crowd.

The audience filed in, unnaturally silent. The orchestra seats filled quickly. The front two rows were occupied by well-dressed men, mostly foreigners, carrying notebooks. Journalists, no doubt.

The stage's high bench faced the audience. The defense table was on the left as the audience faced it, at a forty-five-degree angle to the bench. The prosecutor's table was at the opposite side. There would be three judges, no jury.

Villareal became aware of movement in the wings behind him. Guards were leading in a tall, disheveled man in manacles. The man needed a shave. His eyes, blue and icy, were bloodshot and ringed with fatigue.

There was a stirring in the audience. The four guards led the man to the defense table. They took the manacle from his left wrist and snapped in onto his chair. Villareal noticed that the chair was bolted to the floor.

The two men stared at each other. "You speak Spanish?" the attorney asked.

"Yes."

"I am your defense attorney."

"You must be a brave man."

"I had no choice, señor."

When the man smiled, a broken front tooth showed.

"I meant you must be a brave man for letting yourself become a target up here instead of committing suicide at home in the arms of your loved ones."

Villareal, angry, said, "We have justice in Malanueva, señor, even if the word is unknown in the north."

The man nodded. "Sure."

Further conversation was interrupted by the entrance of the prosecutor. There was a ripple of applause. The prosecutor smiled affectionately at the crowd. Villareal felt a sharp pang of jealousy. That this pig should be cast in such a part!

Then, from the prosecutor's side of the stage marched the judges, wearing black robes and colorful academic hoods.

44

The crowd was looking expectantly toward the empty *Libertador* box. Villareal glanced that way, too, but no one appeared. The court clerk rapped his heavy gavel three times in slow cadence, calling the hall to order.

The presiding judge, in a ministerial tone, read a statement: this was a people's court; order would be maintained; the law would be observed; justice would be served. Then with ringing emotion he declared, *"Viva la revolución!"*

The response of the audience was subdued.

"Is the prosecution ready?"

"We are, Your Honor."

"Is the defense ready?"

All eyes turned to Villareal. "We are, Your Honor," he whispered.

"Speak up, counselor," the judge demanded.

"We are, Your Honor." And then he heard a burst of laughter from his client.

The judge hammered his gavel. "The accused will restrain himself. Counselor, you will advise your client that if he does not behave we will have the guards bind and gag him."

Villareal nodded dumbly. He glanced imploringly at Bradford, who murmured, "Okay."

The judge let the words sink in, then turned to the prosecution. "You may proceed, counselor."

Photofloods were switched on, illuminating the gloomy stage. The prosecutor drew himself up, holding his preliminary statement in both hands, chest high, like a tenor about to embark on an aria.

"If it please the court," he began, "the accused in this grave matter is charged with fourteen specific crimes against the laws and peoples of Malaverde. I shall now read them."

"On or about . . . the accused did with premeditation and malice aforethought . . . in direct violation of penal codes 8 and 9, paragraphs 16 and 24, respectively, of the city of Malanueva and the People's Republic of Malaverde . . . rob, steal, and otherwise misappropriate . . . bring about the deaths of . . . did resist the armies of the People's Republic of Malaverde in military action even while they were led by *El Libertador* himself . . . terrorism . . . cat's-paw of imperialism . . . terrorist . . . poisoning the minds of the people . . ."

45

The prosecutor proceeded immediately to his opening statement.

"The specified crimes are too overwhelming for the People's Republic of Malaverde to accept them with equanimity in order to appease the perverted rantings of a foreign power. Nothing less than a decision of guilty on all counts by this court will appease the people. And justice also demands speedy execution.

"Our national manhood cannot allow us to grovel and appease the great Yankee power of the north, which wants the return of this miserable instrument of its imperialistic policy." He pointed at Bradford.

"But Your Honors, it is not enough to say that a man who has committed crimes stands before us on trial. We must look into the significance of this case, we must look at what the accused symbolizes.

"In my opinion," the prosecutor continued, "the issue to be resolved centers on one, and only one, major question: Will imperialism be allowed to prevail?"

A chorus of "No!" echoed from the balconies and continued until the presiding judge rapped for order.

When the audience had calmed, the judge nodded at the prosecutor to proceed.

"There is little for me to add," he intoned, his voice rising with emotion. "All we ask is justice! Justice for the poor and downtrodden masses, the victims of monarcho-fascist imperialism!" He bowed his head, and made his way back to his table.

The audience, wild, stamped its feet amid the cadenced chant of "Malanueva, *si;* Yankee, *no!*" It gave Bradford's counsel time to wrestle with his own conflicting hatreds—of the gringo beside him and the prosecutor opposite him. That prosecutor's performance would have been hissed from the stage in any melodrama, he mused, but in these times it was a touchstone of revolution.

Villareal sensed that anything less than a holiday execution could hardly be contemplated. Anything he said to contradict it could well make *him* the object of the *campesinos'* wrath.

It took ten minutes for the presiding judge and his colleagues to restore order. By then Villareal had composed himself.

"Does the defense wish to make an opening statement?"

Villareal looked at Bradford, who was watching the audience

with a blank expression. Then Villareal stood, buttoned his coat, and addressed the bench.

"If it please the court," he began. "It is fundamental in the laws and history of our beloved nation that justice be done.

"In most instances," he went on, "this means that a man accused of crimes has the opportunity to prove his innocence." Suddenly, it came to him. He rose to the occasion.

"I realize that it has been the custom of our culture and our heritage to have a devil's advocate—one who defends evil. But such a defense is before God only." He wasn't certain of his theology, but it seemed logical. "The indictments presented by my good friend the prosecutor were not just the image of evil, they *were* evil." He paused dramatically, noting a glimmer of interest from one judge.

"Therefore, it is my intention to present *no* defense against that indictment. If evil exists, it must be expunged. If I were to defend the very personification of evil"—he gestured at Bradford, who was smiling faintly—"then I, too, should be indicted.

"Therefore, Your Honors, I join, as only a true revolutionary can, in declaring before this court and before the People's Republic of Malaverde, that this man must *die!*"

The audience response duplicated—and then surpassed—its response to the prosecutor's opening remarks. It took nearly half an hour to restore order, as the old building vibrated dangerously to the unaccustomed drumming of feet.

"Because of the rapid manner in which the court has proceeded with opening statements," the presiding judge announced when he could finally make himself heard, "this court will adjourn until 2:00 P.M., when we will commence with the prosecution's testimony. This court is adjourned." He rapped his gavel, triggering another wild outburst as the crowd dispersed.

When the guards took Bradford away again, Villareal did not even glance at him. He stood for a long time in the spot where his victory had been won, tears of relief streaming down his face.

7

I

BRADFORD, UNDER HEAVY guard in the dank, low-ceilinged area just beneath the stage of the theater, sat, hands manacled, upon an ancient Victorian sofa encrusted with a bluish-green down of fungus, surrounded by the moldering sets of other ages and by perspiring guards with M—3s at the ready.

It was hot and moist in the storage room, but probably not so hot as Malanueva Plaza beneath the noontime sun. Bradford was grateful that he did not have to return to his cell, partly because it would have been a long hot walk to nothing better, partly because he feared the mob's insanity.

There was a sound at the entryway leading from the area. The door swung open and the white oval shape of DePrundis floated in. He whispered something to the sergeant of the guard and handed him a note. The sergeant scanned it, snapped to attention, and saluted. He motioned DePrundis toward Bradford.

"I fear they have mistreated you," DePrundis murmured. "They are animals." He sat down carefully.

"I thought you had brought me some pipe tobacco or a cold beer."

"My concern was that you not be manhandled."

"Your concern was to no avail, of course."

"You could have saved yourself a lot of trouble."

"I wouldn't give them the satisfaction."

"There is nothing personal in all of this, Bradford. I want you to understand that."

Bradford laughed. "Please. No matter how you try, you will not convince me that you have a conscience."

"I am a businessman. These things are business."

"I'm very tired, DePrundis. If you say black is white, I am not going to argue. Upstairs they tell me I am a monarcho-fascist imperialist. Does anybody listen to that jargon?"

DePrundis ignored the question. They sat in silence for a moment. "You don't look well."

"Concussion probably. I keep drifting into sleep. It's a blessing really." He leaned back and shut his eyes.

"Actually, I have come on an errand of mercy."

"Mercy?" Bradford's eyes opened again. "You?"

"I thought you might want to drop a note to your father. I have brought papers. A pen. I'll see that it is posted immediately."

"My writing ability is curtailed somewhat by these bracelets."

"I'm sorry."

"I'll manage something."

DePrundis handed him the writing materials.

My dear father,

By now you know—probably more than I—what has transpired here in Malaverde. I am on trial, or so they call it. They mean to kill me, of course. Barring a sortie by the U.S. Marines, which does not appear to be forthcoming, I will be dead Saturday afternoon. There is little I can add. However, I do recall a line, an old verse—I cannot remember whose—that says what I want to say. It goes:

When I am dead let fire destroy the world; it matters not to me, for I am safe.

In these hours I long for your wisdom in being able to accomplish the impossible. More than that I long for one opportunity for the two of us to make our good-byes.

With all my love,

D.J.

Bradford folded the letter in thirds. "No envelope?" he asked DePrundis.

"An oversight. Regrettable. However, you have my assurance that it will not be read. It will be enveloped and on its way within the hour."

Bradford handed DePrundis the note. "It makes no difference. We never were a sentimental lot."

DePrundis maneuvered himself to his feet ponderously and glided out.

II

Gaspar Villareal had changed his necktie. He sat proudly now, his demeanor stern.

The remainder of the stage scene was as it had been.

"You may call your first witness, Mr. Prosecutor," the presiding judge intoned.

The court clerk shouted a name, the first on a long and unfamiliar list of *campesinos* allegedly victimized, directly or indirectly, by the accused and his instrument, the Bradford Petroleum Company. The scripts ran:

PROSECUTOR: And after the villain from the imperialist oil baron told you that you would have to abandon your home of many years, what did you do?

MAN: I was sad.

PROSECUTOR: Did the oil company give you money?

MAN: They abused me.

PROSECUTOR: How did they abuse you?

MAN: They denied me my rights and prerogatives as a free citizen of the People's Republic of Malanueva.

PROSECUTOR: Did these running dogs of Wall Street physically do you damage?

MAN: They killed my pig. They ran over my pig with a tractor.

And so it went.

The hours droned by. There was no nuance of law to be impressed upon the court. Rather, the prosecutor wove his tedious fabric of words from the tales of dozens of poor, remote individuals who had been displaced, misplaced, pushed aside, injured, or insulted by the construction program of the Bradford Petroleum Company.

The prosecutor, despite his bulk and his perspiration, moved busily to and fro on the stage declaiming questions at this unhappy parade of "witnesses" almost as if they, and not Bradford, were the villains.

Slowly, he created the desired impression: even if the accused did not personally evict the *campesinos* from their homes, did not personally kill the *campesinos'* pigs, did not personally cause the death of a woman struck by a truck, did not personally stoke the pipes and tubes and tanks that belched the smoke and fumes they breathed, he was, nevertheless, the man responsible.

"Even as Adolf Eichmann was responsible for the death of millions though he, personally, did not do the killing, isn't that so?" the prosecutor shouted.

His human vehicle of that moment in the trial seemed surprised. But he nodded vigorously. "Yes, that must be so, Your Honor."

"Thank you, my friend," the prosecutor beamed. "You may step down."

The judges had had enough. "Is it the intention of the prosecution to present many more witnesses? The hour is getting late and we must consider adjournment."

"Your Honors," the prosecutor said, "my apologies. If the crimes were not so extensive, the testimony would be shorter."

"Yes, yes. How much longer?"

"I have only one more witness, Your Honors. He will not take long."

"Proceed."

The name was not on the clerk's list. There was a whispered conversation between him and the prosecutor, who frowned and scribbled a name on a scrap of paper.

"The Court calls Severino DePrundis."

Bradford's eyes widened but he did not stir from his slouch. Villareal watched him and shrugged. He did not know DePrundis.

On the prosecutor's side of the stage he saw a white suit move with surprising agility to the witness box.

The prosecutor stepped forward purposefully, phrasing his first question as he moved. "What is your full name, sir?"

"Severino Ahmed DePrundis."

"And what is your nationality?"

51

"I hold multiple citizenship with Malaverde and several other nations."

"And what is your occupation, sir?"

"I am an entrepreneur."

"Do your entrepreneurial activities include dealing with the oil industry?"

"That is correct."

"And is it true that you have an interest in Petrol/Malaverde?"

"Yes, that is true."

"What was your objective in helping to organize Petrol/Malaverde?"

"It was well known that our country intended to call within a year for bids on new natural resources concessions in the Gran Matto. It was the intent of the incorporators of Petrol/Malaverde to bid on these concessions against foreign interests."

"Were these concessions, in fact, put up for bids?"

"They were not. They were delayed."

"By whom?"

"By representatives of the Bradford Petroleum Company who intervened with agents of the previous fascist clique."

"Who was in charge of Bradford Petroleum's operations in Malaverde at that time?"

"D. J. Bradford."

"Do you see him here?"

"He is that man, the accused." He pointed a stubby finger at Bradford.

"What did you do when you became aware of the improper delays in the bidding?"

"I set about making contact with the correct revolutionary elements who represented the true aspirations of the peoples of Malaverde, personified by our great leader, Jaime Mercado y Suarez, *El Libertador*."

The audience applauded vigorously.

The judges went through the ritual of rapping for order and the crowd calmed down again.

"And how many months before his triumph were you in contact with *El Libertador*?" the prosecutor continued.

"Four or five months."

"During that time, did anything else transpire between Petrol/Malaverde and the imperialist agents represented by the Bradford Petroleum Company?"

"Yes." DePrundis took out his handkerchief and mopped his perspiring neck. "As I indicated earlier, I and certain of my colleagues made contact with the revolutionary movement. It soon became apparent that the true aspirations of the masses would not be denied, no matter in what direction the imperialist lackey clique turned.

"The Bradford Petroleum Company realized that if the peoples of Malaverde seized control from the imperialist clique, then their days of exploitation of the masses would quickly come to an end.

"Thus, about ten days before the culmination of the people's aspirations, I received a personal telephone call from the father of the accused."

There was a murmur in the audience. "What did he want?" the prosecutor demanded.

"He proposed that Petrol/Malaverde and Bradford Petroleum Company merge." DePrundis pursed his lips distastefully. "He offered extremely generous terms."

"What did you do?"

"I rejected the very thought."

D. J. Bradford's expression now was pensive. He remembered large purchases of Petrol/Malaverde equities in his own name, in his father's, in Simon's.

"Did you end the conversation?" the prosecutor asked.

"Not immediately," said DePrundis. "I wanted to know to what extremes the other imperialists were willing to go to thwart the revolution. I continued with the conversation, pretending all the while that I was a fish who had taken the bait."

"What was their scheme?"

"First, I was to receive a personal payment—a bribe—of three million dollars.

"Next, I was to persuade the stockholders and management of Petrol/Malaverde to accept an exchange of stock, whereby our company would become a vassal company of Bradford Petroleum.

"Finally, D. J. Bradford's oil-field men would secretly drill a test hole to determine whether future bids on the tract under consideration would be advisable.

"If the tracts open for bidding turned out to be sound, Bradford Petroleum could assure a high bid that would win the award. If the tracts were not promising, they intended to rig an elaborate arrangement—it is much too complex to explain here—to profit by the knowledge that the concession was worthless."

The prosecutor was baffled by this but did not pursue it. "It was a kind of swindle, was it not?"

"That's correct."

"What happened next?"

"Naturally, I declined such a barbarous scheme." His self-righteous act was almost believable.

"Thank you, Señor DePrundis. I have no more questions."

The presiding judge turned to Villareal. "Do you wish to cross-examine?"

"I have no questions for this witness, if it please the court."

"The witness is excused."

DePrundis stood, body turned toward Bradford. He seemed to shrug, but it was hard to be sure. Then he turned and walked back into the obscurity of the wings.

"Does the prosecution wish to call any more witnesses?"

"We have no more witnesses, Your Honor. However, at this time, if it please the court, I would like to introduce into evidence three items."

"Proceed."

From a folder he produced a slightly soiled paper. "As Exhibit A I would like to introduce the holographic confession of the accused, in which he discusses his crimes relative to specifications 1 through 8 of the indictment."

"Does the defense object?"

"No objection, Your Honors." Villareal did not bother to examine the paper.

"Next, as Exhibit B, I would like to introduce a document which declares that the Bradford Petroleum Company with Mr. D.J. Bradford as its agent provocateur illegally acquired properties and oil concessions in Malaverde. This document also reassigns to Malaverde all rights to said properties. It is signed by the accused and witnessed and sealed by the state."

"Any objection?" the judge asked.

"None, Your Honors."

"I thank the defense counsel," the prosecutor said, bowing slightly. From beneath his table he withdrew a stack of flat round tins bound together with black tape. "As Exhibit C I would like to present films taken at the time of payment of an indemnity by the Government of the United States to Malaverde for damages involving the Bradford Petroleum operations. It is the opinion of the prosecution, Your Honors, that these films constitute both a confession and an acknowledgment by the United States that economic crimes were, indeed, committed by one of their jackal agents. These films relate to the remaining indictments."

"Does the defense object?"

"No objection, Your Honors."

"Does the prosecution rest its case?"

"We do, Your Honors."

The presiding judge turned a disapproving eye on Villareal. "The defense indicated earlier in these proceedings that it did not feel it had any grounds for defense against the indictments presented. Does defense counsel still so feel?"

"We do, Your Honor."

The judge looked at his watch. "It is now late afternoon. In order to expedite this matter, we will reconvene here at 8:00 P.M., at which time the prosecution and defense may make their closing statements. Following the traditions of the Court of Malaverde, this tribunal will make its decision and pronounce sentence," he smiled, "*if* any, immediately. This court is adjourned."

III

The stocky blond man riffled a sheaf of penciled jottings.

"There is no code apparent here, Monsieur DePrundis."

"You are certain?"

"Absolutely." The blond man hesitated. "That is, I am certain that it is not a cipher code. It is quite possible that it is a book code. That is, a certain word, a sequence of words, has some correlation to a specific phrase in a code book. However, this sample is much too brief to lend itself to analysis from that perspective. Perhaps, if you can get me a more substantial sample . . ."

"That will not be possible."

DePrundis took the paper from him and stared at it:

When I am dead let fire destroy the world; it matters not to me, for I am safe.

Even if this were not a code, DePrundis was certain that it held a meaning beyond a written phrase and that meaning was of significance to his future.

"Do you want me to destroy that message?"

"No," said DePrundis, almost absently. "I have an envelope. We will forward it to its destination." Carefully he removed his pen and unscrewed the cap. On the bottom of D. J. Bradford's note he wrote:

"We could have done business." He underlined "could" and then drew a stylized *D*.

IV

Beyond the mildewed walls of the theater the tropic sky was streaked crimson and gold. From time to time the darkening sky glowed with lightning, and thunder rumbled. Inside the theater everyone was seated, awaiting the final act. The banners and slogans hung still in the lifeless air. The judges entered and took their seats behind the bench.

"The prosecution may proceed with its summation," the presiding judge said.

Villareal noticed that his client seemed strangely subdued. He seemed already to have resigned himself to his inevitably unpleasant fate.

Villareal himself was far more concerned with how he would phrase his closing speech. He paid scant attention to the prosecutor's summation.

"And so, if it please the court, we come to the culmination of this unswervable line of logic, and that is that the accused, D. J. Bradford, is guilty as charged on all counts. I am confident that this court will see its way to the only logical result of these proceedings: the accused must go to the gallows." He returned to his chair.

"Thank you, Señor Prosecutor," the presiding judge said. Three pairs of judicial eyes turned on Villareal. "The defense may proceed with its summation."

Slowly, Villareal stood.

"As I said to this court at the outset of this trial, the indictments against the accused virtually precluded a defense. Indeed, as the day wore on, we heard the sounds of our people, their cries of anguish at the oppression of the imperialist exploiters." He had learned some of the jargon. "Brick by brick the mausoleum of our countrymen's suffering at the hands of the Bradford Petroleum Company has been built. And, as our good friend the prosecutor has urged, that mausoleum should house the corpse of the symbol and the perpetrator of these crimes."

The great hall was silent. As he paused, Villareal looked around at the bench, the prosecution table, the journalists, the box of *El Libertador*, the—

Villareal, his hand trembling slightly, reached into his inside jacket pocket and produced his amber glasses. He put them on and peered up at the box.

Yes. Jaime Mercado y Suarez had quietly slipped into his seat for this final act of the drama!

His moment of triumph was at hand.

"It is customary at this point in a trial for the defense counsel, even if he has conceded the guilt of his client, to make a special plea for mercy.

"If this were an ordinary trial, that is exactly the course I would take, for we Malaverdians are a merciful people and justice without mercy is a sin.

"But the crimes we have heard recounted here today shout at us that there is only once course of action that can be taken." His voice rose.

"Therefore, I, Gaspar Villareal, not only ask, I *demand*, that this tribunal return a verdict of guilty as charged on all counts. I further demand that the maximum penalty be imposed upon this villain." He pointed at Bradford without looking at him. "He deserves to die." He moved his pointing finger up slowly until it was aimed at Mercado. "Would our beloved *Libertador* have it any other way?" he shouted.

All eyes turned toward the box. A great cry swept the audience. From the amalgam of sound a chant began, picked up and resounded: "MERCADO—MERCADO—MERCADO—MER-CADO!"

A spotlight turned toward the box and picked him out. He stood regally, raising one arm, then the other. His teeth glinted in the brilliant light.

The tumult lasted many minutes.

The judges never pronounced a formal verdict or sentence. It had been decided for them.

8

I

A BRASS BAND WAS playing somewhere. The deep thump of its Turkish drum could be heard even inside the palace.

From above, the masses in the plaza looked like shoals of many-colored tropical fish. Near the center of the plaza there was a roped-off area where workmen were putting the finishing touches on the gallows.

Actually, the prefabricated scaffold, a contribution of the Malanuevan chief of police in 1923, had for many years been in readiness in a storage chamber of the Castle. It had only to be transported to the spot where the execution would be carried out, and assembled like a huge tinker-toy. The apparatus could accommodate as many as six customers at once.

Once or twice a year, the gallows was bolted together in the prison exercise yard and a backlog of felons was disposed of at once in the name of efficiency. However, the Bradford hanging was a special event, a national holiday.

Mercado turned reluctantly away from his window above the plaza.

"This is a day of triumph for all Malaverde," he said to DePrundis.

DePrundis spoke from the depths of a large wing chair. "You will keep the legal papers safe? I am counting on it."

"Never in the history of Malaverde has there been such a crowd to witness an event." Mercado selected a claro meduro corona from the cut-glass humidor of his late predecessors.

"I would like to have notarized copies of those papers," DePrundis said softly.

"There must be a hundred thousand people out there." Mercado's eyes glowed.

"I don't know whether I told you," said DePrundis. "We will have the first tankers in port day after tomorrow."

Mercado disliked this talk of business—figures, loadings; they bored him. What did it all matter, weighed against the power and excitement of this day?

"You have trained my people well enough to operate the refinery?"

"Some. I have brought others in. The refinery is operating."

"As before?"

"Well enough. We will easily be able to fill the ships as they come in and still have enough product left over for the storage tanks and for refining."

"These things make my head hurt." Mercado frowned, then smiled suddenly. "Come now, DePrundis, would you hurt Mercado's head?"

"I need the papers."

"I don't understand."

"It is possible that the first shipload will be challenged in the courts. It will be consigned to Antwerp."

"Consign it somewhere else, then." He puffed angrily on his cigar. A thought occurred to him. "You know, DePrundis, the crowd will be very excited, they really should have some reward."

DePrundis had his handkerchief out, mopping. "Give them all cigars. They will love you."

"No, it is important for them to participate in this event, like the taking of Mass. Malaverde will wash away imperialism by abusing the corpse of the gringo."

Mercado shouted for an aide. "Listen, in the prosecutor's office, the copies of the papers that the officers brought there the other evening, bring them to me."

"But, sir," the aide murmured, "today is a holiday. The government offices are closed."

"Goddamn you, don't question my orders! Get those papers! And when you have done that, bring them here to this room and give them to Monsieur DePrundis."

60

"*Claro, Coronel!*" The aide saluted smartly and left.

"You see? Things can be accomplished quickly, DePrundis, when I choose that path."

"You are amazing, *Libertador*," said DePrundis. "My colleagues and I knew we were backing a winner when we offered you our support."

Mercado, eyes half-closed, savored his cigar. "You have talent for choosing wisely, DePrundis."

DePrundis held up a portfolio that had been tucked beside him in the chair. "But my debt is not quite fulfilled, *Libertador.*"

"Nonsense, you have done too much."

"In this folder are stock certificates representing, under certain circumstances, one-half of the Petrol/Malaverde corporation. It is the least we can do."

Mercado took the portfolio. "I am touched. Truly." He looked inside the folder at a sheaf of engraved papers. "I am most impressed. They are beautiful."

"They also are very valuable, and they will become even more valuable as time goes by and more oil is discovered in Malaverde."

"I am a simple man," said Mercado. "I do not understand these things."

DePrundis extracted one of the engraved sheets from the portfolio. "As you can see, this certificate, and the others, are written in French. Each is for ten thousand shares of Petrol/Malaverde special convertible preferred stock." DePrundis knew from Mercado's glazed expression that he might as well have been speaking Chinese. "Look." He pointed at a number of printed squares on the bottom of the certificate. "Each of those squares must be trimmed off on the date printed on it and presented to a bank."

"What bank?"

"Any bank. Say, a Swiss bank. Each square is a coupon, like a check, payable on that date. You will get money for it."

"And when the squares are gone?"

"At that time this certificate can be exchanged for one share of common stock, which represents direct ownership in the company."

"Please," Mercado whined, "tell me only what each of these certificates is worth."

DePrundis chuckled. "Right to the heart of the matter. At present world market prices, each of these certificates is worth a half-million U.S. dollars." He sighed. "And the price is rising."

Mercado quickly riffled the certificates. "I am a very rich man."

DePrundis smiled. "Of course, as with the indemnity payment made by the Bradford interests, these securities are yours to hold in trust for the benefit of all the struggling peoples of Malaverde. It was the least we could do for the revolution."

II

From the prison side of the plaza a spearhead of armed troops threaded into the crowd in two lines, each militiaman carrying a heavy post chained to the post behind him. The murmur of the crowd intensified as they worked their way to the gallows in the middle of the square. Then the lines of soldiers eased the crowd back until a wide path was cleared. Two lines of armed soldiers came to reinforce them.

The same process was repeated from the palace side of the square.

Now a new group of helmeted and armed soldiers appeared, surrounding D. J. Bradford. The noise from the crowd rose in pitch and intensity. Thousands of bodies leaned toward the pathway and the militiamen leaned back. The supporting troops held their rifles at high port, butt up, ready to bang the first head that might vault through the line of chain-and-post bearers.

Bradford, hustled by his guards across the plaza to the foot of the gibbet, kept his eyes straight ahead. To those at the edge of the pathway it was apparent that his face was puffy and warped. One eye was swollen nearly shut. The visible eye was dull and unconcerned with what went on about him. He wore a fresh khaki shirt and a red armband. His hands were manacled in front of him.

Slowly, without hesitation, he climbed the steps of the gallows. His guards moved up with him. As they took their places, apart from the prisoner, he became visible to the throng and, suddenly, a great wail went up.

The guards seemed concerned. Some moved to the front railing of the platform, as if to protect Bradford from attack, but the vast assembly seemed content to shout its rage and wave its banners.

From the direction of the palace came the wah-wah of police horns, and the crowd turned as one in that direction and became silent.

A six-wheeled personnel carrier with a squad of helmeted, polished infantrymen, each with his arms folded smartly across his automatic rifle, rolled quickly down the open path toward the scaffold. It was followed by a double column of a half-dozen motorcycles, each streaming red ribbons from its handlebars.

Behind them came an ebony Mercedes. The Malaverde flag flew from its left front fender; the right was decorated with a red flag. A red streamer flew from the limousine's radio antenna.

The personnel carrier pulled around behind the scaffold, and the soldiers jumped out to take positions between the structure and the crowd. The motorcycles rumbled up. One column peeled off to the right, the other to the left. The limousine stopped at the steps of the scaffold. Guards leaped from the front seat to open the door leading to the steps.

The first to emerge was a small gray-haired man with a woebegone face. A murmur went through the crowd. The executioner. Next, black robes fluttering, came the judge who had presided over the tribunal at Bradford's trial. Following the executioner, he climbed the thirteen steps like a crow picking its way on the branches of a dead tree.

Finally a small man emerged, wearing a powder-blue uniform and a tall hat and carrying a swagger stick.

The crowd watched the wide blue back with the stumpy legs climb to the top, step up on a special elevated dais, and turn slowly around. Sun sparkled from gold buttons and polished leather. He faced them and the chant seemed to explode: "MERCADO—MERCADO—MERCADO—MERCADO!"

The pale-blue idol stood supreme before them, accepting their booming adulation.

III

In the long run it took the electronically amplified personal entreaties of the judge and *El Libertador* himself, plus menacing gestures by the militia and guards, to quiet the masses.

Jaime Mercado y Suarez turned his huge head this way and that to survey the entire plaza. Then he began speaking slowly. He had no prepared text, no notes.

"I will tell you a story." He spoke softly, like a master equestrian gentling a nervous mare. His soothing voice rebounded eerily from the horns of loudspeakers placed at the corners of the plaza.

"Once there was a land of peaceful people," he said, and he described a people strong and without fear, a land of men and proud women, and their many children. The idyllic land he described seemed never to have disease, poverty, filth, or predatory governments that changed with each tide in the Rio Paraná.

"This land," Mercado said, "was part of the blood of the people, and the people were part of the land. And this land that I speak of, you know it well in your hearts. It is our own Malaverde.

"What happened to this marvelous land? Where did it go? Where did the happiness of the people disappear to?

"I will tell you."

His face hardened and he took the neck of his microphone in both hands as if to strangle it. "We were betrayed," he whispered.

Then, suddenly, his face turning livid, he shrieked: *"We were betrayed!"*

The crowd responded with an avalanche of sound that roared across the plaza and rebounded again and again from the walls of the buildings, was picked up, amplified, and projected again from Mercado's microphone.

Mercado raised his arms to quiet the crowd.

They stopped their shouting to hear what would come next. Again his voice resumed its soft quality.

"We were betrayed by jackals and perverts who sold the sacred manhood of this country for silver, who traded its very treasures, our natural resources, for a chance to lick the Yankee boot, who finally sold our entire nation like cheap whores to the gringo for the Yankee dollar.

"We will not be betrayed!"

Again the crowd surged, and again he gentled them. Carefully, pulling a fact here, ignoring another fact there, he told how the Bradford Petroleum Company had first started its operations in Malaverde. He quoted from the trial. He read excerpts of the indictments.

"And so, my beloved people, my own *campesinos*, we come before you today. The time has come for *justice!*"

"Justice" was the prearranged signal for the executioner to slip a hangman's noose around Bradford's neck and maneuver him into the middle of the trap. The American did not appear to focus on these events. Instead, he stood, slightly swaying, as if he might topple over stiffly with the slightest shove. His numb face was streaked where sweat had made the cosmetics run.

"Before you today is a—I cannot use the word "man"—an *individual* who personally was responsible for many of the atrocities inflicted upon you.

"But more that that, *he* is the symbol of repression. *He* is the symbol of the Yankee dollar. *He* is the symbol—" the voice dropped sharply—"of imperialism itself.

"And so I say to you—imperialism must *die! Death to imperialism!*"

The crowd roared back: *"Death to imperialism!"*

The executioner sprang the trap, and D.J. Bradford fell silently to an abrupt death.

9

I

FAR BELOW HIS TOWER, Houston, the city of oil, exuded heat. Even at dusk, its sounds vibrated in a thousand overtones. People scurried and vehicles moved silently within view of his huge window. There was a discreet sound behind him. He turned from the window to face Simon.

"News?"

"The worst."

"Expected, wasn't it? Sit down, Simon." Disaster was something he had used, and had been used by. It was almost a part of him. "Tell me about it."

"There was a call from the State Department." The office was dimly lit and he had to hold his notes at an angle to read. "A Mr. Guy conveyed the message. He knew you."

"We had talked."

"We . . . lost D.J. at 12:20 P.M."

"You mean he was hanged at 12:20!" He spoke sharply. "You don't have to soften it with euphemisms, Simon. They don't change the facts. We're speaking of death, not slumber."

Simon took a deep breath. "Sorry. It's just that D.J. and I were quite close in our own way."

"Get on with it," said Bradford. "The harsh way is a purging. It hurts, but we can grapple with the pain. We forget that sometimes."

"Right." He riffled his notes. "Mr. Guy said the Department's

66

account came via a Swiss observer. Our own consulate there has been under guard and our people restricted to it."

"They couldn't have done anything at the execution anyway," said Bradford. He turned slowly in his chair to stare once again at the city. "We'll have to work out some arrangement for retrieval of the remains. Did Mr. Guy make any reference to that?"

Simon was hesitant. "From what Mr. Guy said, we apparently will not be able to retrieve the body."

"What do you mean?"

"Mercado ordered the body turned over to the mob."

"My God!"

Bradford grasped the edge of his desk, then slowly regained composure. "Where is the body now?"

"Machete men hacked it to pieces. People were seen running off with fragments. The . . . the head was put on a stake and paraded around all afternoon. God knows where it is now. The rest of the body is . . . gone."

Bradford looked down at his hands, clasped tightly together in his lap. It was quite dark in the room now.

After a time Simon asked, "Shall I turn on more lights?"

"No," said Bradford. "But I have instructions for you. Can you see to make notes?"

Simon nodded.

"First, there is the matter of Petrol/Malaverde shares."

"Wouldn't you prefer to do this tomorrow?"

"We'll do it now." His tone was emphatic. "Petrol/Malaverde—what is our relative situation?"

"I priced the securities that we have acquired relative to our purchase price. On average we now have a 110 percent gain. That is, we bought at an average price of 25 in a range from the opening at 20 up to 33, when we quit buying. The price now is 51 bid, 52 asked."

"Good. Order our agents to begin selling the shares on the rise only."

Simon made a note.

"Second, we are going to do something—as The Chairman would say—something fiscal, something monetary."

"The Chairman?"

"An allusion. Forget it. Find out where Hugo Wolfram is."

"Wolfram?"

"That's right. I doubt you know him."

"The name is familiar. Where would I begin to track him down?"

"Wolfram has a company called Firebird. He puts out oil-well fires, gas fires. His is one of the few organizations that can handle something big."

"And when I find Mr. Wolfram of Firebird?"

"That's part three. Go personally to wherever he is and bring him here."

"What are you contemplating, G. B.?"

"I have a proposition to put to Mr. Wolfram."

"You know, G. B., I cannot for the life of me see what purpose Wolfram's presence could serve."

"*Must* you see?"

"It's not a question of *must*, it is the image of what I can project. I don't like the look of it."

"And what do you see?"

"I see revenge."

"Call it retribution," he said softly.

"It's not your style, G. B.," Simon pleaded. "Look, you've been through a hideous shock. Both of us have. Even your company has. But this . . . reject it. Cast it aside."

"No." The word was nearly inaudible.

"Then at least give it time. Wait a week, then look at the idea again."

"I'll have a week or more. By the time you get back with Wolfram I will have had all the time required. I am not approaching this lightly, Simon. It goes beyond my personal feelings."

"Then it is just a larger madness. If we resort to this kind of primitive reprisal, we are no better than they."

"You don't have to stick by me, you know. If your feelings are that strong, I free you from it. I will go and get Wolfram myself. I can't trust anyone else."

"Nonsense!" snapped Simon. "I'm with you, G. B." His voice fell. "However, I am against the idea, not only on philosophical or moral grounds, but also because it is bad business."

Bradford nodded. "Perhaps you're right. Bad business it surely is. Whether it is profitable business remains to be seen. But, then, maybe the idea *will* die. No matter what comes of it, thank you for standing by me."

Simon stood. "I'll try to get back to the State Department just in case some way opens up of retrieving D. J.'s remains." He paused as if awaiting some further word, then left.

G. B. Bradford watched as the heavy office door opened and closed silently behind Simon. From the middle drawer of his desk he removed the limp and soiled last letter of his son and read:

When I am dead let fire destroy the world; it matters not to me, for I am safe.

And then G. B. Bradford broke into wracking sobs, sobs without tears.

Later, in the gloom, he picked up one of his telephones and dialed a number he would never forget. As he waited through the muted beeping of electronic relays, he took the silver cigar lighter form his desk and ignited the stained letter with its obscene addendum by DePrundis. The flame bit softly at one edge and then flared, leaving behind only black ashes.

On the telephone a metallic voice said: "The Grain Exchange and Merchant's Trust Company."

"The Chairman, please."

10

A *HOWLING VORTEX OF* orange flame jetted from the North African desert floor. It fed a spiraling column of dense black smoke two thousand feet high. The column rose in great clouds, widened, and dispersed, to disappear forever in the flawless desert sky. The droning sound of the vortex seemed to rumble from the bowels of the earth.

Around the base of the column the debris of an explosion littered the sand in random patterns. Close to the flame, steel structural members, melted into odd, drooping shapes, glowed in colors from white to straw to cherry red.

Through this scene a man-sized shapeless pillow of white moved awkwardly but with apparent purpose. It would waddle slowly to a distance from the flame, retrieve a box, then move to a specific point near the vortex, and place the box carefully, piling loose sand over it, then move back to retrieve still another box from a large pile of them. The boxes were placed just so. Occasionally the form would place a box, then come back to it, and move it a few feet.

The careful placement of boxes went on for an hour.

Simon stood near, but apart from members of the drilling crew that had tapped the pool of oil feeding the flame. Behind them was an assortment of earth-moving and drilling equipment, tents and Quonset huts, each with a throbbing diesel engine to run its electrical and cooling systems. Beyond the encampment, the Bradford Oil Company jet rested, gleaming white.

Now the white apparition came toward the drilling crew and raised both stumpy arms. A truck motor started somewhere. A large tanker with canvas hoses moved toward the column of smoke, followed by a smaller truck that contained additional figures in the white pillowy suits, hooded, each with one large cyclopian eisenglass eye in the middle. Awkwardly they unlimbered hoses from the tank truck and arranged themselves facing the fire.

The first white figure lumbered back toward the center of its web, where a gray box, a smaller box than those clustered near the fire, was connected to the many wires he had just arranged. The figure raised an arm.

One by one, the other figures raised their arms.

Suddenly, the first figure's arm sliced down. A torrent of water began rushing from the hoses of the tank truck and then, like lightning, there was a vivid white flash followed by an enormous, stunning *crack!* that knocked Simon to his knees.

Incredibly, the vortex of orange was gone and only the howling remained, a different pitch now, lower. Steam billowed in huge puffs, hissing around the base of the wellhead where water from the hoses hit glowing fragments of steel. The white vapor rose swiftly, overtaking the last vestiges of the black oil clouds, dispelling them. From the middle of the steam cloud a jet of ebony liquid plumed three hundred feet into the air.

Accompanied by the throbbing of many engines, heavy equipment moved forward like an armored battalion to complete the battle against the well fire.

The premier figure in white moved toward Simon and the members of the drilling crew. Several men trotted up to it and grabbed it by the head, laughing, talking. Quickly, they removed the blunt headdress to reveal a remarkable head and face, straight from an El Greco painting—a long, narrow visage with skeptical eyes. The jaw was large, the mouth hard and humorless, the nose hawklike. The head was crowned with a shock of long hair as white as the man's asbestos suit.

"Nice job, Hugo," the drilling foreman said.

"It was a *perfect* job," the man said matter-of-factly. "Get me out of this armor."

Simon followed the group into one of the air-conditioned huts, where Wolfram stripped off the asbestos gear and his sweat-soaked undergarments and put on clean white coveralls. When he was settled with a cold beer, Simon approached him.

"Mr. Wolfram. I believe you received a message about me. I'm Bernard Simon."

Wolfram quaffed beer before he replied. "Bradford sent you?"

"That's right."

"I got his message." The skeptical eyes studied Simon. "You don't look like his type."

"I'm a financial man, not an oil man." Simon smiled. "Your fireworks display out there was impressive."

"Routine."

"How did the fire start?"

"Like they all do, a blowout." His voice had a growling quality. "A well blows out when the pressure in the formation down below is greater than the pressure in the well bore. That means oil comes bubbling to the top, out of control. A spark can set it off. Often there is gas associated with the oil. That increases the potential for a fire."

"And when they have a fire, they call Firebird."

Wolfram nodded.

"Then what?"

"We follow a set of procedures that we've worked out by experience. Basically, what we do is blow the fire out, just like you'd blow out a candle. Exactly the same idea. We use high explosives. Today we used three hundred and twenty pounds. Sometimes we use less, sometimes more, depending on the flow from the well."

"It was quite a bang. It knocked me down."

Wolfram smiled. "Sorry." He sipped more beer. "That well is flowing more than thirteen hundred barrels a day. That's a lot of money to let burn up."

"How much did they lose?"

Wolfram shrugged. "It took me eight days to get my crew and equipment here. They'll continue to lose production until they recap it and they can't do that until everything has cooled down. Another twenty-four hours. In this area the wellhead cost is about a dollar and a quarter a barrel. You're a financial man. You figure the cost."

Simon said, "If you're ready, we can get going."

"Water is the critical thing. In the desert we have problems assuring that we'll have enough water to cool the steel down enough to keep it from reigniting the product."

"Your crew can handle it, can't they?"

"Sure, it's all technique. It's not just the cooling effect of the water, it's the steam from the hot metal. Blocks out the air, prevents oxidation."

"We're not going to be delayed, are we?"

"We had to calculate, almost to the pound of water, how much we would require to provide enough steam, just enough, and yet cool the metal down fast enough. We had to fly the water in."

Simon nodded without interest.

Wolfram held up his fingers. "A whole handful of variables, you see? The cost of freighting in water against the cost of lost production if there wasn't enough water. Thousands of gallons of expensive water against thousands of gallons of cheap oil. A very complicated equation."

"I'm sure," Simon murmured. "Are you trying to tell me we can't leave immediately?"

"No, just the opposite. I'm telling you why we *can* leave now. I figured the equation correctly. This fire is out." He stood up. "Let's go."

II

The corporate jet circled once around the oil camp. Snowy clouds of steam floated above the extinguished fire. The plume of oil glistened blackly like some abstract fountain.

"We'll refuel in Tangier and Miami. Then to Houston," Simon said. "Scotch?"

"Of course."

They settled back and watched the bleak North African desert unroll beneath them like soiled beige carpet. On the horizon to their right the Mediterranean was a green smear behind a screen of haze.

They flew in silence for a time. Finally, Wolfram started the conversation. "How long have you been with Bradford?"

"Something over ten years."

"You took a degree in finance?"

"No, philosophy. Then Harvard Law School. When I came out I was at loose ends, didn't want to join either a Wall Street firm or the government. So I answered an advertisement in the *Wall Street Journal:* 'unusual excitement, opportunity for the right man.' After a lot of bizarre screening and psychological testing, it turned out to be Bradford. He needed an assistant. It was as simple as that."

"Was it?"

Simon sipped Scotch before he replied. "It certainly was opportunity. I'm a senior officer in a major oil company at a relatively tender age."

"All the more unusual. You didn't come up through production or marketing," said Wolfram.

"That's right." He pondered a moment. "Actually, other things being equal, I wouldn't be where I am. It just happens that Bradford owns his company. I developed a rapport with him, a way of working. I got to know his son. My progress was as much personal relationship as it was professional skill—in fact, more so."

"I heard the news about Bradford's son. Too bad."

Simon stared out at the arid landscape thirty thousand feet below. "Some of that was ancient Carthage, Wolfram."

"Which part?"

"I don't know," he replied. "I guess that's the point of the story. Carthage is indistinguishable from the rest of the land. It's nothing."

"They butchered him, didn't they?"

"The land all looks the same from up here."

"I heard they chopped him into hamburger."

"Don't discuss that with Bradford."

"Of course not."

"Do you know Bradford?"

Wolfram looked into his glass. "Did he tell you that he knew me?"

74

"He . . . indicated that he knew you. Or, at least, he knew all about you. That would be like him, you know, to learn all about a man he hasn't met."

"Tell me what you think of him."

"I've worked so closely with him day in, day out, that I find myself identifying a great deal with him and what he's doing. He's twice my age, but in many ways we think alike."

"Were you with Bradford in 1968?"

"Yes."

"I mean, I understand he was on some other business—with another company for a time."

Simon shook his head. "I don't . . . oh, yes, he went to Montreal for six weeks." He smiled. "It was my first taste of running the company. He left me in charge. Fortunately, he also left everything running smoothly. I managed to golf every day."

"Montreal?"

Simon shrugged. "He was always vague about it. Nothing involving the oil company. Apparently, he went up there in an advisory capacity of some sort for a company belonging to a friend." He frowned. "I remember, a construction company."

Wolfram nodded slowly. "The Cosmo Construction Company?"

"Perhaps. Yes, I think that's it. Funny name."

"Is there any more Scotch?"

"Ummm." Simon refilled the glasses. "And you. How did you get in the fire business?"

"It was the classic case of filling a need. People like Bradford, they've always needed somebody who is good with fires, either to put them out or to start them."

"Surely you didn't get started as . . .?"

"A torch?"

"That's it."

Wolfram sipped slowly. "As a matter of fact, I did." He smiled at Simon's surprise. "Not to worry, though. I did it in a proper cause for Uncle Sam."

"Wartime?"

"You might say that."

They didn't speak for a time.

"Does it haunt you?" Simon broke the silence. "Fire, I mean."

"Haunt?"

"Doesn't it strike you as something that almost has a mind of its own, that wants to devour, to get loose like a wild beast and rampage?"

"In my early years it seemed that way sometimes. That was when I was young and things had a mystique about them. It's easy to imagine when you're young that the sea has a soul, or that fire is a wild beast, or that God speaks through thunder. The young believe in such things."

"You don't?"

"I believe in technique." His hard face was almost expressionless. "I know fire. I know *how* fire could destroy me, but it is nonsense to ask *why* fire would do it. There is no magic in it."

"You never want to know why?"

"Never. In fact, I have a stock response to philosophical questions: Never ask *why*, only ask *how*."

"The consummate technician," said Simon sadly.

Wolfram raised his glass. "To technique."

11

I

OIL BUILT HOUSTON. It seemed a paradox that so much metallic glitter could be extracted from stinking black petroleum.

They had spent the night at a plastic-and-wallboard motel
by the airport. Now, very early, Bradford's chauffeur drove them
along the Eastex Expressway. Thin haze and smog curtained
everything, covering the harsh, dry scenery and its raw
construction.

It was too early to talk. Both studied the bleached panorama
as they approached the BRAPCO Building. The "white" side of
Houston was a boom town. New office buildings were under construction alongside those recently built. Square miles of stainless steel and aluminum and glass siding, steel and mortar and
multicolored brick, all new, flanked the streets. There appeared
to be no end to newness.

The "black" side of town was an emerging ruin.

The limousine eased onto an expressway ramp and from there
through the shimmering reefs of new buildings. It rolled down
Dallas Avenue to Fannin, then turned right. Soon it turned again
down a long concrete lane sloping to a tunnel.

"This takes us to the parking area under the BRAPCO
Building," Simon announced.

It was like the interior of a fortification: raw concrete, steel,
iron doors, and low ceilings, all dimly lit by incandescent bulbs
in heavy wire cages. The chauffeur pulled up in front of a steel
elevator and opened the car doors for them.

"Has he come in yet, Stephen?"

"Yes, sir," the chauffeur said. "He came in very early today."

"Thank you."

The chauffeur nodded and returned to the driver's seat. The car pulled away down the long, echoing garageway. Simon pushed a button; there was the whine of cables and the clank of an approaching elevator.

Wolfram looked around, as if sizing up the mean thickness of the walls, the gauge of steel, the probable strength of the concrete mix, the bearing members.

He was dressed in an olive-colored washable suit, a pale blue shirt, and nondescript tie. Only his narrow hatchet face and shock of white hair were remarkable. His eyes were hooded, and he had complained that he hadn't had enough sleep.

"We'll head right up to his office," Simon said. "He likes an early start."

Simon pushed buttons on a panel. Doors closed softly on the garage bunkering. They rose swiftly. At the twenty-third floor the elevator stopped and the doors slid open to reveal a broad expanse of sea-foam green carpeting. Great window panels offered smoking vistas of table-flat land brightening under the new sun.

The office area was unpopulated. The widely spaced desks were devoid of papers. Office machines were tucked away inside eighteenth-century housings. It looked like a large, well-illuminated reading room where there was nothing to read.

"Who did the designing?" Wolfram inquired.

"This?" Simon seemed surprised. "A committee." He smiled. "In an oil company every nonessential decision is assigned to a committee. The theory is that a committee is the most likely way to come up with the least offensive solution."

They were at a wide brass-fitted door in the paneled wall. Simon rapped briskly and then opened it.

G. B. Bradford sat behind a wide, sparsely accoutered antique desk with his back to a huge window. His office was very large, and thickly carpeted in sea-foam green. A single leather chair of the same green faced the desk. Another leather chair was close to the nearest paneled wall. Opposite the desk, the wall framed an eighteenth-century credenza, an original. Above it hung a portrait of some earlier Bradford. The other walls were bare.

78

There were no books, no other pictures, no charts. In spite of the bright morning sun, the room seemed arid and bleak.

Bradford watched dourly as they crossed the space between them. He made no move to rise.

"G. B., I'd like you to meet . . ."

"I know him."

"It's been a long time." Wolfram said it as if it had not been long enough.

Simon was surprised. "I didn't realize you two had met. Hugo, you said . . . "

"I didn't say anything."

Bradford raised a cautioning hand. "It's all right. It makes no difference."

"Listen," Simon persisted, "if I've tramped on someone's toes, I apologize."

"Obviously, Hugo, you didn't discuss our—relationship."

"That's your prerogative." Wolfram shrugged.

"Simon, Wolfram and I first met in . . . what year was it, Hugo?"

"You know as well as I do. 1943."

"Of course. World War Two." Bradford leaned forward, elbows on his desk. "Hugo was younger then. We all were." He paused and smiled briefly. "We were both in OSS. That was about it."

"I see," Simon murmured.

"And then our paths crossed again," Bradford continued. "When was that, Hugo?"

"I forget," Wolfram said deliberately.

Bradford smiled. "That was Operation Heike."

Wolfram motioned toward Simon. "Has he been cleared? Operation Heike is still classified."

"Yes, yes, Hugo. I know." He looked at Simon. "Sorry, we can't tell you about that one. Sometime later, perhaps."

Simon remembered snatches of conversation on the plane . . . somehow it seemed that Bradford and Wolfram were members of some obscure fraternity, closing him out of their ritual.

"Well, here we all are again," said Bradford abruptly.

Wolfram said nothing.

Bradford's synthetic smile faded. "I can't inoculate you with enthusiasm, can I, Hugo?"

"Enthusiasm is some guy with plastic teeth pushing gelatin desserts."

"Are things going well with you, Hugo?"

"Exceptionally." He nodded at Simon. "Your man here caught me on the crest of a fifty-thousand-dollar wave. That was the net collection for dousing that Libyan fire. My company has more like it lined up, one—two—three."

"I'd like to interest you in a little project of mine."

"I'm a businessman, G.B. You have at least a fair idea of my rate schedule. What's the project?"

"This is a special project."

"They all are."

"This one will require very special skills. In fact, the job may be impossible."

Wolfram's eyes narrowed. "I'll be better able to decide that when I hear the details." He glanced at Simon. "Does this job require a clearance?"

"For this project he *is* cleared. However—except for you, of course—we will not want anyone to know for whom he is working or why."

"Who would I be working for?"

Bradford smiled. "Me, of course."

Wolfram studied him for several minutes. With the sun behind Bradford, it was difficult to tell what was in his eyes. But Wolfram knew that any project managed by Bradford would have one critical hallmark—there would be no skimping on material or funding. He was intrigued. "What part of the world are we talking about?"

"South America."

"This is a project related to your son?"

"Perhaps."

"In Malaverde?"

"Perhaps."

"Why are we playing twenty questions?"

"You haven't agreed to do the job."

"How can I agree or disagree? I don't know what it is."

"Goddamn it, Wolfram," said Bradford, suddenly angry, "have I ever conned you?"

Wolfram shook his head.

"Then why, for Christ's sake, can't you just say yes or no?"

"All right," snapped Wolfram. "I'll say yes. Maybe. But I still have to know what the job is."

Bradford relaxed and leaned back in his chair. "Thank you." He sat silent for a moment, then said, "Remember your Shakespeare, Hugo?"

"No."

"Then I'll remind you of a line from *Romeo and Juliet:*

"One fire burns out another's burning.

One pain is lessened by another's anguish."

"You mean 'an eye for an eye.'"

"That's about it."

"Then we are talking about your son. I was sorry to read about it. And they gobbled up your property down there, too."

"Now you have the motive and the place."

"Revenge." Wolfram savored the word, as if it were the first time he had said it.

"Does it trouble you?"

Wolfram glanced at him and laughed. "My God, Bradford, it would be the first purely human motive that I have ever operated for. Everything I have done professionally—every military job, every agency job, every commercial job—all have been for *mechanical* motives." He laughed. "I'm fascinated! I've blown up trains, sunk ships, blasted oil operations, and not once was there a hint that the job had some direct human affiliation."

"People got killed," Bradford said quietly.

"People got killed," Wolfram conceded, "but that was because they were in the way of the job. Their deaths were incidental, just like you might step on an ant walking to the store."

"Would the change in perspective, the human motive instead of the—as you say—mechanical motive, change your perspective?"

Wolfram was thoughtful. "Perspective is one of those vague words like 'overview' and 'conceptual.' I'm really quite disappointed to hear that you have drifted into that kind of flabby language, G. B. It's not like you. But then it's not like you to build a job around a human motive, is it?"

"World War Two was scarcely a humanistic endeavor, Hugo."

"But BRAPCO's oil operations in Malaverde were?"

"That's not fair, Wolfram," Simon interjected. "It was his son. It was my friend. What stronger motive could there be?"

"Hugo is a technician, Simon, and frankly, I didn't invite him here to cry with us about our loss."

Wolfram smiled sardonically. "You're the man who made me what I am today, G. B. The callow youth of yesteryear transformed into the mechanical man of today."

"That's nonsense. You were born a technician. All you needed was the training. You were like a good steel knife that only required to be honed for cutting."

Wolfram nodded. "Sometimes I wonder if I've missed something by being so good at what I do."

"Perhaps you've missed being human," said Simon.

Wolfram rubbed his chin. "Perhaps." He said it with faint amusement. "G. B., you asked whether this so-called human motive would change my perspective on doing a job. I'll give you a technician's answer.

"First, my expertise is useful only against property, not people. If you want to kill a man—say, the man who killed your son—get someone else. If you want to kill lots of people, hire lots of assassins. Hire an army. They can be gotten easily these days.

"Second, assuming this *is* a mission against property, there is the matter of authorized covert operations versus unauthorized covert operations. As you know, the latter are far more costly, far trickier. If this revenge thing is your personal approach, you have to remind youself that it could cost millions."

"The money?" Bradford asked. "You never seemed concerned about it before."

Wolfram took a slow, deep breath. "One has to face the facts, Bradford. Or at least ask the questions. Can you implement a cash flow like that without having government auditors ask embarrassing questions? And can you keep me insulated from exposure?"

Bradford nodded. "I'll answer your questions in the same order. One, we have the cash. Sure, we took a great loss in Malaverde, but it was plant that virtually all had been paid for. Meanwhile, we made gains elsewhere. Two, implementation. We have reactivated the Cosmo Construction Company of Montreal, and that also covers your third question. You can install all the insulation you require."

"Cosmo? But isn't that . . .?"

Bradford interrupted. "There is a temporary arrangement. A personal favor to me, a repayment, more or less."

Wolfram snorted. "That's good enough for me. I know where the money is."

Simon looked from one to the other. "What the hell are you talking about? I sit here listening, but it's like hearing a foreign language."

"It's an arrangement, Simon, a very special arrangement."

"If I'm to be of any use to this project, I must have all the pertinent information."

"This isn't the corporate decision-making process," said Wolfram. "We're not playing the Harvard marketing game."

"Easy, Wolfram, easy." Bradford turned to Simon. "What Hugo is saying, Simon, is that we are planning to carry out a very different kind of program. Essentially, it is a clandestine operation of the type, in many respects, that Hugo and I participated in for the government.

"Consequently, we must employ fundamentally different techniques. Information and communication in this kind of operation are almost exactly the opposite of a corporate staff operation. In this case it is imperative that as few of us as possible know details that don't directly concern us. Our communications must be circuitous instead of direct."

"But where does this construction company fit?" Simon asked. "Whose company is it? Shouldn't I be briefed on these things?"

Wolfram snorted. "My God, you fairly reek of amateurism."

"Do I? Hell, I don't have enough information to know whether I should even be in this room."

The other two watched him for a time. He shrugged helplessly.

"Well," said Bradford a moment later. "Well, we know where we stand. As a matter of fact, Wolfram—as I told Simon before, I think—he will have no direct hand in this at all."

Wolfram laughed shortly but said nothing.

"His function, really, will be to help *me*. As far as you are concerned, he will see to it that any and all information you might require about the company—the size and nature of facilities, for example—is provided. In addition, should something happen to me, he will act in my place. He may handle other details."

Wolfram exhaled noisily. "G. B., I hate to belabor the point, but you have not yet told me what the target is, where it is, when it is to be hit, and so on."

"I know, and there is a reason. I don't know what the target is, not precisely. I only know what I want to accomplish."

"You'd better explain," said Wolfram. "All of it."

Bradford pressed his palms together. "There are several key elements. Initially, there are two men: DePrundis, an international economic menace, and Jaime Mercado y Suarez, the murderer of my son.

"Then there are two broad sectors of operations: the former BRAPCO oil properties in Malaverde and the Government of Malaverde itself. DePrundis controls the former; Mercado controls the latter.

"Finally," he meshed his fingers, "these components fit together into an economic whole. What interests me is destroying the power of those two men. I want to wipe them out. I mean it, Wolfram."

"You mean economically?"

Bradford shrugged. "Fundamentally, yes, but if either or both of them get in the way, like your ants, then that's all the better. However, they are incidental to the main objective."

Wolfram was nodding his head. "DePrundis," he said. "How well we know that name."

Wolfram's and Bradford's eyes met, and once again Simon felt like an outsider. They sat like that for a time. Finally Bradford said, "Hugo, what I want is a devastating solution. *Delenda est Carthago.*"

"Meaning?"

"Meaning economic murder. Meaning that economic murder is as old as Cato, two centuries before Christ. Cato ended every speech he made with the line 'Carthage must be destroyed.' Eventually it was. Not the people, the economy."

Wolfram smiled. "The Romans really belonged in the twentieth century, didn't they? Damned fine technicians. They didn't do much for the soul, but a lot of their buildings are still standing. And Carthage? Not a rock."

"I want a Carthaginian solution, Hugo."

Wolfram stood up slowly. "Agreed. Under the circumstances

it will be my pleasure. You should have dropped the DePrundis name earlier."

"One more thing . . . "

"What's that?"

"This . . . Carthaginian solution. It must look like an accident. A massive, devastating accident."

Wolfram studied him for a long time. Then he said, "That's very difficult to bring off."

"You did it with Operation *Heike*."

"That was one ship in one place, not a whole economic complex."

"Didn't you tell me once that complex things are the easiest to wreck?"

"Possibly. But I would have been referring to a machine, a key component."

"An oil economy is nothing more than an immense machine."

"And if it can't be made to look like an accident? Suppose I figure a way to jam this economy, but it would be something overt. What then?"

"Try the accident approach first. If it simply can't be done, we'll work on something else."

"I can't draw up a proposal until I have a lot of information—details, thousands of them. I need to know *how*."

12

LATER WOLFRAM AND Simon met in the BRAPCO board room, a large chamber without windows. The paneling of the walls, the color and depth of the carpet, the square yards of rosewood table, the thick, padded cowhide of the roomy swivel chairs, created the impression of power.

At the far end of the table from where Wolfram and Simon sat in leather chairs, a wall screen had been revealed from behind a sliding wood panel. Between the two men was a black slide projector with a round magazine, a chrome decanter of coffee, and china cups. At Simon's right hand there were three dark-blue leather folders, with "Malaverde" printed in gold on the cover of each. Wolfram held a yellow legal pad.

"If you'll turn down the lights, Hugo, we'll proceed." Simon switched on the projector.

"The arrangement of these slides is roughly chronological from the inception of our operation in Malaverde eight years ago through our channel-deepening project completed just two months ago. All these pictures were taken by us either for record purposes or for use in our annual and quarterly reports."

The first slide clicked into place. "This is an overview of the harbor taken from a plane about 5,000 feet directly above the airport. We are looking east toward the city of Malanueva. Between us and the city you can see the Rio Paraná. The harbor, of course, is on the left. At the time this picture was taken, neither the pipeline nor our refinery had been built."

The projector clicked again and Simon described the initial exploration and discovery of oil in the Gran Matto. Pictures of one, then three, then dozens of oil derricks, appeared on the screen.

"Tell me about the wells," said Wolfram. "What kind of wells, what kind of oil, the formations."

Simon fumbled in his blue-covered folders, then found the papers he was looking for. "The field you see in this picture was developed from discovery well G4–101. It tested at 33,000 barrels per day."

"That's awfully high for a South American formation," Wolfram observed.

"Of course. A typical South American well produces only in the neighborhood of 300 to 350 per day," Simon said. "Actually, this well tested a pattern more typical of Libya. As you can imagine when we got into production, as you see it in this picture, our typical well was producing at a rate of something less than 20,000 barrels a day. Still awfully good. The oil is good grade, 35 degrees gravity. Low sulfur."

"How deep?"

"This field came in a range of 600 feet in the pay section at a depth of 9,300 to 9,900 feet."

"What are the reserves of the field?"

"Our best estimate, counting the most recent test wells, is that our Malaverde fields have about 1.5 billion barrels," Simon said.

"Let's move away from the fields," Wolfram murmured, making some notes on his pad.

"Naturally, we had to get our oil from the field to a port facility. The distance to oil port facilities in Venezuela was prohibitive, though we did consider that." A slide clicked into place. "Instead, we did this." The picture showed teams of laborers digging trenches, surrounded by piles of rust-red tubing. "We built a 40-inch pipeline extending 111 miles to Malaverde's principal city, Malanueva. This line cost us about a half-million dollars a mile, in place. When our operations were taken over by Mercado and company, we were producing about 200,000 barrels a day from our operating field. Actually, the line is capable of handling up to 850,000 barrels per day."

"Why all the extra capacity?"

"Eventually, we anticipated bringing new fields on stream. We never got the chance."

"So the pipeline cost upwards of fifty-five million dollars."

"That's correct."

"If the pipeline were destroyed, how long would it take to replace it?"

Simon stammered. "That depends on a lot of things."

"Jesus!" snapped Wolfram. "That's my whole point in trying to get information, isn't it? *Everything* depends on a lot of things."

"All right. Let's say the pipeline was destroyed, every yard of it . . ."

"That's possible," Wolfram muttered.

". . . it would take more than seven months to build a new one."

"Seven months using what kind of equipment and labor?"

"American, of course," said Simon defensively. "American equipment and operators. Native hand labor."

"Native skilled labor could *not* do it in seven months?"

"Definitely not. There's another thing, however." Simon smiled coolly.

"What's that?"

"The pipeline material itself. Tubing, pumps, valves. The whole thing. There is always a substantial lag between ordering and delivery. Sometimes it can run to months."

"What would be your best guess?"

"With DePrundis ships for transport, it shouldn't take more than a month."

Wolfram nodded and made some notes.

"Naturally, a pipeline goes somewhere." Simon was back into the board-presentation style. "This is where it goes." Another aerial view from the same position as the first one flashed onto the screen. This time, however, there was a mass of something in the foreground that looked like snarled fishline. "You can see the pipeline runs in from the right. It passes underground for a distance, reemerges, and goes into the port of the refinery."

"Why does it go underground for a distance? It looks to be about a mile."

"It is scarcely noticeable from the altitude of this picture, but there is a low ridge there." He walked to the screen and indicated the ridge with a pointer. "At the time it seemed more feasible to have the pipeline continue on a downgrade toward the harbor, here, than to construct additional pumping facilities on the ridge. So we just chopped through the ridge. The ridge isn't even a hundred feet high there and mostly sand and loose rock. It was a relatively easy job."

"Do you have any closer picture of the terminus of the pipeline?"

Simon clicked ahead through slides until he found one showing a thick round pipe approaching the foreground where it suddenly split into four smaller pipes, each with its own valve. "This is the initial terminus. Here we can regulate the direction of the crude. We can either divert it all into harbor loading facilities or divert all or part of it into crude storage tanks. The tanks can service either ships or our refinery."

"Show me the tanks."

Rapid images of pipes and sand flicked by, until an aerial view came on showing an oil-tank farm. "Twelve 600,000-barrel tanks." Wolfram scribbled notes as Simon recited more facts. "Each tank is 260 feet in diameter and 65 feet high."

"What kind of top?"

"A floating roof." Simon was startled that Wolfram would ask such an obscure technical question. "The unloading rate from these facilities is about 120,000 barrels per hour."

Wolfram stared intently at the picture of the tanks. "Do you have a close-up of that loading facility?"

Slides clicked by until Simon found the one he wanted.

"What is the arrangement here?" Wolfram asked.

Simon walked to the screen again. "The offshore terminal—here—is 600 feet out. The channel there originally was 50 feet, but we dredged it deeper and widened it."

"How deep?"

Simon referred to his notes. "Sixty-five feet."

"Is that measured at mean low water?"

Another referral. "That's correct. Also," he added, "that is the shallowest point in the entire channel. At the harbor entrance, the channel is a natural 75 feet as a result of strong tides. However, the channel is rather narrow everywhere. There is only a usable 250 feet."

"What size ships can be accommodated?"

"The biggest handled under our management was 200,000 tons," Simon said. "However, I understand that DePrundis has four or five tankers in the 250,000-ton range."

"They could use the harbor?"

"Yes. However, not under their own power."

"How do they get in?"

"A pilot would bring them into the lower harbor, that is, the north, where they are picked up by heavy-duty tugboats and pulled into place like big barges. When they're full, they are towed out of the harbor."

"How do they turn around?"

"They don't." He pointed. "The ships are brought more or less around the rim of the harbor, following the channel, in a counterclockwise direction. When they leave, they continue moving counterclockwise until they come into the ocean channel heading out."

"It sounds tricky."

"Not really," said Simon. "There is a system. Since the oil ships are virtually the only craft that go into Malanueva, except for an occasional tramper, there aren't any serious complications."

"Would you say that the harbor is vulnerable?"

"You mean to destruction?"

"Something like that."

Simon stared helplessly at the projected picture. "I don't know," he said. "I hadn't thought about it." He laughed mirthlessly. "You know, Wolfram, some of us get so used to solving problems by *making* something, it is virtually impossible for us to think of solving a problem by *destroying* something."

Wolfram nodded. "I've run into the syndrome before. It can be fatal."

II

It was mid-morning.

Wolfram wanted to know how much oil the pipeline held.

"It took about 800,000 barrels," Simon replied. "That would be a full day's capacity, if we tapped other fields."

"Tell me about the pumping arrangements."

90

Simon found a slide showing a silvery corrugated metal building in a yellow desert landscape. The pipeline ran to it and from it. "This is a 10,000-horsepower pumping station," he said. "We were planning another one, again contingent on tapping new fields."

Wolfram stared at the picture. "Very vulnerable," he muttered. He made more notes.

"Well," Simon continued, "that leaves us with the refinery itself."

What had appeared in an earlier picture as snarled string was brought into closer focus. Now it looked like tangled cable interspersed with vertical shapes like elongated tea kettles.

"We are—or *were*—very proud of this refinery."

"Why was it located there in Malaverde?" Wolfram asked. "Isn't crude usually brought to the refinery closer to the market?"

"Generally, yes. Several factors dictated our decision to locate it at the harbor. The first was marketing. The production from this area was sold mainly abroad because of the rather stringent U.S. import quota restrictions.

"Then, of course, this way we could ship finished products directly to foreign markets without having to go through the process of off-loading crude, refining it, and then transshipping it somewhere else. It was very profitable."

"Until now," said Wolfram. "Let's hear about it."

"This is a refinery with a capacity of 100,000 barrels a day. The plant covers 155 acres, not counting the tank farm you saw earlier. The main processing units consist of atmospheric and vacuum distillation units for crude. There is also a catalytic reforming unit for the production of high-octane gasolines, a catalytic desulfurization unit, and gas-recovery facilities for the production of liquid petroleum gas."

"Your refinery capacity is smaller than the output from the fields. How come?"

"First, we were handling an increasing direct demand for our crude, since our production was low in sulfur content. Second, we intended to expand the facility when we brought the other fields on stream. In fact, plans were in the works."

"I'd like to know some of the details of those plans. Will you get me the engineer's proposal?"

"Certainly."

Wolfram poured himself coffee. "You haven't talked about communications. How are they conducted between, say, the field and the port, or between the pumping station and the port?"

Simon referred to one of the blue folders. "There is a regular telephone-line system connecting all the facilities in the harbor area. The line follows the pipeline to a point about twenty miles out, where there is a station that converts the line signals to radio signals, which can be received easily at the field or at exploration sites. And the signals come back by radio the other way for communication with the port."

"Is it a standard radio-telephone linkage?"

Simon shrugged. "I can't give you an authoritative answer. However, I suppose it is. We have a policy of getting standard equipment wherever we can for maintenance reasons, particularly in the remote areas."

"I'll want the precise specifications of that system."

"Right." Simon made a note.

"Have we covered all of it?"

"I think so, but let's finish these slides in case something comes up."

The screen changed rapidly. Tubes and towers and ships connected by rubber umbilical cords to shore, valves with heavy steel wheels on top, tanks—the peglike ones for oil and balloon-shaped ones for gas—and intricate webs of pipe.

"Wait!"

"What is it?"

"In the background. Is that a helicopter with the company logo?"

"Yes, of course. It's virtually standard around oil operations these days."

"What kind?"

"I don't know."

"Find out."

Simon nodded and made another note. Then he flicked through the remaining slides. "That's it," he said.

"Go back two slides," said Wolfram.

A picture of the offshore lines and the edge of the harbor appeared. In the foreground there were buildings and a long pier.

"What is that pier for?"

Simon scrutinized the picture. "That pier was constructed when the refinery was being built. The buildings are warehouse facilities."

"Can it handle an oceangoing ship?"

"Oh, yes. We dredged up close to the harbor edge when we put the pier in. It is—or was—used for unloading equipment. In fact, all of the equipment for our last test well was unloaded there and trucked into the Gran Matto."

"How large a ship can it handle?"

Simon pursed his lips. "It definitely could not handle one of the giant tankers. However, I have seen smaller tankers in there. As you can see, down the edge of the pier, there is a pipeline. We can employ that if we choose to. And, indeed, we have."

"What would you say is the biggest ship that pier could handle?"

Simon shrugged. "I'm not that up on ships. However, when the U.S. Government was building the superhighway between Malanueva and the *airport*, they unloaded something like 40,000 tons of cement from one ship."

"That's fine. Just fine." Wolfram scribbled another note, then stood up and turned on the lights. "How much did that oil refinery cost to build?"

"Slightly more than 104 million dollars."

"And how long did it take to build?"

"The initial construction from contract to production took more than a year," Simon said. "It has been expanded since then."

"I need a good naval chart of the Malanueva harbor," Wolfram said softly. "Then I need those other things that I mentioned, and time. I'll want this tray of slides and the use of this room the rest of today and tomorrow. Book me a hotel room."

"Anything else?"

Wolfram looked around the boardroom absently, as if there might be something tucked away and forgotten. "Make an appointment with Bradford. Day after tomorrow. Right here at 10:00 A.M."

"You're sure, Wolfram? You're absolutely sure?"

Wolfram's eyes focused on him. He laughed abruptly. "I'm sure, Simon. I know *how*."

13

THEY WERE AT THE boardroom at precisely 10:00 A.M. The rosewood double doors were closed. Simon knocked softly and Wolfram invited them to enter.

The long room was arranged as if for a review of middle-management marketing problems. The movie screen was exposed. To the right of it stood a large easel covered by a red cloth.

At one end of the table the slide projector was in place. Its circular magazine held perhaps a dozen slides. A long remote-operation cord snaked to the screen end of the room. Wolfram stood behind a wooden lectern to the left of the viewing screen.

"Please, sit where I've placed the background papers."

Bradford and Simon sat down at the designated places.

"The trick," said Wolfram, moving around the lectern to reach for his coffee cup, "is not just to blow something up willy-nilly." He smiled at them. "Anybody can cause an explosion. The trick is to make your explosion do exactly what you want it to do."

He lifted his cup.

There was a sharp crack. Wolfram's saucer sailed into the wall and smashed. "It takes talent to blast the saucer from beneath a cup." He sipped coffee.

"We recognize your expertise," Bradford said dryly. "Let's get on with it."

Wolfram nodded. "Pardon the histrionics. They are germane to my lecture."

Wolfram leaned on his lectern. "To men who build things—like

94

the two of you—men who destroy things—like me—are a suspect lot. Contrived construction requires thought, planning, and skill in implementation. We want to do so much and no more. Now we'll get on with it." Briskly he moved to the easel and threw back the covering sheet. In heavy black lettering he had written the words "TARGET" and ACCIDENT."

"There are two key problem areas we must examine in evaluating this mission, and they are interconnected." He indicated the top word with the pointer.

"The target in this assignment is the cornerstone of the economy of a small nation.

"The key problem is that our mission must be implemented in such a way as to appear to be an accident."

He flipped another page. There were a number of words arranged under the heading "TARGETS." "In the broadest sense we could say that *the* target is the oil company: Petrol/Malverde. But, as both of you know, an oil company is a microcosm of the whole industrial economy. Unlike most other basic industries, oil companies tend to have integrated functions all the way from exploration for their basic raw materials to complex consumer products."

Wolfram tapped his pointer on the easel display. "The more sharply defined operation is the more attractive target, because one or several of its elements represent a greater proportionate impact on the whole. An oil complex, on the other hand, is a series of interconnected targets that, with one exception, are not necessarily interdependent."

"I don't agree," said Simon impatiently.

Wolfram smiled. "Let's go through the list on the display here." There were four words under TARGETS. "Exploration? You could wipe BRAPCO's exploration operations off the map today and you could replace them, or hire an independent agency, tomorrow.

"Production? You can buy all the crude you want on the world markets.

"Distribution? Tankers, train equipment, trucks—even planes—all readily replaceable.

"Marketing? There are companies, big names in the field, that do little more than refine and sell. And so on."

"All right," Simon conceded. "They're not necessarily interdependent. But profitability suffers in direct proportion to the limits on integration."

"You put your finger on an important word, Simon. Profit. It is precisely what we want to expunge on this mission. We want *negative* results.

"As we go over this set of words, we recognize that almost any single element can be destroyed and the economy will survive. I emphasize the word *almost*. Moreover, not one of these functions could be attacked in any meaningful way without its being readily apparent that the attack was contrived. We could create sporadic 'accidents' here and there. But they wouldn't *do* much.

"That leaves us only one area that I haven't discussed—manufacturing. Specifically, the harbor refinery. That refinery is the heart of the Petrol/Malaverde oil economy. If you stop it, you interdict the flow of crude from the fields and cut off the supply of refined product abroad."

Bradford poured himself coffee from the decanter. "You just don't go in and place a dynamite charge in a refinery and destroy the whole thing, Hugo. A refinery doesn't explode like a can of gasoline. There are all kinds of cutoffs and valves and bypasses, not to mention a wide range of firefighting and safety mechanisms."

Wolfram flipped another page on the easel. "What I have in mind is this." The word "BOMB" was printed huge and black.

Bradford and Simon regarded him suspiciously. He stared back triumphantly.

"A blockbuster, you say?" Simon was sarcastic. "Hell, ten blockbusters would scarcely dent that refinery! Besides, it would be so obvious! Or are you contemplating a fleet of BRAPCO B-52s? Nothing overt, of course."

Wolfram studied them a moment. "A bomb, gentlemen, does not have to be something in a cigar-shaped metal cylinder with fins. Nor does it have to be a plain leather suitcase filled with plastique."

"Just what *do* you have in mind, Hugo?" Bradford asked.

"I have in mind a device of 40,000 tons of explosives." He turned another sheet on the easel. "FORTY THOUSAND TONS OF EXPLOSIVES WILL DESTROY *EVERYTHING* WITHIN A ONE-MILE DIAMETER."

"Jesus!" Simon blurted. "He's talking about an atomic bomb!"

"Even if my financial resources allowed it, Hugo, I most certainly do not have access to that kind of policy weapon."

"Who said anything about atomic devices? I'm talking about more or less . . . conventional explosives."

"Conventional!" Simon responded. "What the hell is conventional about putting 40,000 tons of explosives on the doorstep of a refinery?"

Wolfram was enjoying himself. "The actual amount of material I have in mind, as we conventionally measure it, would be equivalent to approximately 17,000 tons of TNT." He smiled. "Or, to put it another way, the equivalent of ten to twelve tactical atomic warheads."

"He's serious!" Simon exclaimed.

Bradford was morose. "There's no way, Hugo. I can see no way."

Wolfram brandished his pointer. "On the contrary. Not only is there a way, but the technique has been demonstrated. I might add that it was demonstrated *accidentally*."

"Demonstrated?"

"That's what I said. A bomb similar to the one I contemplate—but smaller, only about 20 percent the size—actually was detonated to perfection."

"How?"

"It will all be in my detailed report, if we proceed. Suffice it to say that it can be done." Wolfram referred to some notes. "I calculate, conservatively, that the bomb I contemplate would obliterate the refinery and everything within one mile of it. It probably would sink every ship in the harbor within two miles, or set them on fire." He looked up. "Part of my plan includes making sure that the harbor is full of shipping. Thus, we strike at transportation, too."

"What about casualties?" Simon interjected.

"Minimal," Wolfram said blandly.

"How can you say that? A major blast will kill hundreds—scores at the refinery alone." He turned to Bradford. "You said there wouldn't be any heavy casualties. It was part of the specifications, wasn't it?"

Wolfram shook his head emphatically. "Let's look at the target. Will you dim the lights, Simon?"

The first slide showed the aerial view of the refinery from

a mile up with the Rio Parana beyond it and the city beyond that. "The river, here, is slightly over a mile from our explosion area."

"Is that housing—those buildings on this side of the river?"

"According to the charts and maps Simon provided for me, those buildings are the barracks of the Malaverde Navy. The piers by those buildings accommodate naval vessels. You can see two vessels at the docks." Wolfram squinted at the picture. "The BRAPCO files indicate that Malverde has three old U.S. corvettes and a half dozen or so launches.

"The part of Malanueva City that is within the two-mile limit is the downtown area that includes the central park, the government palace, the prison, the opera house, and a variety of office buildings."

"There would be a lot of people in them, wouldn't there?" Simon pursued.

"We can time the blast when there wouldn't be," Wolfram replied. "We could trigger it at night, during siesta, on a Saturday afternoon when everyone goes to the beach, on Sunday. Whatever is suitable."

"And the crews of the ships?"

Wolfram smiled cryptically. "I have a plan for that. The crews probably will not be on board."

"You mean to tell us you can get a gigantic bomb, do the appropriate job, and not kill a great many people?" Bradford sounded unconvinced.

Wolfram nodded. "It sounds far more complicated than it is." He held up his fingers. "One, there is the bomb. Two, there is the timing. Three, there is the scope."

"Scope?"

"The size of the bomb and what peripheral targets we will attempt to include within the blast area."

"Such as?"

"Shipping, bridges, the pipeline. A number of possibilities. For example, the airport is slightly more than two miles from the refinery. Would we want to rearrange our actual blast site farther away from the city toward the airport and wreck it?" He smiled. "Extras."

"How would you make this bomb?" Simon asked.

"I'll tell you all about it in due course, as I said before."

"And you can do all of this covertly—as an accident?" Bradford asked.

"You should know, G.B., that I have done such jobs, such accidental jobs. You more than anybody else should know."

Bradford nodded.

"As I indicated before, this will be costly."

"We can handle it," Bradford murmured.

"I will also have to make extensive use of Cosmo Construction."

There was that name again. Simon shifted uncomfortably in his chair.

"Cosmo is at your service," said Bradford.

"You're giving me the green light?"

"Tentatively."

"It can't be tentative," Wolfram said. "I have to know definitely."

"Hugo, how much *is* this going to cost?" Bradford wanted to know.

Wolfram shrugged. "I'll have to develop a bill of particulars. Roughly, I would say about three million, give or take fifteen percent."

"What would be the biggest area of expense?"

"The explosives, of course. Dynamite runs around thirty cents a pound. A ton would cost something like six hundred dollars."

Bradford winced. "And forty kilo tons, then, would cost"— he paused to calculate—"eighteen million dollars." His eyes narrowed. "Where did you get a figure of three million?"

Wolfram smiled. "Sorry to frighten you, G.B. Actually, the material I would use would cost about ten percent of that."

"But that much explosive," Simon injected. "Wouldn't it be easily traceable?"

Wolfram was getting irritated. "I said it can be done. I know *how* to do it. The plan is here." He tapped his temple with a forefinger. "If you want me to go so far as put it down in a prospectus, I want a definite commitment from you that we'll go ahead with the plan."

"You want a contract, Hugo? From me?"

"Your word is good enough."

Simon exploded. "I think it's insane!" He turned imploringly to Bradford. "Let's scratch the whole idea. Even if it worked—and that's a big if—we are on dangerous ground. It could boomerang horribly."

"There is no if about its working," Wolfram growled. "And the tracks will be covered. Your hides will be safe."

"That attitude is uncalled for," Bradford declared.

"Sorry," said Wolfram.

Bradford sat silently with his chin cupped in his hand. Finally, he asked, "Would a smaller blast be effective?"

Wolfram nodded slowly. "We could devise a smaller blast, say, half the size. It might wreck the refinery, but ships in the harbor would probably escape. You did say, however, that you wanted a Carthaginian solution. Are you hedging now?"

Bradford shook his head. "No. Just asking. You're right. If we do this job at all, it must be shattering." He paused, then spoke again. "From that perspective, wouldn't a larger blast be still more effective?"

"Not significantly. In dealing with explosive force there is an optimum effect in each case. Increasing or decreasing the amount of blast usually does not provide a proportionate effect in terms of damage."

"I don't understand." Simon was still annoyed.

"It's simple," said Wolfram. "Blast is a three-dimensional rapid expansion of gases, a release of energy. However, we employ a large-scale blast on what is fundamentally a two-dimensional plane." He paused momentarily. "In other words, to double the effective area of a blast, one would have to use eight times the amount of explosive. For this . . . exercise . . . I based my calculations on a one-mile diameter of total effectiveness."

Bradford saw the point. "Suppose, then, the explosion occurs. What keeps them from repairing, say, the pipeline terminals in a few weeks and pumping crude for sale to other refineries?"

"A harbor full of sunken ships."

"How long would it take to clear out the wrecks?"

"Perhaps a year. It would depend on how many ships were in the harbor. Let me show you something." He flicked through various slides until he found an aerial view of the Malanueva region taken from a very high elevation. "In this picture you can see the ship channel very clearly. It is the thin, dark stripe of water going around the harbor."

"That is about the only real weakness in that facility," Bradford observed. "Navigation."

"Right," Wolfram replied. "There is no ship-mooring area, no parking lot, if you will. All the cars have to park in the street."

"So?"

"So all the wrecks will be in the channel. Every scrap of wreckage would have to be cleared before one tanker could use that facility."

Bradford shook his head. "Ingenious."

"The effect would be very fiscal," said Wolfram, significantly.

Bradford looked at him sharply. "It would, wouldn't it? And very monetary, too, wouldn't you say?"

"The Malaverde escudo wouldn't be worth a cent."

"It is scarcely worth that now," Simon observed.

Bradford cupped his chin in his hand. Wolfram stood immobile beside the easel.

After what seemed a very long time, Bradford said, "All right. We're going in."

14

I

THEY WERE ENGROSSED in the mechanics of obliteration.
They continued to use the boardroom. Wolfram seemed to like
the absence of windows and the relative seclusion. He bent over
a special folder labeled "Cosmo Construction." From time to
time he would ask Simon to lower the lights and silently switch
on the projector, select a slide—usually an aerial view of the
harbor and the refinery—and stare at it thoughtfully.

Occasionally, he would ask Simon to secure certain documents,
charts, or engineering drawings. A copy of *Lloyd's Register*,
several chemistry reference works, or an almanac.

Most of the time Simon sat watching. On demand he would
secure the required texts or order sandwiches. Occasionally, he
would answer a question.

"Do tourists visit this Castel Mala shown on the map at the
mouth of the harbor?"

"No."

"Are people allowed to go there?"

"It's used by the Malaverde Coast Guard. The harbor pilots
quarter there and run in and out in a launch to pick up ships
entering the harbor. There's also some kind of garrison. Customs,
I suppose."

"Can visitors go there? Could they have free access to, say,
the channel at that point?"

"There's some kind of filthy public beach there by the channel. It's not used much because of fear of sharks. Also, the currents are fairly strong on the change of tides."

At another point Wolfram asked, "Is the bridge across the Rio Paraná from Malanueva to the refinery a suspension span?"

"There's only one bridge," Simon said. "A drawbridge that carries the road to the refinery. The same route serves the airport further out."

"A double-span drawbridge?"

"What do you mean?"

"Do two sections go up?"

"No, only one. It's an antique."

"Seems to be a bottleneck," Wolfram observed.

"Unless one goes by fast launch, there's no other way to get to either the airport or the refinery from Malanueva."

The afternoon wore on. At 4:00 P.M. Wolfram looked up suddenly and said, "All right, Simon, we're ready."

"From all this you've extracted something . . . fiscal?"

Wolfram stared at him. "You don't know what that means, do you?"

"Not the way you and Bradford use it."

"Perhaps some day he'll explain it to you."

"When do you want to see him?"

"Now."

Simon glanced at his wristwatch. "Out of the question. Bradford leaves at precisely 3:30 P.M. He's been gone nearly an hour."

"Where does he go?"

"A round of golf at his club. Dinner there, usually with friends, then early to bed."

Wolfram's expression didn't change. "No matter."

"Tomorrow morning all right?"

"Of course. Make it here. Ten o'clock."

Simon glanced at his wristwatch again. "May I take you to dinner?"

"No. I need my beauty sleep." Wolfram's face crinkled into a smile.

"Wolfram," Simon said softly.

"Yes?"

"No more exploding saucers, if you please."

II

The next morning Bradford and Simon were on time. Everything was just as it had been before: projector, screen, easel, lectern, coffee cups and saucers. There were yellow pads and pencils for making notes.

Wolfram wore a dark-blue suit, red tie and, in his breast pocket, a coordinated handkerchief. He looked like a Vice President for Marketing.

Bradford sat down carefully and poured himself a cup of coffee. "All right, Hugo."

Wolfram extracted from his suit pocket a plastic sandwich bag filled with some powdery material. "I promised Simon no more exploding saucers. I did not promise to leave my explosives behind." He emptied the bag on the table in front of them. The contents were grayish, crystalline grains, like coarse sand. "This is the way we'll complete the mission."

Bradford picked up one of the pencils and poked the pile of material. "What is it?"

Wolfram's smile was broader than usual. "That, gentlemen, is plain old garden-variety chemical fertilizer."

"Fertilizer?" Bradford was momentarily puzzled. Then his brow lifted in recognition. "I get it. You call it fertilizer, but it is actually explosive."

"We do both, G.B." He walked back to his lectern.

"You see, gentlemen, Simon touched on a very important point at our previous seminar. An individual, a company, cannot just go out and buy up, say, 40,000 tons of some explosive and have it go unnoticed." He paused. "Consequently, we intend to purchase 40,000 tons of ordinary materials on open markets. The world won't notice. At least not that part of the world that watches commerce and worries about things.

"The material we will purchase above board and consign openly to the Cosmo Construction Company Agricultural Project for delivery in Malanueva harbor is," he pointed at the tiny pile of chemicals on the table, "fertilizer."

104

Bradford shook his head. "You mean you substitute explosives later for the fertilizer?"

"Of course not. That would mean acquiring 40,000 tons of explosives and we would have the problem all over again." Wolfram enjoyed being mysterious. "Besides, this must be a bona fide accident."

Simon disliked being made to seem the fool. "Get to the point, Hugo! How do we acquire a shipload of explosives and what do we do with 40,000 tons of fertilizer?"

Wolfram studied them briefly. 'I *do* believe you really don't know."

"That's right!" snapped Simon. "You've been sputtering about amateurs. Let's hear your professional word."

He was unchastened. "So that you'll grant me a little credibility, I will have to give you a very short lecture on explosives."

Simon sighed.

Wolfram ignored him. "Virtually all useful explosives, particularly military explosives, are variations on the same theme—nitrogen." He picked up a felt-tipped red marker and wrote $C^6H^5CH^3$ on the easel. "You oil barons should recognize that formula."

"Toluol," said Bradford.

He wrote on the board HNO_3. "Simon ought to know that one."

"Nitric acid," Simon muttered.

"Very good," said Wolfram. "Now toluol—or toluene—when treated by a certain process with nitric acid becomes . . . " he wrote on the easel, "TNT."

"Definitely *not* fertilizer," Simon declared.

Wolfram shrugged. "We treat glycerin," he scrawled $C_3H_5(OH)_3$, "with nitric acid, plus some sulfuric acid, and we get nitroglycerin. Dynamite, our favorite commercial explosive, is nothing more than nitroglycerin soaked into some absorbent, like sodium nitrate and wood pulp. Glycerin, as you oil men know, comes from the hydrolysis of oil."

"None of which is fertilizer," Simon interjected.

"Not exactly," Wolfram conceded. "But we have had oil products employed so far, haven't we?" He didn't wait for an answer. "Okay, my point is that nitrogen is the basis of most high explosives. Oil helps.

"Now, it also happens, coincidentally, that nitrogen is the basis for critical life processes in green plants. As a result nitrogen is built into the most commonly used agricultural chemical fertilizers. And, within that group, the most common product is," he wrote NH_4NO_3, "our old friend, ammonium nitrate."

"Are you trying to say you can convert ammonium nitrate into an explosive?" Simon asked.

"I am trying to tell you that ammonium nitrate *is* a high explosive!" Wolfram announced triumphantly. "By itself, ammonium nitrate has a relative effectiveness as an external charge equal to about 42 percent that of TNT. Of particular value to this exercise, its velocity of detonation is relatively slow, about 11,000 feet per second, compared with, say, 21,000 feet for TNT, or 26,000 feet for some of the plastic explosives.

"That relatively slower velocity gives more of a push-blast effect, as opposed to a shattering effect. And the push is what we want."

Bradford was fascinated. "But why isn't this stuff blowing up all over the farms of America?"

"First, it takes a professional with professional skills and technique to detonate this stuff. Actually, it is quite safe to handle. A lot safer to ship, store, and use than gasoline. And, frankly, it's one hell of a lot safer than liquid propane gas.

"Second, this material is very hygroscopic. When it's wet, its effectiveness is minimized or eliminated. That means our buyer is going to have to make certain he buys his bulk bagged."

Simon regarded Wolfram with grudging admiration. "It's unbelievable."

"That may be," Wolfram nodded, "but it is so."

"Forty thousand tons—what kind of a blast will it be?"

"Equivalent to fifteen or sixteen tactical atomic warheads." Wolfram held up a cautioning hand. "That is not a completely valid comparison because the nuclear explosion has such a fantastic velocity. But the total energy equivalents are about right."

Bradford shook his head wearily. "I feel as if I have had one weight removed from my shoulders only to have a heavier one placed there. I really didn't think this could be done to my specifications. I'm not sure I wanted it to be."

Wolfram said nothing.

"I'm not informed about fertilizers," Simon commented. "Is this stuff readily available?"

"Readily. Especially here in Texas. It is also cheap." He shrugged noncommitally. "I believe it's less than fifty a ton."

Wolfram continued. "Cosmo Construction will have to produce back-dated communications ordering this material, G.B. We will also want a back-dated file of correspondence in Spanish that, hopefully, we will be able to slip into the cabinets of the Malaverde Department of Agriculture."

"Does this company really exist?" Simon asked. They talked about it as if it were an old friend.

"I'll take care of that personally, Simon," Bradford told him. "There are . . . some special considerations. Hugo, you must give me the specifics as soon as feasible."

Wolfram nodded, then looked at each of them for a moment. "Let's get on with it," he said at last, and flipped the easel pad for a fresh sheet. "All right, we have the explosives. Now we need a package that can be delivered. A very large suitcase."

"The DePrundis fleet has three bulk carriers that could handle this tonnage. The real prize would be the *Empress DePrundis*, 56,141 deadweight tons. This ship cost DePrundis nearly five million dollars, and he has it mortgaged up to the gunwales." He wrote the ship's name on the easel. "The problem is, the DePrundis fleet manager probably would not want to tie up that much capacity on a forty-kilo-ton load."

"It would be quite a plum," Bradford commented.

"There's more," said Wolfram. "There is the 44,500-ton *Queen DePrundis*, slightly older, a less costly ship, but still worthwhile, and the 42,300-ton *Mother DePrundis*, older still and the least juicy target of the lot. Actually, any one of them would be suitable."

"DePrundis is devoted to his own name, isn't he?" Simon noted.

"All of his ships have his trademark on them," Wolfram said. "The Greek letter 'Delta.' Incidentally, his tanker fleet consists of twelve ships, mostly new. Five are in the 100,000-ton to 200,000-ton range."

Wolfram moved back to the lectern. "In addition to the fertilizer, I want the ship to be deck-loaded with one hundred tons of magnesium ingots. The price of the stuff at Freeport, Texas, is now thirty-six cents a pound. If it cannot be deck-loaded, then interior loading."

"What would that be for?" Simon asked.

"I'll explain it shortly." He paused for a few seconds to allow Bradford, who was taking notes furiously, to catch up. "All right," he said. "We have our goodies and we have our package. The package transports itself to the pier beside the refinery at Malanueva. Let's look at that."

Simon switched off the lights, and Wolfram illuminated the screen with the now-familiar aerial photo of the onetime Bradford facilities. "This is the pier," Wolfram said, indicating it with his pointer. "Notice the crane and sheds. Apparently, this is the only pier in the entire port capable of handling the kind of bulk cargo we are shipping."

"Right," Bradford injected. "We had to build the pier and crane so we could unload our bulk supplies for construction of the plant."

"Just picture the *Empress DePrundis* moored at that pier with a cargo of explosives," he said softly. "We push a button." Wolfram flicked the projector switch and bright, clear light flashed on the screen. "It's all gone."

"That's the plan, isn't it?" Bradford sounded almost unsure.

"That's *part* of the plan. Get the ship to the pier." He switched on another slide, a map of Malanueva Harbor. "The top of your picture is the open sea, which is north. The airport, here, in the west; the city in the east; the harbor." He drew his pointer in a circle around the nearly oval harbor. "A critical point: This harbor has only a relatively narrow channel to the sea. Try to picture this. We have our shipload of explosives at the pier by the refinery, which will take care of that facility, But we must also make sure the harbor is clogged by ships sunk by the blast. That means, of course, that there has to be shipping in the harbor.

"Which brings us to the second phase of the plan." He paused. "I want Cosmo Construction to acquire a ship—an old Liberty or Victory would be ideal. That ship will take on a cargo of gravel or cement aggregate, ostensibly for a construction project in Malaverde. It will reach this point," he indicated the narrows

108

between the sea and the harbor, "where it will have an accident and sink in the channel."

"Is the channel so narrow that one ship could block it?" Bradford asked.

"According to the charts. The blockage is compounded if any of the over 100,000-ton DePrundis tankers are in port. Those ships are dangerous elephants in any harbor.

"The reasons for blocking the harbor are twofold," he went on. "First it will keep shipping bottled up. Empty tankers will probably proceed with loading, so there will be several large accumulations of flammable product.

"When the blast comes, it might trigger a secondary blast in one or more tankers. It is far more likely, though, that it will stave in their sides, swamp them, and sink them where they lie, namely, in the channel." Wolfram turned to Simon. "You asked about the deck-loaded magnesium. Magnesium oxidizes readily at high temperature. It is a main component in such things as incendiary bombs and flares. Each ingot of magnesium will be ignited by the blast and hurled like a huge incendiary bullet. Most of them will fall on oil tankers in the harbor and set their cargo on fire, augmenting the effect of the initial blast."

Bradford grimaced. "Incredible. How long would it take to clear out a wrecked ship?"

"It depends on the nature of the sinking," Wolfram replied. "Some ships get little holes that can be patched and the ship refloated. Clearance of a bad wreck can take months. The ships we sink by blast will probably be unraisable."

"Our freighter's sinking must look like an accident, too," Bradford reminded him.

"Right," Wolfram replied. "It has to be a *plausible* sinking—an obstruction perhaps—which means the ship might be refloatable. That's why I want a cargo of gravel or something like it. Delay the refloating. In any event, we will trigger our blast before it is raised. After the blast, the whole question will be academic. But the extra couple of days will allow for the filling of all ships in the harbor, crude storage tanks ashore, and all refined product tanks."

Bradford poked idly at the granules of ammonium nitrate with his pencil. "Fertilizer," he said softly. "Ashes to ashes."

Wolfram's Clan

15

I

ALL AROUND THERE was silence.

At the huge ancient wooden gate behind Hangan's house, Yuranosuke stood alone beneath an orange paper lantern, his face contorted with grief. Slowly, precisely, he withdrew from his kimono and raised before his eyes the bloodstained dagger, the instrument of his master's death. Upon it he swore to carry out his master's last order: vengeance. In the background the chanting of *joruri* added gravity to the gloomy scene.

Then, with the clacking of sticks, the curtain closed.

Yuranosuke's expression of anguished dedication relaxed as he hurried toward the wings of the stage. From the shadows a gravelly voice murmured *"Heike!"* Slowly the kimonoed figure, still holding the bloody knife, turned toward the shadows. "Wolfram?"

The gravelly voice became a chuckle. "The very man." The long, saturnine face emerged from the shadows. "It's good to see you, Harada. You were very convincing."

Harada smiled faintly. "You *enjoy* Kabuki, Wolfram?"

"I enjoy watching the mastery of technique, Harada."

Harada bowed. "When I got your wire, I did not expect that you would come to Tokyo just for the theater."

"I'm pained, Harada," Wolfram said. "I have a deep respect for your art."

"Did you know this play?"

"More or less. *Kanadehon Chuchingura*, was it?"

"Wolfram, you tease me." Harada chuckled.

"Perhaps," Wolfram conceded. "But the stories of the forty-seven *ronin* are known to some of us, even in the west."

"You came to Tokyo to talk about the forty-seven *ronin*, then?"

"Indirectly, you might say."

Harada rubbed his chin thoughtfully. "The last time we met, I told you no more adventures, no more 'operations' like *Heike*."

"It *was* a success, Harada—and you were the key man."

Again Harada bowed. "As you say, I have learned to master certain skills. But . . . my love is this." He gestured at the stage.

"Don't you know the Shakespeare line 'All the world's a stage . . . ?"

". . . 'and all the men and women merely players.' " Harada laughed.

"You don't believe it."

"I believe that all the world's an audience." His smile turned rueful. "An audience forced to watch a bad scene."

"But with the proper technique a man of honor can change a bad scene into a good one, can't he?"

"A man of *honor*, did you say?" Harada was scornful.

Wolfram seemed irked. "Why not? There is honor in technique."

"Perhaps." Harada gestured again at the stage. "Out there technique is only the mechanism for the story. With you everything is technique."

"I have my ideals, Harada."

"Ideals and honor are for out there," he pointed at the stage, "not back here."

Wolfram shrugged. "Revenge is the story, isn't it?"

"What story?"

"The forty-seven *ronin*. All of the plays and stories are built around their quest for revenge for their warlord."

"That's right."

"I want to talk about revenge," said Wolfram seriously. "I want to tell you a story. I need your help."

"I'll listen to a story, Wolfram. Only listen."

"You *do* owe me that."

"Yes, I do owe you *that*."

Wolfram scribbled the address of a nearby bar and handed it to Harada.

II

It was one of those boxes wedged between the Kabuki theater and the Ginza-Tokyu Hotel. Fishnets and glass-ball floats hung from the low ceiling. Dried starfish were glued to the walls and rafters, and behind the bar a mammoth stuffed sea bass swam among amber bottles of Suntory whiskey.

The place was jammed with tiny tables, almost all of them occupied. Wolfram found a booth. Harada appeared in a correct pinstripe, and a tie the crimson of Shinto temple lacquer with a small, intricate gold figure. A matching handkerchief blossomed from his breast pocket.

Wolfram squinted at the tie. "That's your family crest, isn't it?"

Harada smiled. "You have a good memory."

Wolfram ordered drinks. He mentioned the humidity of Tokyo and the polluted air.

"There is some kind of plan," said Harada. "Somewhere there are special men—technicians—studying a design for destruction."

Wolfram mentioned the most recently published novel by Mishima. He wondered whether the translation did the original Japanese justice. He inquired casually if Harada had any time off from the theater.

"I'm planning three weeks at my place on Lake Biwa. I leave in a week."

"Great," said Wolfram.

Harada looked around the crowded, smoky room, then spoke without looking at Wolfram. "You were going to tell me a story."

"It can wait."

"A story, I believe you said, about revenge."

"No hurry."

"Wolfram, what is the story?"

Wolfram shrugged. "What can I do? If you are so anxious to hear this . . ."

"You do not fool me. You are baiting a hook for me and I know it."

"Very well. I wasn't fooling when I told you that I would tell you a story of revenge." He signaled the waitress for more drinks. "There is an organization, which shall be nameless, that has suffered badly at the hands of a man named DePrundis."

"Do I know him?"

"Not by that name. He is . . . an evil man."

"Ah, the *demon*." Harada was delighted. "There *must* be a demon."

"Yes, and this demon was instrumental in the torture and cruel death of the son of the head of the organization I referred to."

"A motive. Proceed."

"These events occurred in a country called Malaverde in South America."

"A 'banana republic'?"

"At one time, yes. Now a small oil republic." The waitress arrived with their drinks. Wolfram waited until she left. "De Prundis helped engineer the overthrow of the legitimate government of the nation. The young man I mentioned was seized at that time and executed as part of the so-called revolution."

"He was innocent?"

"Completely."

"But you said he belonged to a nameless organization."

"I will rephrase that. He worked indirectly *for* the organization, but not knowingly."

Harada frowned slightly. "Forgive me, but revenge is not the function of . . . a nameless organization."

Wolfram smiled coolly. "You're right, of course. However, it is effective personal motivation, don't you think?"

"I don't buy it, Wolfram. You would destroy this evil man because one of *your* front men got trampled by him. That isn't the way things are done."

"I haven't finished the story," said Wolfram. "This man, our demon, controls an oil company, and he also owns a fleet of tankers to carry his oil to markets. Do you begin to see a familiar plot emerging?"

116

"Go on."

"These ships all go into the main port of Malaverde, called Malanueva, pick up cargoes of oil, and leave. If this harbor is blocked . . ."

"Then the oil goes nowhere," said Harada. "I hear an echo of Operation *Heike.*"

"There are similarities."

Harada was puzzled. "But in *Heike* we were only buying time, a few weeks. In this case it would seem that time is of no consequence. After all, a sunken ship can be removed."

Wolfram's planning did not include briefing each member of his team about the destruction of the refinery. That would be his personal surprise. "You are right, of course," he said smoothly. "We plan to sink several ships."

"Must this look like an accident, as in *Heike?*"

"That's right."

"Several ships sinking all at once would certainly strike anyone as more than a coincidence."

Wolfram shrugged. "That can be arranged. The channel is narrow and long." He took out a small notebook and a pen and drew a sketch of the Malanueva Harbor. "We 'accidentally' sink our own ship here." He indicated the narrow harbor entrance. "Naturally, that will block a number of other ships in the harbor channel. A day, two days, three, after the first sinking, there will be another kind of accident. A fire, perhaps, since most of the blockaded ships will be loaded tankers."

Harada's eyes narrowed as he stared at the paper. "But I still fail to see the significance of this. Two ships, even three, can be removed, in one month or two months, if expedited. They could be refloated. The channel soon could be cleared. Then the oil flows again and this . . . demon . . . is where he was before."

Wolfram smiled. "Ah, but this man is an international financier, as well as a backer of revolutions and espionage. That means he has borrowed heavily to finance his operations, particularly his ships. If his oil fails to reach market for, say, six months, he is ruined. He will not have funds to pay his creditors."

"But he will still have the property."

"No." Wolfram sought a rationale. "A company that cannot pay its bills, regardless of the value of its assets, must go bankrupt.

Bankruptcy is a loss of control, which is what this . . . nameless organization . . . wants."

Harada shook his head. "It's very strange."

"It is an exercise in revenge." Wolfram used his final tool. "We destroy the demon using his own tools. It is classic."

Harada laughed. "You haven't told me what I would do."

"You haven't told me you would join."

"I told you, no more adventures."

"I didn't believe you."

"Why?"

"Because you have, as you said, certain skills. You would want to use them again sometime. It's the curse of the technician, the need to exercise skills."

"All right. Perhaps I'll join. What can I do?"

"First come with me to my hotel room, where I'll brief you and give you money."

III

The rain in Tokyo was heavy. The drops were large and warm and they slashed in great planes. Inside Wolfram's room the only evidence of the storm was the drumming on the windows and the streaming water that turned the dark view translucent and abstract. Wolfram had chosen a Western-style accommodation instead of the traditional Japanese room. The chamber was as plastic and featureless as any Texas motel.

A large chart of Malanueva Harbor lay open on the bed.

"This is the best we have."

Harada scanned the chart. "It is incomplete."

"That's why we need you."

"The depth indications are misleading. There aren't enough indications of the kind of bottom."

Wolfram offered no comment. Harada was a master of channels and harbors. During World War II he had participated in Japanese naval operations against the Americans. His specialty was planning the hit-and-run attack, the use of terrain and reefs and special craft, and tides.

"This channel is poorly arranged, you know," said Harada.

"I doubt that anyone ever took into consideration military or naval probabilities."

Harada used his pencil as a pointer. "There is this fortress."

"I have been told that it is used only as a service area for harbor pilots." Wolfram looked closely at the chart. It seemed to show a paved road leading to the fort. "That is one of the things you would find out."

Harada studied the depth indications at the harbor entrance. "Is this chart accurate?"

"As far as the channel is concerned, it should be. It is the standard chart used by ships in the harbor. I understand that, because of the narrowness, all ships are brought in by pilot."

Harada grimaced. "This chart fails to show even the kind of channel markers."

Wolfram made a note on a pad. "That, I suppose, brings us to your assignment."

Harada backed away from the chart on the bed. He looked at it with distaste, then sat down in the cheap hotel-room chair. "All right. Let's hear it."

Wolfram went to his suitcase and took out a gray office envelope. "One, Malaverde currency, the equivalent of ten thousand dollars, U.S.

"Two, a passport in the name of," he glanced at it "Shojii Gosho."

Harada snorted. "You were that sure of me, weren't you?"

"Three, an airline ticket to Caracas. From Caracas you will secure passage on the daily feeder flight to Malanueva.

"Four, two sets of papers and appropriate counterfeit correspondence." Wolfram held up a sheaf of scuffed-looking papers. "This file identifies you as the Shojii Gosho recently retired from a position in the Kobe Harbor Service. The file indicates that it is your intention to go to Malanueva to start an independent career operating fishing boats and a tackle-and-bait shop."

Harada scowled. "I sound like a moron."

"Gosho is a perfect cover for taking a boat around the harbor." Wolfram walked over to the chart. "Now, it is not vital, but it might be helpful if you can acquire a facility in the area of the refinery." He indicated a space on the chart.

"What refinery?"

"It is not shown on a harbor chart," Wolfram explained, "but when you get to Malanueva, one of the first things you'll acquire—I hope—is a decent map."

Harada laughed. "Wolfram, you're charming."

"That's your cover," Wolfram continued. "The money ought to be plenty, but there's more if you have a problem."

Harada nodded. "What is the other file of correspondence?"

"As an enterprising Japanese businessman with an eye on the main chance, Gosho has approached several companies, offering his services as their representative in the Malanueva Harbor area."

Harada nodded.

Wolfram riffled the papers, a variety of recognized corporate letterheads, plus some mythical companies. "All these companies turned down your offer."

"How sad."

Wolfram held up a single letter. "This company accepted." He handed the letter to Harada, who chuckled softly.

"Cosmo Construction Company, Montreal." Harada smiled sardonically. "They always liked my work."

"There is always a job at Cosmo for a good man."

"What do I do as their representative?"

"That will be explained at the time you make your first report."

"On what?"

Wolfram put all the material back in the gray envelope and handed it to Harada. "You must draw up a precise tide schedule, paying particular attention to the maximum velocity of the tides through the harbor entrance.

"We will need to know how large a ship will be required to block the channel."

"I can tell you that now, if that chart is accurate."

Wolfram picked up his notebook. "Go ahead."

"A freighter or bulk carrier in the class of 10,000 gross tons and 6,000 to 7,000 deadweight tons. An old American Liberty or Victory. They are readily available on the maritime markets in a price range from, say, $150,000 for one sailing for the scrap yard to $200,000 for one with a few more voyages in her."

"You're sure that size ship would be adequate?"

"More than sure, Wolfram." He stood and walked over to

the chart. "This channel is little more than a deep ditch, very narrow. A sunken rowboat would be an obstruction in it."

"Good," said Wolfram.

Harada smiled. "You see? I have earned my money already. By the way, you haven't discussed my fee."

"How does fifty thousand in U.S. cash or securities sound?"

Harada whistled softly. "They do take this seriously, don't they?"

Wolfram nodded. "But not me. I work on a cost-plus, fixed fee basis, the same as you. This is a priority job."

"Apparently," said Harada. "But we were talking about my assignment. What else besides setting up a front and charting the harbor?"

"We'll need to know, of course, the kinds of channel markers. Also, whether the pilots ever bring in ships after dark, and, in line with that, the moon schedule."

"All easily done."

"One more thing." Wolfram pointed at the Rio Paraná. "There is a drawbridge here. I'll need to know how it works and how it can be jammed."

"I'm not an engineer."

"No, but you're a first-class saboteur. The problem will be to break the bridge—accidentally."

"For the fishing business cover, do you require any special kind of craft?"

"A sturdy inboard launch for the water—and a good panel truck. We'll probably be able to use it."

"You won't require small craft for this . . . accident in the channel?"

Wolfram pondered it. "I'm afraid we will have to try something different this time. I haven't worked out just what. However, it'll probably be something aboard the ship, or maybe a way to run aground against the side of the channel."

"What was wrong with the *Heike* system?"

Wolfram turned again to the chart. "Nothing, except I fear there isn't any cover on either side of the channel. It's probably marsh, not jungle."

"Then that leaves only one thing," said Harada.

"What's that?"

"When do my tickets tell me to depart?"

"They're open tickets. The sooner you leave the better."

Harada stood. "In that case, I am virtually on my way."

"There's an item sheet in the envelope recapping most of the points we discussed. Also, where you will meet me in two weeks."

"Where is that?"

"Freeport, Texas. Fly to Caracas; Caracas to Houston; drive Houston to Freeport."

"It sounds hideous."

Harada turned and left.

16

TO HIS LEFT, FAR away, the masts of a freighter loomed, marking the location of an unseen river. The ship appeared to glide across the land. Closer by was the blacktop at the northern end of the airport. From time to time, huge jets soared across his view.

A veil of kerosene-streaked haze hung over the busy facility. The sun flashed against the control tower and terminal. The whole dreary panorama shimmered in heat waves and smelled of turbines and metal.

Wolfram leaned casually against the corroded hurricane fence that segregated him from the abandoned earthworks of what had earlier been an antiaircraft battery. Moving toward him now was a helicopter, its glassine eye flashing in the last rays of the sun.

The craft settled quickly in a sudden burst of dust. The rotary wing slowed, its turbine engine winding down in pitch. The craft's small door snapped open and a long, disjointed man disengaged himself from the controls.

Carefully, the pilot packaged up his clipboard and put aside his radio earphones. Disembarking, he walked toward Wolfram. His expression was glum, but he put out his hand. "Hello, Hugo. Good to see you." He didn't mean it.

"Are those the call letters of your . . . what is it? . . . a radio show?" Wolfram pointed at large painted letters on the side of the helicopter.

"I give traffic reports." He seemed reluctant to talk about it. "I tell them that the bridges and approach highways are crowded at the rush hours."

"You have to go up in the air to learn that?"

"Sometimes there are accidents." He looked around him, as if searching for another person. They were alone. A hundred yards away a mechanic wheeled a piece of equipment on a dolly around a private plane.

"Philadelphia certainly has become a busy place," Wolfram muttered genially. A jet shrieked above them and they both cringed involuntarily. "You're looking fit, Jock," Wolfram said as the jet passed them by.

Jock Kinsey shrugged. It was an awkward motion, like that of a gawky adolescent. Kinsey was four inches over six feet, and thin. Perhaps he was twenty-eight, or thirty-eight. It was hard to say. His hair was sparse. "It's a quiet life. I'm in the air twice a day. I tell them about the traffic."

"You always liked that, didn't you? The flying, I mean."

"It's a comfortable living. Useful, I suppose."

"You got my wire?"

Kinsey nodded. "Frankly, Hugo, I'm happy with this. There's no pressure."

"I'm glad you have kept up your skills. Flying choppers."

Kinsey looked still more glum. "I did bring *that* back from Southeast Asia."

"You miss it, though, don't you?"

"Miss what?"

"You used the word yourself—pressure." Wolfram smiled. "You miss the pressure of duty."

Kinsey flinched. "I did my part."

Wolfram agreed. "You were the key man, Jock."

"I was frightened." Kinsey himself seemed surprised at that. "Did you know that, Hugo? Operation *Heike* scared the wits out of me."

"A figure of speech, Jock. Your wits were all right when we needed them."

"I suppose they were."

"We need them again, Jock."

"Once was enough."

"I need a key man, an experienced man, who can fly one of those," he gestured toward the helicopter.

"I'm happy here."

Wolfram patted him on the arm. "Okay, Jock, if you say so. But I can buy you a drink, can't I?"

Kinsey had not stopped frowning. "One drink."

Wolfram chuckled, but the sound was drowned out by still another jet lunging across the field.

II

The airport bar was a kind of waiting room, stamped out of shiny alloy and high-impact vinyl, riveted together like the interior of an aircraft.

The drinks tasted of jet fuel. Wolfram waited for Kinsey to speak.

"What have you been up to, Hugo? Since Operation *Heike*, I mean," the younger man said finally.

"I still have my own firm, you know."

"But you work for The Company, don't you?"

"I work for my own firm. We do special assignments, yes." Wolfram lifted an eyebrow sardonically. "In any event, we couldn't break security, could we?"

"In *this* place?" Kinsey glanced around scornfully. The crowd in the bar matched the decor: salesmen wearing brown eighty-seven dollar suits, carrying black plastic dispatch cases. "They wouldn't know what you were talking about, Hugo. They wouldn't even know what part of the world you were talking about."

"You sound bitter, Jock."

Kinsey sipped his drink. "I suppose I am." His lean face creased in concern. "It was a dirty rotten war—like pushing a lot of gunmen into a vacant house to shoot things up." He laughed shortly. "The survivors come out of the house and stroll down the street just as before. The house catches fire, but no fire engines come. It burns to the ground, and the town complains about the smell of smoke."

"So, you wanted some glory after all."

"Glory? My God, Hugo." He thought about it. "Maybe. I

think we just want someone to know what we went through."
He glanced sharply at Wolfram. "Did you think I was after glory
when you recruited me before?"

"You volunteered, Jock, and you didn't do it for the money.
You already were in the Army. You could have gone home."

Kinsey shifted uneasily. "There was nothing there. Home,
I mean. I guess I never mentioned that to you before."

Wolfram had known from the beginning that Kinsey was an
orphan. It was one of the reasons the computers had selected
him for Operation *Heike*.

"Your skills, Jock. We need them."

Kinsey looked at his hands. "I'm not sure I'm up to it."

"It's a simple mission."

"You said the last one was simple."

"In retrospect it was," said Wolfram. "It was a piece of cake."

"We lost Sam."

"It was an accident."

Kinsey swirled the ice in his drink and stared at it thoughtfully.
"Good old Sam, the scuba man."

"Forget it!" snapped Wolfram. "He's gone."

Kinsey glowered.

Wolfram bored in. "No one could fault you, Jock, for building
a relatively secure life around . . . traffic reports. As you said,
it's *useful* work."

"Come on, Wolfram," Kinsey said defensively. "There's still
a lot of adventure in flying, even for traffic reports. Why, the
other day . . ."

"Sure. I'm sorry, Jock. I'm not a flier. But it struck me that
a lot of guys wearing white silk scarves and leather jackets are
like taxi drivers. There seems to be a lot of buckle these days,
but no *swash*, if you know what I mean."

"I can't argue it much, Hugo. There's a lot of aerial motorboat-
ing on Sundays."

"Damn shame." Wolfram shook his head. "It dilutes the real
achievement, the *duty*, if you will, of what flying is all about."

"Duty," murmured Kinsey. "I don't know what the word
means."

"On the contrary," said Wolfram. "I know the opposite to
be true. That's why you'll join me for this mission.

126

"I won't go back to Southeast Asia, Wolfram."

"The mission is not in Southeast Asia. If you come in, you'll learn about it." Wolfram knew he had him. "I can tell you this much. The mission is not in hostile territory, at least as that phrase is usually defined."

"How would it stack up against a mission like *Heike?*" His voice dropped.

"Basically simple." Wolfram sipped his drink. "In fact, we will operate openly through a cover enterprise."

"A friendly country? Why?"

"The Company has its reasons. From what I know of them, I would say they are good reasons."

"It's hot. The air-conditioning must be on the fritz." Kinsey pulled out a rumpled handkerchief and mopped his face. "Let's get out of here. Walk."

"Sure, Jock. It's not an easy decision. Let's walk it out."

III

They strolled like lovers, each with his thoughts on the other.

"I have vacation due," Kinsey said.

"How long?"

"Two weeks."

"You're in, then?"

Silence.

"I can tell you this," said Wolfram. "The element of danger has been reduced to the playing of roles. If each member of the team plays his role properly, the necessary action will take care of itself."

"Roles?"

"It is vital to the mission that we each be someone else. Like a play—we will have lines to recite, cues. We step on and off the stage."

"I'm no good at remembering lines."

Wolfram was impatient. "Not *precise* lines—situations. Scenarios."

"What kind of flying?"

"Can you handle a Bell 204B helicopter?"

Kinsey snorted. "In my sleep. That's the commercial version of the Hueys."

"Could it carry a small group of people?"

"How many?"

"Six."

"It could handle ten. It has a 1,100-horsepower T5309A shaft turbine, or maybe a later modification."

"How does the commercial version differ from the military?"

Kinsey thought briefly. "It has a tail boom that is slightly longer than the military to provide more cargo space, and some civilian extras—passenger steps, outside lights."

"Range?"

"Over three hundred miles."

"We might have to steal the chopper." Wolfram was casual about it.

Kinsey looked at him abruptly. "Guards?"

"Sure. But the plan we have will . . . but why don't you join us, Jock? It's right up your alley."

"How much?"

"Fifty thousand."

"They really *are* serious."

Wolfram nodded.

"It puzzles me."

"And it might right up to the end," said Wolfram. "It's a strange mission—not difficult."

Kinsey stopped short. "I'm in." His smile seemed strained. "What next?"

Wolfram took out a small notebook and a ballpoint pen. He wrote an address and a date on one page and tore it out. "This is in Freeport, Texas," he said, handling Kinsey the scrap. "It's hot as hell there."

17

ACROSS THE SOMBER harbor the city crouched behind its screen of smog. Crosscurrents ripped, piling hedges of water on the East River. Coiling rainbow skims of oil pocked with seaweed lapped against the timbers of the pier where Wolfram stood.

He watched the approach of a stubby green tugboat. It shouldered its way through the turgid waters easily, leaving a long muddy wake of churned saltwater behind. As the boat drew nearer, Wolfram heard the thudding of its diesel engines. It seemed the craft would crash into the bulkhead, but at the last instant it swung agilely to portside, then yawed gracefully up beside the pilings with a solid thud. A crewman leaped onto the pier and another threw him a bowline. Expertly, the man on the dock twirled hitches around the mooring cleat, then went astern to make it fast there.

A tall bearded blond youth in a Navy turtleneck and watch cap swung off the tugboat and strode purposefully in Wolfram's direction. He loped past with little more than a nod.

Behind him came a short bullnecked black man. He wore a tattered sweat-stained fedora with the brim turned down all around and a scuffed leather jacket. He stopped before Wolfram. His face was expressionless.

"Magraw," Wolfram reached a hand out tentatively.

The black man studied the hand a moment, then reached quickly and took it. "Wolfram." He glanced at the sky. "Bad weather follows you."

"Why don't you wear a peaked cap like all the other skippers?"

"I had a skipper's hat once. A blue hat." He didn't smile. "It blew overboard."

Wolfram hunched his shoulders inside his trench coat. "Let's go somewhere."

"There's a good little place down the line here. No sailors." Magraw laughed abruptly. "I wouldn't want to have to associate with crew, you know. Me being an officer and gentleman, you understand."

"You got my wire?"

Magraw stepped back suddenly and looked him up and down. "Man, you look like the guy from the syndicate, come to collect the installment." He chuckled, a gargling sound deep in his throat.

"I'm the man who has come to pay out, Magraw."

They headed back up the pier. The dockside area was a wide lumpy avenue of Belgian block worn smooth by countless sailors' feet and iron-rimmed wheels from the time of sailing ships. The place still smelled of tar.

"You enjoy skippering a workboat?"

"I enjoy it."

"Don't you miss the sea?"

"There's plenty of excitement in the harbor, and when *this* ship sinks, Wolfram, it's only a short swim to shore."

They strolled slowly. The buildings needed paint. The brickwork was soot-streaked and crumbling with age. Even the torn posters advertised events long past, a wrestling card for April 22, 1967, a Hubert Humphrey campaign poster, its flag colors now faded to pink, pale yellow, and blue.

They turned down a charcoal street and the dank, gusting wind caught them face-on with fly ash and newspaper scraps. Among the bleak, rumpled shops ahead, a broken neon sign announced "EATS."

Wolfram and Magraw edged through an ancient slatted door and took their places in a side booth. From the shadows at the back of the room a glum, thick man in a denim shirt approached. Wolfram ordered coffee, and Magraw asked for a double shot of rye and a can of beer.

"So early in the day?" Wolfram asked.

"I've been up for hours," said Magraw.

130

They fell silent again as the proprietor returned with a round, rusty tray. He thumped the coffee and drinks before them, then returned to the shadows.

Wolfram skipped the amenities. "Operation *Heike*, Magraw. The ship was the important thing. You were the key man."

Magraw nodded. "I suppose so." He bolted half his rye, then sipped some beer.

"It was an important job, very important."

Magraw shrugged, then bolted the remaining half of his whiskey.

Wolfram spread his hands. "It's a sad thing, Magraw, but we all still live in the same world, don't we?"

Magraw looked around the dim saloon. "It seems very much the same." Again he sipped delicately at his beer.

"We make the big gestures, like Operation *Heike*," Wolfram went on. "It doesn't seem to change anything."

"You want to replay Operation *Heike*," Magraw said matter-of-factly.

Wolfram went on as if there had been no interruption. "But we must keep struggling, mustn't we?"

"You want me to do something with a ship," Magraw said. "Something dangerous."

"That's right."

"Tell me about it."

"Let me talk around it," said Wolfram. He signaled the man at the back for another round. "Give me a double rye, too," he said. From an inside pocket he drew some papers and a ball-point pen. On the back of an envelope he drew a fat *C*, and pushed it toward Magraw. "Harbor, narrow channel, like Operation *Heike*. We want to sink a ship in it."

Magraw nodded. "Get me aboard. We can work it the same way."

Wolfram held up a finger. "But there is a difference."

"There usually is."

"This time we will not have a crew in position to carry out the . . . *accident* to the bottom of the ship."

Magraw looked interested. "But it still must look like an accident?"

"Right."

"How wide a channel?"

"Relatively narrow, but very deep. It can handle all but the very largest oil tankers."

"Are you going to tell me *where?*"

"In due course."

"I could swerve it into the channel bank."

"Another problem. You will have to pick up a pilot outside of port."

Magraw laughed abruptly. "An ice pick, Wolfram. I run to the hold with this large ice pick. Then, very carefully, I punch holes in the hull, you see?"

The proprieter returned with drinks. When he had left, Magraw asked, "This ship, will I be a deckhand, like last time? Will we have some prior access to the vessel?"

"Good question," said Wolfram. "As a matter of fact, we—that is, our little group—will own the ship. You'll be the skipper."

"Then we can arrange an accident, can't we?"

Wolfram nodded. "To the extent that prior access allows it. But remember—no bombs, no opening the seacocks. For practical purposes this must be an accident."

Magraw scowled. "Explain that."

"You tax me, Magraw."

"You can always get someone else, Wolfram."

Wolfram held up a hand. "Forget that talk. You still have your master's papers, don't you?"

"For all the good it does me."

"Good, that saves one step. You'll be operating under your own name."

Magraw chuckled. "You want me to wreck a ship under my own name! Hell, man, what do I do for a living after *that?*"

"*You* won't wreck the ship in the channel, Magraw. The pilot will."

"How?"

"That's the problem, isn't it?"

Magraw leaned back against the wall of the booth. "Will you have access to the channel?"

"I hadn't planned on it. We aren't going to attack the underside of the ship from the outside as in *Heike*. What kind of access are you talking about?"

Magraw shrugged. "I would have to see the charts, but

undoubtedly there are channel markers." He smiled. "If the markers are moved . . ." He made a crunching sound to simulate a ship hitting ground.

"Running aground won't do the whole job," said Wolfram. "The ship could be pulled away too easily. The bottom is mud. There couldn't be enough damage to sink her."

Magraw studied his beer can intently. "Suppose, just suppose, we had a thing fastened to the bottom of the ship like a gigantic can opener. When the ship starts to move aground this big can opener punches a huge hole up into the ship." He pointed at the top of the beer can. "Like this."

Wolfram was impatient. "Be serious."

Magraw was suddenly angry. "Goddamn it, I *am* serious." At the back of the room the proprietor stirred like a bird moving on its roost, disturbed by the sound. Magraw's voice dropped again.

He pointed again at the beer can. "We weld or bolt to the bottom of the ship something like a right triangle made out of steel I-beams." He took Wolfram's pen and he drew a right triangle on the paper, a horizontal side up. Across the horizontal side he sketched the shape of a ship's hull. "Now," he said, "the ship is moving up the channel, probably at a net speed of four knots. When the ship hits the side of the channel, this lower point connects with the bottom, too. The pressure there, multiplied by the leverage, drives the opposite point of the triangle right through the bottom of the ship." He smiled. "Just like a churchkey punching a hole in a beer can."

Wolfram looked at the sketch. "Why wouldn't the triangle just stop the ship?"

"A ship is a big, heavy thing, Wolfram. Even at four knots it carries enormous momentum. Suppose, for example, you have a five or six thousand deadweight ton ship. You apply the energy of that many tons, multiplied by the speed, against one area of a few square inches, representing the point of the triangle. The result, my friend, is precisely the same as opening a can."

Wolfram nodded slowly. "I think that's our answer." He studied the sketches a moment. "It means we'll have to have a scuba man to move the channel markers. I hadn't planned on underwater work this time."

"Underwater work can be dangerous," said Magraw. He stared

hard at Wolfram. "Isn't that so, Hugo? A man can get—shall we say—stuck on the bottom."

"If that's supposed to be a snide comment about *Heike*, I'll ignore it. All work is dangerous. A man can get cut down crossing the street."

"Skip it," said Magraw.

"You haven't asked about pay."

Magraw laughed abruptly. "I trust you, man, I trust you."

Silently, Wolfram wrote the Texas address and the meeting date. Then he stood and quickly left Magraw alone in the dark saloon.

18

I

FROM THE PLACID depths, twin columns of crystal bubbles rose and shattered against the bright Caribbean air. Wolfram, peering over the side of the swaying orange barge, could see clouds of fish flickering in and out of the coral. At the bases of the columns of bubbles, he could make out black shapes suspended weightlessly, then growing larger until, in an explosion of drops, they returned to the surface. The shapes pushed back face masks and Wolfram saw the square, dark-jowled face of a man and the fine-featured oval face of a woman. Both were deeply bronzed by the tropic sun.

Stripes of fluorescent yellow outlined the arms and legs of the black scuba suits. Twin air tanks swung from their backs as they made their way awkwardly to the ladder of the barge and scrambled up, their swimming fins flailing. Out of water these shapes lost their gracefulness, like game fish brought to gaff.

Assistants on the barge rushed forward to assist in dismantling the scuba people. Gradually they emerged from their black rubber skins: a muscular man of middle height and age, and a well-formed woman of an indeterminate age, perhaps thirty.

The divers and their assistants spoke rapidly in Spanish. There seemed to be an agreement of some kind. The assistants broke away and moved to various tasks. The dark man finally noticed Wolfram.

"Hugo," he called, and strode across the barge deck. He clasped Wolfram in an *abrazo*, then waved an arm at his female companion. "Juanita!" She moved closer, regarding Wolfram warily. "This is the man I tell you about. Hugo Wolfram." The man laughed. "Sometimes he makes me rich. Maybe he wants to do it again." He turned back to Wolfram. "This is Juanita Huerta."

"How do you do," Wolfram said stiffly. Women, like the depths of the sea, were another world to him. They made him uneasy.

"Jorge tells me you are a big man with the fire business." She didn't shake hands.

"It's been a long time, Esposito," said Wolfram. "How many years?"

The dark man shrugged. "Five years." He waved his arm toward the horizon. "An offshore drilling rig in the gulf."

"You were the key man on that job, Jorge. The key man." There was irony in Wolfram's voice. "But come on! I have a fast boat. Let's go ashore and talk about this with a rum flavor."

"Sure, why not?" The three of them moved to where Wolfram's speedboat was moored.

"We're lining up underwater locations for a movie—fancy coral and places to moor the cameras. She and me, we are going to be in this movie, but not the stars. We just do the work."

Wolfram nodded. "You got my wire. Are you available?"

"Well, there is this one thing, Hugo."

"There usually is, Jorge."

"I'm free for the job, you understand, though I don't know what it is." He nodded in the direction of the woman. "She and me are partners, though, Hugo. We work together."

"I don't get it. You mean you can't do the job because of that?"

"I mean if *I* go, she has to be counted in, too."

Wolfram stopped abruptly. Then he spoke almost inaudibly. "We must talk about *that*, Jorge. But first I must get you away from your element. It puts me at a disadvantage."

Wolfram signaled to Juanita to step into the speedboat. Jorge scrambled in beside her. Wolfram climbed into the wheel seat, started the powerful engines, then maneuvered the craft away from the barge and gunned for shore.

They sat beneath a cupola of grass perched among many under the palms. A gentle breeze shifted the heat around, but did not cool. Wolfram had ordered planter's punch and they all sipped gratefully at the frigid rum.

"The mission is in a hot place, too," said Wolfram. "Hotter than this, in fact."

"Far?" Esposito inquired.

"No."

Esposito sighed. "About this partnership."

"We'll have to work around it." Wolfram smiled at Juanita. "It's nothing personal. It's just the way these things get planned. We design for so many people and that's about it. We don't need one more. We can't use one less."

"If it is the money, Hugo, we can . . ."

"It's not the money!" snapped Wolfram. "It's the mission. We have it planned for X number, not X-plus-one."

"I am as good a diver as any man," she said. "Better than you."

Wolfram laughed. "The average Arab would be better than me. It's not my game. That's why I am here talking to Jorge. I need a great diver. *One.*"

"Listen, Hugo," said Esposito. "Maybe we can work her into the mission. She can dive like a man, I tell you."

Wolfram sipped his drink silently. Perhaps his thinking was not flexible enough. Esposito went on to say she could handle different types of equipment underwater, was fearless.

Wolfram tapped his forefinger on the table, then smiled guardedly at Juanita. "Tell me, how did you gain all this expertise underwater?"

She shrugged. "About six years ago I was with some friends in the Bahamas who had scuba equipment. I tried it."

"But a hobby does not always become a vocation."

"I had friends, men around boats. They liked me to dive with them."

Wolfram sipped his drink again. "But moving from that to this—professional diving."

"Him." She gestured at Esposito.

Wolfram leaned back and smiled grimly. "And now you want to bring your arrangement along on my mission. That it?"

"Look, Hugo," Esposito said. "It's not quite like that. There's other things, too. I mean she and me are good friends and partners, but we are not love birds, you know what I mean? She is not my wife."

"I still don't quite understand," Wolfram persisted.

"Look, Hugo, a diver, any diver, should never go down alone. He should always have a partner with him. Too many things can go wrong. You get down a little low and you get nitrogen narcosis. You come up too fast, you get the bends. You get caught on something, there's somebody to unhook you."

"At least that is a valid reason to bring her along. But this is a dangerous mission, Jorge."

"I don't want to go down alone, Hugo."

"This job isn't deep."

"I'm thinking about Sam, Hugo."

Wolfram's eyes narrowed. "How do *you* know about Sam?"

Esposito turned to Juanita. "Please, honey, would you get us some more drinks?"

She stared thoughtfully at the two of them, then stood and walked toward the outdoor bar not far away.

Esposito clenched his hands together on the table. "Operation . . . what you call it . . . hike?"

"It's still classified."

"I *know*, Hugo. I have clearances, too."

"Explain."

"The agency recruited me for a mission in Southeast Asia, but it got scratched when they began to wind down out there." He looked up. "Anyhow, as part of the briefing, they gave me the report you wrote on this hike operation."

Wolfram smiled faintly. "That's pronounced high-kay. It's a Japanese crab."

"I got to hand it to you, Hugo. It was a hell of a job—only one thing."

"Sam?"

"I knew him, Hugo. We did Navy work together underwater. He was the best."

"He was a pro."

"If there is one thing that haunts a diver, Hugo, it is the thought of being caught underwater to die."

"And, of course, that is what happened to Sam."

"If he had someone underwater with him, it might not have happened."

Wolfram scowled. "Jorge, the odds against a clandestine mission rise in direct proportion to the number of people involved in it. Each additional person multiplies the probabilities of discovery, or accident, or failure to get away."

"I can imagine Sam's eyes looking at me from his face mask, trapped eyes, but silent, because there is no sound down there."

Juanita returned with a tray of tall glasses. Carefully she placed them around the table and sat down.

"Well?" she said. "Are we hired?"

Wolfram picked up his drink and sipped it slowly, then placed it back on the table. "Okay."

Esposito grinned. "That's great, Hugo! Believe me, you won't regret it."

Juanita smiled ruefully. "How do we know that, Jorge? We don't even know what we are to do."

"One thing you *will* do is collect fifty thousand dollars each when the job is completed." Wolfram looked at Juanita. "She's counted in for a full share."

Esposito raised his glass in a toast. "She'll earn it."

Juanita raised her glass slightly and murmured, *"Saludos."* She did not sound convinced.

From the pocket of his white jacket Wolfram took out a folded paper. "Some instructions—where to meet, when. I'll see you there."

19

I

HE FOLLOWED the drill.

The metallic female voice at the other end of the line said, "I'm sorry, but the number you have dialed is not in service. Please check the number and dial again."

The recorded message repeated itself three times. He waited. There would be an answer.

"Yes."

Wolfram did not identify himself. Electronic devices would verify his identity elsewhere. "Cosmo Construction Company is ready to proceed with its contract."

"Thank you. We'll notify the customers."

Wolfram hung up the telephone in the booth on the beach and stared back through the clusters of thatched cabanas at the couple he had left only a few moments before. The woman worried him. He had never conducted an operation that included a woman as a key support element.

He told himself he would not let her upset his plan.

II

Two days later Bradford handed Simon a legal advertisement from a newspaper pasted on a sheet of white paper.

"This came by messenger from The Bank."

"What bank?"

"That isn't important. Read the notice."

Notice of Marshal's Sale
of
S/S Salvager

The United States steam screw SALVAGER of 8,228 gross and 4,829 net tons

WILL BE SOLD

"as is and where is" and free and clear of liens and encumbrances at public auction on July 12, 1972, at 10 A.M. by the United States Marshal for the Southern District of Texas (Houston Division) at the Office of the Marshal, Room 10130 United States Courthouse Building, 515 Rusk, Houston, Texas."

"Tomorrow."

"Read on."

The purchaser shall be a United States citizen as defined at Section 2 of the Shipping Act of 1916 . . .

Simon skimmed the legal details to the last paragraph:

The vessel is lying afloat at City Dock No. 1, Brazos River Harbor Navigation District, 1001 Pine Street, Freeport, Brazoria County, Texas, and may be inspected by appointment with the United States Marshal.

He looked up expectantly.

"You're going to buy that ship in the morning," Bradford said.

"I'll have to track down the price we should pay, get a certified check, and so on."

"It's all been taken care of. The Bank took care of it." From the middle drawere of his desk he took an envelope. "The details are all in here, the appropriate identifications, the certified check, everything."

"What if we aren't the high bidder?"

"We will be. The Bank has arranged it."

Simon took the envelope from Bradford. "This bank you refer

to must be quite an organization. Maybe we should be giving them our corporate business."

Bradford chuckled. "Believe me, Simon. *No* one gives business to The Bank. The Bank takes what it wants." He paused. "Why don't you skim through that material? You might have some questions."

Simon emptied the envelope on Bradford's desk. All the papers seemed in order. "We're buying this in the name of the Gluck Transportation Company. I never heard of it."

"Gluck is a Delaware corporation. It is closely held by a . . . consortium."

"I see."

"It has already been arranged to charter the ship to the Cosmo Construction Company. A cargo has been ordered."

"What kind of cargo, G.B.?"

"Gravel, Simon."

III

In Washington a clerk handed The Chairman a carbon flimsy. "This confirms that we have completed the sale of the Malaverde currency for Swiss francs."

The Chairman nodded. "How was the market for Malaverde escudos?"

"Firm, sir. No sign of weakness. Malaverde closed on a slight uptick."

"Good, good." He glanced sharply at his clerk. "Starting immediately, we want to begin daily borrowings of Malaverde funds and conversions as quickly as possible."

"Conversion to hard currencies, sir?"

The Chairman pursed his lips. "No, I think not. We are well hedged in hard currency. Instead, I suggest we trade in South and Central American and Caribbean funds. On a speculative basis they will be softer relative to Malaverde." He smiled. "A little extra margin for us."

20

I

WOLFRAM HAD chosen Freeport.

The region reflected its stained commercial labels: Nation's Largest Basic Chemical Complex; Fastest Growing Industrial Community in Texas; Shrimp Capital of the World.

In the interests of industrial development and quick profit, a band of Chamber of Commerce brigands in Stetson hats had threaded together Freeport, Clute, Richwood, Quintana, and other minor wastelands, into one matrix of tacky housing laced with oil and chemical tubing. The committees had rechanneled the river to create a straight, high-flow tide of pollutants into the Gulf of Mexico.

Wolfram gazed through a fly-specked window of a jerry-built Freeport motel at the bleak landscape and found it reassuring. Behind him, in scarred Danish modern chairs, Harada and Magraw sat waiting. They held tall rum drinks and puffed thoughtfully on cigars.

"It's time, gentlemen," said Wolfram, not turning from the window.

Harada went silently to the closet and extricated a large black briefcase, from which he removed a stack of papers bound with a thick rubber band. He pulled out a marine chart and unfolded it carefully on the room's single bed.

"This is the scene."

Wolfram turned from the window and looked at the chart,

while Magraw pulled his chair closer. Harada used a yardstick as a pointer.

"I obtained this chart from the Coastal and Customs Service of the Malanuevan Port Authority." He glanced at Wolfram. "As with everything else in Malanueva, it cost a small bribe. Parts of it are hopelessly inaccurate."

"Malanueva!" Magraw snorted. "A boil on the earth's backside."

"You've been there?" asked Wolfram.

"I took a couple of ships in."

Harada picked up a small ringed notebook and flipped it open to pages littered with Japanese characters. He touched the left side of the chart with his stick. "North is the top of the chart. The stick is at west." He made a circular motion with the yardstick. "This is the delta of the Rio Paraná. The single channel of the stream coming from the east divides into a number of relatively shallow channels that create marshy islands."

He tapped the chart at an island with a jumbled grid pattern. "The city of Malanueva. It is set off by channels roughly to the north and south. The south channel is navigable for small freighters."

The Japanese glanced at his notes. "Across the south channel drawbridge—here—is what these people refer to as the Navy Yard."

"Navy?" asked Magraw.

"Two badly maintained American-made corvettes from the Second World War—armed, however—some tugboats, an assortment of other workboats, dredges."

"How many uniformed men?" asked Wolfram.

"About five hundred, many more than required for their craft. However, this is a military state, and the Navy is one of the components of the power base."

"What do they use their corvettes for? Customs duty?" asked Magraw.

"Previously, yes."

"What do you mean 'previously'?"

"The current dictator is very ill disposed toward . . ." he turned apologetically to Wolfram, ". . . the United States. Two days ago, he announced a two-hundred-mile territorial limit. As

144

you know, that runs counter to United States policy. It is probably only a matter of time before one of the corvettes seizes a United States shrimp boat or creates some other incident."

Harada proceeded. The yardstick slid from the Navy Yard area down the line marking the edge of the land. "The channel widens out here into a shallow bay. At low tide most of it is covered by only three to five feet of water."

How far from the Navy Yard to the refinery?" asked Wolfram.

The northern edge of the complex is about a half-mile from the southern edge of the barracks and continues" the yardstick slid along the shoreline, "for more than a mile."

Wolfram nodded. He had seen it before.

"This river channel between the city and the Navy Yard," Harada continued, "carries the main flow of the river out to sea." The yardstick drew a line through the bay and between two smaller islands at the left edge of the chart. "Here, on this seaward island you can see the landmark Castel Mala.

"It is occupied by the Customs Service, which also supplies the pilots who bring ships upchannel and into the dock area." He smiled at Magraw. "There are military patrols around this island and some of the other seaward islands—on the lookout for smuggling, primarily—no real military interest." His stick tapped the chart. "The fortress island is served by a bridge and road from Malanueva."

Magraw tapped a forefinger on the refinery area. "How do ships serve the facilities here?"

"A very deep, narrow channel has been dredged in a semicircle through the bay, roughly following the southern shoreline."

Wolfram walked slowly across the room, pondering. Finally, he sat down in the one remaining chair. "Tell us more about the ship channel."

Harada again referred to his notes. "The depth is seventy-five feet. It is relatively narrow, one hundred meters." He glanced up. "That is one of the main reasons they insist on their pilots handling the ship. Both edges of the channel are marked by light buoys anchored at relatively close intervals."

"You mean they take ships up that channel in the dark?" Magraw was incredulous.

"On nights of high tide, most assuredly. The tide gives them a bit of extra maneuvering room. Since I have been there the ship traffic has been most heavy." He referred to his notes. "The ships primarily are of Greek or Liberian registry, all under the ownership or lease of the DePrundis interests." Harada glanced at Wolfram. "The refinery works around the clock. The workers rent my fishing boats."

That reminded Wolfram. "Just where is your establishment?"

"Here." Harada pointed to a place between the Navy Yard and the northern edge of the refinery. He shrugged ruefully. "The noisy activity of the planes and the ships keeps me awake, Hugo. The cracking towers are illuminated like giant Christmas trees."

"It won't be much longer, my friend."

"What now, Hugo?" Magraw asked.

"You brought the tide and moon charts, Harada?"

"Of course."

"Good." He looked at Magraw. "Now we get down to serious planning."

II

Mist hugged the pocked macadam and eroded cement of the old cargo wharf, and the smell of hydrogen sulfide hung in the early morning air.

Above the three men, a forty-ton container and general cargo crane was poised. A rusting hulk was moored by limp, tarred hawsers at the end of the wharf.

They had breakfasted on lumpy eggs and sodden toast at a diner near the motel. They still squinted from the all-night fluorescent lighting.

Wolfram, hands thrust in pockets, observed, "It's not much, but it'll look as good on the bottom as any other iron."

Magraw chuckled. "I've sailed in a dozen like her. She's a Liberty. From the quality of her rust I'd say she was built about 1941."

Wolfram nodded. "Right on the button."

"The ship rides low," Harada said.

"Her cargo is already aboard," Wolfram replied. "The Cosmo

Construction Company does not waste time. A crew of drunks and drifters has been signed and, it is hoped, most of them will report for duty about this time day after tomorrow, as will her master, Captain Abdullah." He glanced at his watch.

"Who?" asked Magraw.

Wolfram smiled in fragments. "That's you. We have papers showing that you are a citizen of Trinidad. I decided there was no point in risking your own name and master's papers."

"But *Abdullah,* Wolfram! Should I show up in a turban?"

"Just appear as your own gracious self."

"What is the cargo?" Harada inquired.

"Gravel." Wolfram frowned. "You see, we want this tub to go down and stay down."

"Ordinary cargo could be off-loaded from underwater eventually," Magraw explained. "The ship could be refloated."

"But gravel can be off-loaded, too," said Harada.

Magraw chuckled. "Not without special work barges—barges that aren't in Malanueva."

"About our plan to open her up," said Magraw. "Can we accomplish it all tomorrow, before the crew arrives?"

Wolfram pointed at a stack of heavy I-beams and equipment, loosely covered by a heavy tarpaulin. "There are the raw materials." He glanced at his watch. "In exactly three hours you will meet the rest of the team. Our Kabuki friend here will return immediately to Malanueva."

Harada nodded assent.

Magraw frowned slightly. "Sometime, Hugo, I would like to know *why* I sink freighters in odd places."

Wolfram smiled, clapped Magraw on the shoulder, and turned to Harada. "My two key men. The mission centers on you. You'll know everything you need to know. Count on it."

21

WOLFRAM WATCHED KINSEY get out of a rented sedan and make his way into the motel. He winced visibly as he strode into the chilled and musty gloom of the air-conditioned entry.

"Welcome to Freeport." Wolfram got up from his chair and approached.

"What a godawful place."

"You won't be here long—two days at the outside."

"Are there others I should meet? *Have* I met them?"

"Why don't you sign in?"

They went together to the vacant registration desk and rang for attention. An elderly clerk appeared from a rear room. Kinsey signed a dog-eared registration card. Silently, the clerk flipped him a room key chained to a huge plastic paddle, then moved back toward his inner chamber. "Check-out, 2:00 P.M.," he muttered over his shoulder.

"You have a bag?" Wolfram asked.

"In the car." Kinsey shivered involuntarily.

Wolfram gestured toward a dim hallway. "Second door on the right. We have a meeting room. Luncheon has been laid on. Noon."

Kinsey nodded, then went out to retrieve his bag.

Outside, heat waves ruffled the horizon. Faint smudges of ocher smoke moved slowly across the sky. Another automobile

148

pulled up outside. Wolfram made out the profiles of Esposito and Juanita, each wearing dark glasses. Esposito was driving too fast, and he braked too hard. He moved the convertible into a parking slot and got out, stretching. From the opposite side Juanita appeared.

Wolfram met them at the door.

"It ain't Miami Beach," Esposito said.

"It's not supposed to be." Wolfram turned to Juanita. "I'm sorry it doesn't suit."

"Who cares?"

Wolfram summoned the clerk from his secret place.

"Separate rooms?" he demanded.

"That's what I reserved," said Wolfram. "One for the lady. One for the gentleman."

The clerk tossed the two plastic-paddled keys onto the counter, muttering something unpleasant.

"I need a drink," said Esposito. "It's a long hot drive from Houston."

Wolfram led them to the deserted bar just off the lobby. The room smelled of old mops and spilled beer. The middle-aged bartender seemed in no hurry to serve them.

"A double Jamaica rum for me," called Esposito. "And a glass of water." Juanita declined a drink. Wolfram had a Scotch. "Here's to it," said Esposito, downing half his drink quickly.

"We won't be here long," Wolfram said. "Today, tomorrow, and out the next day." He glanced at Juanita. "I didn't pick it for style."

"You don't have to explain," she said crisply.

Esposito tapped his glass. "Another, *por favor*."

"We have a luncheon laid on for noon," said Wolfram. "After that we have an afternoon of discussion, a seminar."

"And tomorrow?" she asked.

"We'll discuss tomorrow after lunch." Wolfram glanced at his watch. "We only have a half-hour or so before our get-together. I suggest we adjourn to our rooms until then."

"To meditate?" she asked. "Pray, perhaps?"

"Why not?" murmured Wolfram. He dropped cash on the bar, and they walked out together.

They lunched on jambalaya and made small talk.

Wolfram worked at affability, wearing it like a too-tight collar. He recited Chamber of Commerce facts about the fishing off the coast, the shrimp industry, the petrochemical complex. Magraw told stories of the sea. Silent, Kinsey watched the woman. Esposito drank too much.

At the end of the meal a team of Mexicans cleared the table while the five of them stood by.

"Is this place secure?" asked Kinsey wryly, looking around the austere room.

"Secure enough," said Wolfram. "I've retained the cell on the other side of this plastic concertina." He tapped the folding wall divider.

When the Mexicans had left, Wolfram motioned the group to sit down. From the corner, he produced an easel with a chalkboard and a thick, old-fashioned briefcase. He withdrew a map from the briefcase and taped it to the chalkboard. It was the same chart Harada had used the day before to explain the harbor of Malanueva.

He turned to them. "A few words in general," he said crisply, looking intently into each face. "This is a need-to-know mission. I will tell you nothing that you do not *need* to know to carry out your specific duties. In addition, I will sketch in for you just enough about the mission to give you a certain amount of flexibility." He smiled grimly. "Inevitably, there will be twists and turns in our plans that we do not foresee."

He pulled from his pocket a telescoping chrome ruler and extended it. "One other thing—most important—this is a mission against property, only property. I tell you that in case you have any qualms. We will not be armed on the mission itself, nor will we carry any arms at all. Our mission will take us into areas where any sign of serious arms—pistols or shotguns—subjects the bearer to instant trouble. We want none of it.

"You are denied the answer to only one question from me regarding your specific assignments. That question is *why?*"

He paused again and looked into each face. "I am not sure there is even an appropriate answer to 'why.' In any event, you do not need to know why this target was chosen or why we are undertaking this mission. Suffice it that you are being handsomely paid, and then some, for your particular talents." He smiled. "Any questions about that?"

There were none.

"Very well. Now to the mission itself." Wolfram turned to the chart and tapped it with his pointer. "Our target is here, the harbor of Malanueva.

"The key to this mission is to sink a ship here." He indicated the sea channel. "The purpose is to block the channel and cut off commerce in and out of the harbor. The ship must sink in precisely the correct place at the correct time and in such a manner that it will look like an accident. Captain Magraw will explain the technique to you in a few minutes.

"As for the rest, it is a matter of making a critical temporary adjustment in the channel markers."

Wolfram pulled from his briefcase a rumpled red-and-white plastic object, like a deflated beachball, a pneumatic cartridge, and a black canvas sack. After arranging his display on the table, he proceeded.

"Our friends Esposito and Juanita will go to Malanueva, posing as honeymooners. They will travel with these Venezuelan documents." He tossed an envelope to Esposito. "On the afternoon of the correct day, they will travel," he pointed to the map, "from Malanueva's Gran Hotel Bolivar, across the West Bridge, out along the road to Castel Mala, which is beside the ship channel that we are interested in. There is a sandy beach by the Castel where they will camp." Wolfram paused. "Incidentally, our honeymooners will have a small panel truck provided by our man already there, whom you will all meet later."

Esposito stirred. "This Castel Mala, it is an army post?"

"Not really," said Wolfram.

"How do we explain our equipment?"

"Your scuba gear, you mean?"

"No, this other stuff you have here."

"I'll explain that in a moment. Any other questions before I continue?" Wolfram looked around briefly, then went on.

"At the channel beach the honeymooners will make no pretense of concealing their scuba gear." Wolfram shrugged. "It's not an uncommon thing for people to dive, is it?

"When darkness falls, they will get down to business. In their truck they will have," he held up the plastic object in one hand, the black sack in the other, "six of each of these. Taking three sets each, they will swim into the channel and, first, place a black sack over the existing light buoy, then swim west seventy-five yards, more or less, and . . ."There was a sudden whooshing sound and the red-and-white plastic ballooned into a large striped sausage. "Presto! A brand-new buoy!"

From the bag, Wolfram produced a small road lantern and turned its blinker on. "These will be the lights." He pointed to a noose on the bottom of the inflated buoy. "A heavy cord will go through here and attach to a light weight. You'll be in quite shallow water.

"What we will have done is to move the marked channel seventy-five yards to the west. Any ship following the new markers will run aground on the west bank of the channel. On the night in question we know that a certain freighter will arrive at twilight off the coast and request a pilot. Because this freighter is relatively small, the pilot will bring it in at night."

He held up a cautioning finger. "We cannot be sure how long this will take. But we know this—as soon as the freighter appears, our honeymooners must be near their temporary markers. As soon as they see the freighter is in trouble, they must extinguish, deflate, and sink their own buoys as quickly as possible. They they must uncover the original buoys. This will require cleverness and speed on their part, because by that time there will be lifeboats and excitement around the sinking ship." He paused. "I emphasize the word 'sinking.' We cannot merely have our freighter run aground, it must go down. Now Captain Magraw will tell you how we accidentally sink a freighter under safe conditions."

Magraw, puffing thoughtfully at a cigar, moved to the head of the table as Wolfram sat down. He turned to them. "Fellow Rotarians . . ."

Even Wolfram laughed.

Magraw fumbled with the chrome pointer. "If I get this properly adjusted, we can pick up Moscow." His smile was infectious. They appreciated his casualness after the German General Staff manner of Wolfram.

Magraw continued, "My assignment, as Hugo indicated, is

to bring a freighter up to the channel mouth about dusk on the proper day, pick up a pilot, and let him follow the channel markers. He will run the ship into the edge of the channel. And the ship will sink.

"Because I need your help tomorrow morning to assist me in preparing the ship, I am going to explain to you now how we can make sure that our vessel will fill with water and go down in the channel."

Magraw turned to the easel and drew a silhouette of a ship in profile and proceeded to explain how his "can opener" would sink the ship.

"What about the crewmen?" asked Kinsey, when Magraw had finished his explanation. "They'll be trapped."

"Not at all," said Magraw. "A freighter proceeding down a channel like this makes approximately four knots—about the speed of a man walking at a good clip. What will tear the bottom out of the ship will be the momentum of the vessel, not the velocity." He smiled reassuringly. "Not to worry. The crewmen will hear a loud ripping sound. They'll make for the ladders. And even if they're a little slow, there'll be plenty of time." He handed the pointer back to Wolfram and returned to his chair.

Wolfram stood slowly. "In addition to the gravel cargo in the hold, there will be a small, locked chest on the bridge, which will be retrieved a day or so after the sinking. The bridge will not be far below the surface at low tide and may even be exposed."

"What is it?" asked Kinsey.

"Some explosive devices that will be used to sink another ship in the channel area." He again taped up the chart. "Here in this dock area. This pier is the only facility that can accommodate a large ship. We anticipate sinking one there."

"With an explosion?" said Kinsey.

"I said these were special devices. Ships do have diesel tanks explode. Static electricity. It happens all the time."

"That's the plan?" Kinsey persisted.

"That's as much of it as you need to know."

Wolfram turned to Magraw. "Perhaps you had better explain our work project tomorrow."

Magraw went back to the head of the table. "We are going to fasten on the can opener." He took a small notebook from his pocket. "Heavy-duty electric drills will be aboard. Mr. Esposito, by benefit of his scuba expertise, will be under the ship with six long two-inch threaded steel rods. When the drill punches through, he punches up with the threaded stock. Topside, we stay it in place, caulk it, and so on. When we have the rods in place, we will bolt on a heavy plate topside, and then swing the can opener into place under the ship and position it on the rods and bolt it fast. Simple?" He grinned. "We'll see in the morning."

Wolfram stood up again and removed more envelopes from the briefcase.

"Your expense cash and credentials, tickets, and so on," he explained, tossing them around the table. Then he produced some larger envelopes, each bearing the name of one of the group. After handing out the last one, he said, "Take good care of these. It's your down payment. No U.S. currency, of course. But securities you can turn into cash. I suggest you deposit them forthwith in some safe place." He smiled, as if to himself.

22

"*THE WORD 'TUB' WAS* coined for this one," Kinsey muttered.

Five people stood on the pier beside the old boat. Its new name, *Charon*, gleamed in large white block letters from the bow.

"Who is this Charon?" Juanita asked.

Magraw grinned. "An old friend of Hugo's."

"The crane is the key to it," said Wolfram. "Magraw will run the crane."

"The water is very polluted," said Esposito, peering over the edge of the pier.

"We'll move the girders for our special 'keel' from over there, Magraw. Kinsey and I will bring out the power tools and drill the holes for its assembly."

"Are you going to assemble it here?" Kinsey asked.

Wolfram shook his head. "In pieces underwater. Will you be able to see down there, or is it too murky?"

Esposito shrugged. "Depends on the lights. You have an underwater light for me?"

Wolfram nodded. "On board with your scuba equipment. Also Juanita's." He looked around. "You might as well go aboard and get it." He pointed to a deck cabin door. "Here's a key for the padlock."

Esposito and Juanita headed toward the corroded gangway.

"Will threaded rod stock be strong enough when the vessel impacts?" Kinsey asked. "Why won't it just shear off?"

"That would be a danger with only one or two connections," Magraw agreed. "But we're going to have six."

Wolfram was frowning. "We'll need a stabilizer bolt at the punch end of the keel, won't we, Magraw?"

"Right. One should be enough."

"Let's get started." Wolfram walked over to the stack of materials covered by a tarpaulin and began to peel the canvas back. Kinsey assisted while Magraw made his way up the ladder of the crane.

II

It took all morning. Magraw maneuvered the heavy beams to dockside while Kinsey and Wolfram worked the heavy-duty electric drills inside the ship.

"It's a bit tricky," Wolfram observed. "If we get the holes through the ship out of sync with the holes in the beam we're going to waste one hell of a lot of time underwater." He found a strip of sheet metal and made a template.

The drilling of the beams took two hours. Kinsey drilled small holes where Wolfram told him to, then, changing bits, reamed larger and larger ones until the job was complete.

Nearby, Esposito and Juanita carefully checked their underwater gear.

"Okay," Wolfram said finally. He handed Esposito the foot-long, threaded steel rods. Each had a thick rubber washer and a hexagonal nut. "They have to go through the beams, through the hull and through a reinforcing plate inside the ship," he explained. "Esposito, you and Juanita wait here until I signal you from the ship. When you're underwater, you'll hear the drilling near the keelson. Keep a sharp eye peeled for the breakthrough and move fast."

As Wolfram and Kinsey struggled to carry their drills aboard the ship, the divers waited at pierside.

III

The bilges smelled of sewage and old oil, but they were relatively dry. A few days at sea would change that.

"I hope to hell Esposito is fast on the trigger with those rods," Kinsey muttered. "I don't want to go down with this rust bucket."

"Forget it," said Wolfram. "This is a piece of cake."

Wolfram adjusted the template and motioned Kinsey to begin. A few moments earlier, he had signaled Juanita and Esposito to go underwater and they were somewhere down there, just the other side of the hull.

Shortly, the drill punched through the side. Water spouted up as Kinsey pulled the drill out, but a threaded rod from below shut it off immediately. Quickly, Kinsey spun a thick rubber washer and heavy nut onto the threaded stock, while below Esposito, presumably, did the same.

The process was repeated for the remaining rods until each was in place and bolted. Wolfram mopped at his greasy forehead, then said to Kinsey, "Next step."

IV

The beams of the underwater spotlight sliced through the translucent olive gloom. Juanita held the light as Esposito maneuvered the heavy, awkward beam.

It had been decided to offset the weight of the steel with empty drums, then drag the combination under the ship by crane and cable until Esposito could jockey the beam into place. Once it was connected to the ship, the remainder of the keel could be attached to it with relative ease.

It was slow work. Esposito would signal Juanita how much the beam-and-drum rig had to be pulled to port or starboard, or forward or aft, and she would relay the message to the surface.

After prolonged tugging and pushing, the beam nestled itself onto the bolts. Esposito attached one nut loosely, then another, a third, the sixth. Finally, the stabilizer bolt at the point.

He went to the surface, emerging with a whoop. "She's on, baby! Hand me a big wrench!"

Wolfram and Kinsey applauded. From the crane Magraw tipped his grimy fedora, while Esposito dived again to tighten the connections.

V

The sun was high and they were sweating, but Wolfram was pleased. He helped Kinsey haul Esposito and Juanita from the water. The divers quickly unharnessed their equipment and peeled away their rubber suits.

"Not so bad," said Esposito. "That first beam was a son-of-a-bitch. The rest, no sweat."

"Plenty of sweat up here," said Kinsey, glancing at the sun.

"I feel greasy all over," Juanita complained. "That water is dirty soup."

"We'll head back to the motel shortly," said Wolfram. "Only a few more things to do here."

Magraw descended from the crane with consummate dignity. "First time I handled this kind," he said.

"Tonight we celebrate," said Wolfram. "Tomorrow, we all come down here and watch Magraw clear the harbor."

"Of course I might sink in the channel if it hasn't been dredged to the depth they say."

"How much clearance is there, actually?" Kinsey wanted to know.

"On the chart, eight feet all the way out to sea. How did it look to you, Espo?"

"About that. Right by the dock the silt had gathered like this," he made a swooping gesture with his hand, "you know, the edges fill in that way."

"Okay, let's clean up here," Wolfram instructed. "Espo, you and Juanita pack your gear in that trunk. Make sure you have every piece of it, because there is no way to get spares in Malanueva." He looked around the pier, then toward the area where the steel beams had been stacked. A steel container marked "Flares" remained. "Kinsey, help me move that aboard."

23

AT 7:15 P.M., Wolfram joined them in the same beige room they had occupied the day before. Now their mood was different: they were partners in an enterprise.

A bar had been set up.

Wolfram poured himself a glass of gin and smiled at each of them. Esposito was already into his third drink.

"This job is going to be a fun job, Hugo, I tell you," he said loudly. "Movies, those are the tough jobs down there."

Magraw brandished a thick cigar. As he told Kinsey and Juanita a story about an alligator, Kinsey was more relaxed than he had been for days.

Wolfram circled around them until he was at the end of the table set for their festive meal. He tapped a spoon against his glass for attention.

"This is the last time we will be together until, as your instructions inform you, we make our—how shall I say it—our return flight." He wore his corporate expression—businesslike, but not unfriendly. "As you know, Magraw sails with the tide tomorrow. We will see him off from the side of the channel downstream. We would like to join him at the pier, but that wouldn't be wise, since we don't want his crew to see us.

"Juanita and Esposito also leave tomorrow to begin their journey via Venezuela to Malanueva. Kinsey and I will be on our way in a few days." He paused significantly and glanced down at his place setting as if looking for a program note, then looked up.

"Our date is Sunday, the fifteenth." He lifted his glass of gin. "Here's to the success of our mission."

Silently the others lifted their glasses and drank the toast.

"Now," said Wolfram, "if there are no questions, let's get this party going." He headed back to the bar for a refill.

II

Incredibly, Wolfram sang. His voice was a clear baritone that showed signs of formal training. After dinner, at his request, a piano had been wheeled in from the luncheon room nearby. Magraw's mellow bass joined in lustily, along with Esposito's rather strained tenor.

"Shall we take a walk?" Kinsey suggested to Juanita.

"Wolfram sings well," she smiled. "You wouldn't think it. His face hardly moves, but this voice comes out."

Kinsey took her arm. "I wish we had a rose garden instead of a sulfur bath. We'll make the best of it."

"I have never been to Malanueva. What's it like?"

"I haven't been there either," he said. "I believe it is just like this."

They strolled down the hallway, through the lobby, out to the parking area in front of the motel.

"This Wolfram," she said. "Have you known him long?"

"One hundred and eight years."

"I'm serious. You knew him before this?"

"Does the word 'Heike' mean anything to you?"

"No."

"It was an operation. It had some elements that are like this job."

"Were you in it?"

"I was flying Hueys—helicopters—with the First Cavalry Division in the central highlands of Vietnam." He took out a packet of cigarettes and offered her one. She declined. He lit up slowly. "I was frightened to death. Our birds were going down every

160

day. My chopper was hit several times, and I lost a crewman once. I lost troop passengers other times. It just seemed a matter of time."

"Wolfram was there, was he?"

"No." He was silent for a moment, then went on. "Finally, I got hit. Nothing very serious, but enough to put me in the hospital for a few weeks. A clean chunk of flak in the thigh."

"My God!"

"I was lucky. The bone was spared." Kinsey was silent for a moment. "Anyhow," he finally continued, "in the hospital I was trying to figure out some way I could evade having to go back to flying missions."

"Who could blame you?"

"They would. That's when I met Hugo. He appeared in the ward one day."

"He was an officer?"

"Who knows what Hugo was . . . or is. He was wearing army fatigues without insignia. Anyhow, he came in and sat with me, very solicitous. At first I thought he might be some kind of chaplain."

"Seems hard to imagine."

"It does, doesn't it? But there he was. He asked me how I felt about going back to combat missions."

"What did you tell him?"

"I told him the truth. I told him I was so scared I got cramps in my stomach."

They had reached the edge of the parking area and stood staring across the darkened desert of Freeport. "Hugo probably was not very sympathetic about that."

Kinsey flipped away his cigarette.

"As a matter of fact, Hugo was very sympathetic." He turned to her. "I'll tell you a secret about Hugo. He is to other people exactly what he wants to be to them—Mr. Nice, Mr. Tough, Mr. Professional, Mr. Heartless. I don't know which one or two or more of those is the real Hugo."

"Do you care?"

"After *Heike*, I never wanted to see him again. But then, a couple of weeks ago, when he appeared at the airport . . . I was trapped again. He has a talent for knowing when your frying pan has gotten so hot that you'll accept his fire." He laughed abruptly.

"What happened the first time?"

"Well, to make a long selling job short, Hugo convinced me that all I had to do was volunteer for a relatively simple clandestine flying mission and I would be excused from further combat, sent home, and given my honorable walking papers."

"So you did?"

"Of course." He chuckled. "Don't get me wrong. I had no illusions that I would not be in danger, but the option was one dangerous mission against dozens. The odds seemed good."

"Did it turn out that way?"

"For me?" He sighed. "As a matter of fact, yes. For some others, no. Some others who deserved better, I might add."

"You sank a ship?" she asked.

"Basically, yes. There was a little more to it than that. It's classified. I shouldn't have told you as much as I did."

"I understand."

"Do you really?"

She smiled at him. "I have been through a lot."

"But not through a Hugo Wolfram mission." He put his arm around her. "You see, Juanita, Hugo's missions are mysteries. Things are not what they seem. The straightforward thing is crooked. The crooked thing is correct. Dumb luck is planned. Planned things don't happen."

"Who is this Hugo? Where does he come from?"

"All part of the mystery," Kinsey replied. They walked back toward the motel. "All I know about Hugo is that he is the consummate technician."

She laughed softly. "Don't ask 'why,' he says."

"That's it. He thinks the word 'why' is the common denominator of all the world's trouble. And he thinks the word 'how' is the common denominator for all solutions."

"Even sinking ships?"

"He thinks very quickly, very surely, in tough situations," said Kinsey. "He can do anything we can do. He can dive as well as you or Esposito. He can fly a helicopter or any other plane better than I. I wouldn't be surprised if he could handle a ship as well as Magraw."

"Was Magraw in this other operation?"

Kinsey nodded. "But not running a ship exactly."

"So the three of you have worked together before," she said. "It is reassuring to know that we are not all professional strangers."

He did not reply. He did not tell her that there had been another diver, and that he was dead.

She laughed. "And Wolfram *sings!* I cannot believe it."

Kinsey laughed, too. "He likes Bach. Would you believe that?"

Inside, the meeting room was still illuminated. They didn't walk that way.

III

It was 1:00 A.M. when Kinsey returned to his room to find the door slightly ajar and the light on. He reached out and pushed it with his palm, standing to one side to see who or what was inside.

"Come in," called a voice. It was Esposito.

Cautiously Kinsey moved inside. Esposito was sprawled in one of the room's armchairs. The Latin's face was puffy, his eyes bloodshot from drinking.

"You're late, buddy," he said. "You take long walks."

Kinsey shut the door behind him.

"I never knew Juanita liked to go for such long walks," Esposito said, smiling strangely. "Only short walks—on streets—you know?"

"What's on your mind?" Kinsey said.

Esposito stood up and moved toward him, swaying slightly, smiling. Kinsey braced for trouble.

"Juanita," said Esposito. "She means something to you, does she?"

"She's all right," said Kinsey. "She's honest."

"Oh?" Esposito's smile spread. "She tell you all about what a good hooker she is, eh?"

"I don't give a damn about that," said Kinsey. He worked at looking calm.

Esposito's smile faded. "Well, I tell you something, buddy boy, I pull that dame off the streets, you understand me? I save her backside."

"Now you think she belongs to you, that it?"

Remarkably, Esposito's anger faded, as if a sudden cloud had passed. He turned and walked back to the chair. "You don't understand," he sighed, slumping down into it.

"Of course not," Kinsey snapped. "I don't know what you're talking about."

Esposito shrugged. "We're Cubans, she and I. Not Puerto Ricans, like we say."

"So?"

"So, I was with Castro when he went into Havana." He smiled. "Those were great times."

"Go ahead."

"Juanita had a pretty tough life as a kid, so she do what lots of little Cuban girls do before Castro, she becomes a hooker. Only Juanita, she better looking and smarter, so she the girlfriend of a big shot in the Battista government."

Kinsey began to relax again. "Was she arrested when Castro came in?"

"Of course." He chuckled bitterly. "She was held for a while, then sent to a women's prison. They called it *retraining* and that's where I get to know her."

"*You* had something to do with the *retraining* of women?" Kinsey laughed at him.

"You don't get it. They put me to running the place because they could trust me." Esposito looked at the floor. "I'm no rooster. More like a capon. Maybe more like a hen."

Kinsey said nothing.

After a minute he looked up again and went on. "So, you see, they figure I am the best one to run the women's jail."

Kinsey began to unbutton his shirt. "I'm sorry I don't have any booze."

"I had enough."

"It's getting late, you know," Kinsey said. He was not unsympathetic to Esposito. "You have a long day ahead."

"I can take it." He stood suddenly, almost aggressively, and Kinsey backed away again. "Juanita and me, we swam out of Cuba—in scuba gear and some floats."

Kinsey was surprised. "Why?"

"It was beginning to turn sour for me under Castro. Juanita knew how to use scuba gear from when she lived with the big shot."

"You mean you just went into the surf one day and began swimming?"

Esposito shrugged. "I arranged for her to be with me because I needed a partner That's all there was to that."

"How long did it take?"

"We were in the water for more than three days. We swam steadily and I had studied the currents, so I knew we would be carried toward the Keys. At night we slept on our floats. I brought enough food, water. We had a small sail."

"That's incredible!"

"We ran into an American fishing boat before we came to any islands and he take us into Key West."

"I never read anything about it," said Kinsey. "You'd think there would have been a lot of publicity."

"Nothing," said Esposito. "First thing ashore, I get in touch with your CIA. I have lots of things to tell them and they work out this Puerto Rican cover for me and Juanita. We go as brother and sister."

Kinsey nodded slowly. "Then you're not lovers?"

"That's why I'm here, buddy."

"What do you mean?"

"We're not, like you say, lovers. But we *love* each other. She's more to me than anything else. We don't go to bed with each other, but we're in love. You understand?"

Kinsey stared at him. "And what's that to me?"

"I tell you. It's two things. First, if you hurt this person, I come from wherever I am and kill you." He ran his forefinger across his throat. "Second, I want you to promise that you will do your best to get her out of this thing, if it goes sour."

"How can I promise that?"

"Of all of them, you are the only one who will put a person ahead of the mission, you know? I feel that. I want that for her, if anything happens to me—insurance. You know what I mean?"

Kinsey nodded. "All right. I'll do that." Why not, he thought. The idea of saving Juanita from a Malanueva firing squad was not repugnant. But, then, he would not see her until it was over, and they all were flying free.

"I promise."

24

I

THE FAINT EARLY MORNING breeze unfurled the Liberian flag at the stern of the *Charon* as the vessel moved into the main channel. Its horn sounded, a flatulent, vibrating sound, and the tugboats responded with derisive hoots. Across the oily water came the steady thrum of the tugs' diesels. A plume of steam rose from a pipe beside the stack of the *Charon*.

"The name stands out clearly," said Wolfram. "Can you see it?"

"The letters look like bones," Esposito replied.

"It's luminous paint. You'll be in the channel after dark, and it might help you to know that you have sabotaged the correct vessel."

They squinted through the gradually brightening haze for some sign of Magraw on the bridge. The horn sounded once more, and the toots again responded. Wolfram's group stood watch on an old pier far downchannel from the old Liberty. Slowly, ponderously, the tugs, one fore, one aft, ushered the ship along the waterway.

The sun was almost over the horizon before the ship glided by them. Even though they could not see Magraw, they waved.

And then it was downstream.

"It's strange to know that she's sailing off to her doom," Kinsey said. "I wouldn't feel half so sentimental if I knew the old barge was going to the wrecker's bar."

Juanita smiled at the flier. Esposito, puffy-eyed from the previous night's revelry, shook his head slowly and said nothing.

Wolfram clapped his hands suddenly, startling them. "Now!" he said. "Now the mission is really under way!"

II

They ate in a diner made of stainless steel and fly specks. Wolfram ordered French toast, orange juice, and coffee.

"You'll rue the day," said Kinsey.

"What day?" Wolfram grinned.

"The day you eat French toast in Texas."

"Who said I was going to *eat* it. I only ordered it."

Esposito giggled. "I tell you, it's a damn shame we have to break this crew up so soon when we're only getting to know each other."

Their orders came. Wolfram held up his glass of orange juice. "To our next meeting."

"You seem very pensive," Juanita said to Kinsey.

He smiled at her. "Missionitis."

"What will become of you when this is over?"

"Do you care?"

She shrugged. "As much as I care about anything or anyone."

"I'll spend time with you." He reached across and took her hand. "Count on me."

Esposito picked up the line. "We damn well better count on you. You're the wheelman, buddy boy. Without you, we no make our getaway."

Wolfram paid the tab, and they walked to the parking area.

"I'll drive," said Kinsey when they arrived at the car.

"Did you check the flights?" Wolfram asked.

Kinsey, starting the car, nodded. "Three P.M."

"The weather will be more pleasant in Montreal," Wolfram said. "Juanita? Espo? Your flights check?"

"Noon sharp to Caracas," said Esposito. "Connecting flight from Caracas at midnight." He laughed loudly. "Some way to spend a honeymoon!"

"I'll say *au revoir* here," said Wolfram. "Drive carefully." He didn't wave as they pulled out.

III

Two hours later Wolfram waited at a vacant concrete pier near the lower turning basin on the Freeport Channel. Through a pair of binoculars he watched a pair of giant cranes deck-loading racks of metal ingots aboard a huge bulk carrier ship, spanking new, painted gleaming white with aquamarine trim lines. The raked-back stack bore the Greek Delta insignia of the DePrundis lines.

He didn't turn around as a dark-blue limousine pulled up behind him. A car door slammed.

"Why must we always be doing something out in the tropical sun?" asked Simon.

"Mad dogs and Englishmen," Wolfram murmured. "You certainly picked a beautiful ship."

"The *Queen DePrundis.*" Simon took out a white linen handkerchief and touched it carefully to his upper lip. "She's 550 feet long, draws 32 feet of water, and can handle a cargo of 44,000 deadweight tons, which happens to be the amount of ammonium nitrate that was loaded aboard her yesterday and the day before. Let me borrow your glasses."

"It looks like they're almost finished with the metal," Wolfram said. "They should have no trouble making their sailing schedule."

"They won't." Simon smiled. "The Cosmo Construction Company boxed them into a penalty clause for late delivery."

"It's the only way to guarantee performance from the DePrundis interests." Wolfram glanced at Simon. "And what did it cost you and Bradford?"

"Actually, we benefited from a soft ship-charter market." He passed the binoculars back to Wolfram. "A year ago we would have had to pay six dollars a ton for this job. Now the going rate is down to a dollar ninety. We paid a premium of ten percent."

"Not bad." Wolfram scanned the ship again.

"Why the trashpackers?" Simon asked. The odd-shaped vehicles were deck-loaded under gray canvas.

"My plan says we will run them over a pipeline at an appropriate moment." Wolfram started to load the binoculars into a black leather case.

"Let's get into the car. At least it's cool."

"No chauffeur?"

"This is a secret mission, I'm told."

Wolfram laughed. It was going well.

"The others," Simon asked him. "Do they know the whole plan?"

"They know everything except the dénouement."

"You mean the blast?"

"That's correct." Wolfram looked out of the limousine window toward the ship three hundred yards away across the channel.

Simon was hesitant. "Bradford. He wants to know if you have any . . . estimate."

Wolfram glanced at him sharply.

"I'll be frank, Wolfram. I wish to hell he'd call it off. There *must* be some other way."

Wolfram snorted. "I'm sure there is. There *always* is. The real question is whether we are going to do it *this* way."

Simon said nothing. He fiddled with the air-conditioning controls.

"Have you been working on him?" Wolfram asked. "Are you chipping away?" He reached across the seat and grabbed Simon's forearm. "I'll tell you something, mister." He pointed at the *Queen DePrundis*. "When that ship sails tonight, the balloon has gone up, unless you or Bradford make up your minds that you are going to tell the whole world . . . what?"

Simon shook off Wolfram's hand. "I did not say the plan would not go through. I indicated only that Bradford . . . well, all of this finally came home to him. He suddenly realized that he was programming the destruction of, perhaps, a whole city, a harbor at the very least."

"Jesus!" Wolfram exploded. "I don't care a hoot in hell if this is right or wrong. But, believe me, if a person, or a group, or the whole damned U.S.A. wants to expunge a maggot like DePrundis, then we are doing it the *correct* way. It may not be all that nice and *right* for your guts, but it sure as hell will happen."

Simon raised his hands, almost imploringly. "Okay, Hugo. The show goes on." He took a deep breath. "But . . . what is your estimate?"

Wolfram did not reply immediately. Finally, he said,

"Maximum of fifty dead. With the harbor blockaded, the ship skippers will let everyone ashore for Saturday night except a small skeleton force. Sunday is not a regular work day at the refinery. Only a small guard force will be on hand."

"Fifty is the absolute outside, then?"

"I can't make guarantees like that," said Wolfram. "For all I know they'll bring a Sunday excursion boat right past the *Queen DePrundis* when she goes bang."

Simon sighed. "My God. If something like that happened, he'd kill himself."

"Look," Wolfram snapped. "Bradford—and others—have retained me to make certain things happen. Molecules of explosives have no morals. Only confused human brains have them."

"We're getting nowhere."

"On the contrary." Wolfram gestured at the huge white ship. "A few more hours and that bomb is on its way."

"Whatever happens, Hugo, good luck to you and your crew —as people, I mean."

Wolfram chuckled. He reached for the car door and got out. Simon put the limousine in gear and pulled slowly away. Behind him Wolfram kept laughing.

25

I

THE STREET-LIGHT SYSTEM had just winked on when Simon entered Bradford's office and padded across the deep carpet. Bradford sat with his back to his desk, staring out across the city.

"Sitting at the top of this tower, Simon, is like being inside the periscope of a submarine," he said. "I keep looking for a target."

Bradford swung around to face him. He pulled a spearlike pen from his onyx desk set and examined it.

"Wolfram said it will cost as many as fifty lives."

Bradford didn't seem to hear him. Simon leaned forward in his chair and spoke more loudly.

"Skeleton crews on ships. Some will be guards at the refinery. Innocent bystanders."

Bradford looked up sharply. "Aren't we all?"

Simon seemed about to reply. Instead, he shrugged. "It's immaterial now. The mission is on its way."

Bradford raised an index finger. "We still have the fiscal side, the monetary side. I want you to go to work immediately. Call our agents wherever the bourses are open around the world."

"And . . .?"

"Begin to take short positions in Petrol/Malaverde." He frowned slightly. "It's going to be tricky. Don't trust the agents. If they ask what we're doing, make up some plausible story."

"I'll tell them we're going short against the box in order to defer taxes against our long profits on the original investment," Simon said.

Bradford was smiling. "That's a damned good story. But will they believe it? They're the same agents who were liquidating our long position a few days ago."

"They'll believe it."

"And out there somewhere are hundreds of rabbits that don't know the eagle is about to swoop down on them."

Simon's expression was somber. "We could still tell them, you know."

"We couldn't turn it around at this stage."

"Not turn it around." Simon warmed to his argument. "Abort it. We get the information out to the public. We make a big splash through some agency. Buy an ad. We could disguise ourselves just like we put this . . . mission . . . together." He leaned toward Bradford and rapped his forefinger sharply on the desk. "As late as the afternoon of Saturday, the fourteenth, we could still wreck it."

Bradford looked at him and shook his head. "There are too many other things at stake now."

"I don't get it."

"You aren't supposed to."

Simon leaned back in his chair. "All along I've had the distinct feeling that there is more to all of this than the mission—as we know it, as I know it. I've had the feeling that someone has been looking over my shoulder, over yours, over Wolfram's."

"Forget it!" Bradford snapped. "Sell short!"

Simon nodded assent. As he moved toward the door, Bradford said to him, "Remember what Pliny said? 'The best plan is . . . to profit from the folly of others.'"

II

Alone again, Bradford dialed a telephone number. Three times the recording told him to dial again. He waited.

"Yes?"

"Board room."

"Name?"

172

Bradford referred to a small card. "George J. Harmon, account number CCC4074."

Click.

Another voice. "Good evening, Mr. Harmon."

"I just wanted to bring you up-to-date," said Bradford. "Our shipments are en route. The financial arrangements have been most satisfactory."

"Are you proceeding with your equity program?"

"Yes, thank you. The first funding has been completed, and we are now embarked on the second phase."

"The Bank always stands ready to assist in these financial arrangements."

"That's appreciated."

"You supplied me with a contract delivery schedule for your shipments. Are those dates still firm?"

"All firm."

"The penalty clause leverage was effective then?"

"My associate is very good at finance."

The voice asked if there were any questions.

"No, sir. I'll say good night."

There was a click at the end of the line, then a second click. A monitor? Bradford smiled grimly.

The coded conversation told him the tale. Through its intricate access to the tellers and cashiers of the world, The Bank had somehow borrowed millions of Malaverde escudos and converted them to other currencies. In addition, The Bank had sold millions more for delivery in the future markets. And when the mission had accomplished its goals, The Bank's debts in escudos would shrivel. In Malaverde an economic desert would result.

26

I

PHOSPHORESCENT PLUMES OF foam curled around the bow of the *Charon*. From the bridge Magraw could easily make out the shimmering edges of the sea even though the moon was now only a sliver among the clouds. Though dark, the sea was snug, not ominous this night. The swells were shallow and the slight wind was warm and benign.

He puffed contentedly on a cheroot and strung together small, dull beads of dialogue with his first mate, a retired drunk, who was manning the helm.

"She answers most peculiar to the helm, Cap'n," he slurred. He'd been at the rum before his watch, but he knew by instinct what most men never learned of the texture of the sea.

After an appropriate time Magraw responded, "She has a special stabilizer keel." Magraw lied easily, effectively. "They were fitted on ships of this type during the Korean War."

"Never heard of a stabilizer keel, exactly."

Magraw puffed a while before saying more. "A number of American bottoms were fitted with them." He leaned against the varnished slat wainscoting that lined the bridge. "The Liberty ships and the Victories are relatively flat-bottomed."

The mate nodded slowly, as if that explained everything.

Magraw went on. "Flat-bottomed ships tend to ride up and over the big swells of the type you find in the west Pacific waters in winter." It wasn't entirely true. He paused to think up technical reasons for the keel. "As the flat ship rides over the swell, it tends to yaw, sliding down the other side, and wallow in the trough."

"Could swamp," the mate conceded. The idea was making sense to him.

"Right." Magraw rummaged for more jargon. "Actually, the most important reason for the keel is roll stability on a rough sea. Keeps cargoes from shifting as much as they might, especially bulk cargoes like we're carrying."

The mate nodded again. The information was stowed like baggage with his other seaman's knowledge. "Anticipate any rough weather, Cap'n?"

Magraw shrugged. "The glass is steady. I think we'll make it smooth as silk."

They stood in silence for a time until the mate cleared his throat. "There's a ship on the horizon on our port side. I can just barely see some lights."

Magraw opened a lower locker and found a pair of binoculars. "Can you make her out?"

Magraw adjusted his focus for a moment and brought into view a large white bulk carrier. "It looks like the *Queen DePrundis*," he murmured. "She was loading in Freeport when we left."

"It doesn't take the new ones long to catch up with old ladies like this one."

Magraw chuckled. "We're wide open doing ten knots. Best this ship ever did was twelve." He put the glasses aside. "A ship like that can make fifteen to eighteen, fully loaded—better with light cargoes."

"Things sure change."

II

Far to the south another boat shared the sea. Harada drifted in a small cabin cruiser, his line dragging bottom for whatever fish might chance by in the near-slack tide.

His craft was a mile off the first channel marker into Malanueva, but even here there was the swampish stench of the refinery.

With a free hand he picked up his binoculars and studied the inshore waters—the channel; the dark, shallow bay water; and, some four miles in, an illuminated line of five tankers to be loaded the next day.

At least three of them would still be in port tomorrow night when the cork went into the neck of the bottle. Two more tankers were due tomorrow afternoon, followed later by the *Queen DePrundis*.

In the darkness Harada rummaged about and found one of the good Havana cigars so readily available in the port. Carefully he lit up, rolling the cigar in the flame until its soft brown eye turned bright orange. He took in a large mouthful of the rich smoke and savored it, then blew it out.

For some moments he puffed thoughtfully, musing.

Suddenly a jolting, persistent tug shook his rod. Harada snapped from his reverie. Chuckling and puffing pungent clouds of smoke, horsing the rod, winding the reel, he brought to gaff a red snapper of some five pounds.

The fish of good fortune for the New Year.

III

From where the honeymoon couple sat on the open side veranda of the Gran Hotel Bolivar, overlooking the dingy harbor, they, too, could see the ships at their moorings.

"Tomorrow this time we go for our swim." He was drunk, but in control.

She nodded. Her last drink was untouched. The tables near them were empty. At other corners of the room couples ate silently. At a large round center table sat an enormously fat man, cutting, lifting, chewing, and swallowing with enginelike regularity.

"Are you afraid?" Esposito's eyes searched her face.

Oddly, she was not. Worse, perhaps, she felt nothing. "Tell me what to fear," she said.

Esposito swirled the ice in his glass. "If I were Juanita instead of Esposito, I would be afraid of *me*."

"Why?"

"Cowardice."

"You don't know what the word 'fear' means. You are like a little child that has had no experience with danger or mortality."

"Why do you say that?"

She laughed softly. "You are foolish and brave. You have done the most dangerous things. You have done them well and have survived. By any measure you are brave."

He shook his head. "I have tried, but that is not enough. There are shapes in the water sometimes, dark and changing. I want to scream. It gets worse the more I do it."

She was looking elsewhere. "Do not turn your head, but there is a fat man at the center table and he puts food in his mouth as if he were shoveling coal. It is incredible!"

"Around the reefs sometimes," he murmured, "there are hidden, shadowed places in the mountains of coral and each has its snakes and monsters."

"I wonder who this man could be," she said. "The waiters are all trying to kiss his ring." She touched the tip of her finger to her lips. "But not, I think, a Malaverdian. His features are not Latin. It is hard to say with all that fat."

"Tomorrow night we will plunge into the dark waters and strong currents." He rattled his ice and looked around for a waiter to order more liquor. "You know, I never liked swimming in dark waters," he said matter-of-factly. "Even in that sewer of a canal in Freeport, I was afraid." He laughed abruptly. "No sea monster could live in those chemicals."

She sat up quickly. "Something is happening!"

At the entry to the veranda stood a squad of uniformed men with submachine guns. On a spoken command, they marched smartly from table to table, passing by the fat man, who ignored them. One of them came to their table. "Identity, please."

"What the hell is this all about?" Esposito demanded.

Juanita said, "Please," putting her hand on his arm. He relaxed. Grudgingly he produced their passports and handed them to the man. Carefully the officer studied the documents. "What is your business in Malanueva, señor?"

"We are newly married. This is our wedding trip."

The officer handed the documents back to Esposito. "Welcome to Malaverde."

"What is this about?" Juanita asked politely.

"You will see shortly," the officer said. He turned on his heel and clacked away briskly. The other machine gunners took stations at various points on the veranda. The fat man ate on.

Through the entry stamped an incredibly short man in a powder-blue uniform decorated with multicolored ribbons. For a moment he stood in the doorway, thumbs hooked in his belt, then strode quickly and noisily toward the center table. Distracted, the fat man struggled to his feet to greet the other man, then returned to his feeding. Two waiters wrestled a huge chair under the uniformed man. Another team of waiters brought a bucket and champagne.

"Who is it?" Esposito asked hoarsely.

"Another of our great Latin heroes, *muchacho*. *El Libertador* himself."

"Should we leave?"

"No. Let's look at this snail so that we might savor the meaning of our swim in his channel tomorrow night."

Mercado, still wearing his hat at table, glanced her way.

She smiled enticingly, professionally.

He raised his glass.

She nodded.

IV

She is completely overwhelmed by the presence in person of her *El Libertador*, Mercado assured himself. He lets his smile linger benignly upon her as he slowly returned his glass to table.

She continued to stare at him. A lesser man, he thought, would become embarrassed.

Turning, he motioned to the maître d'hôtel, who scurried over. "The lady and the man over there!" Mercado said curtly. "Who?"

"A honeymoon couple, *Libertador*. From Colombia, I believe."

"How very charming! Send them a bottle of champagne with my compliments."

The maître d' bowed away. When *El Libertador* looked back at the couple, they were engaged in earnest conversation. I could impose myself, he thought, perhaps even take her for myself.

Undoubtedly she regrets the presence of that lout while *El Libertador* is so near. A belch beside him interrupted his reverie.

"DePrundis, you are a monument of flesh that is ever building itself at the expense of others."

The fat man chewed and smiled, and, finally, put down his utensils. "Since all monuments eventually disappear, *Libertador,* I just want to arrange that my own dissolution not be too quick." He carefully removed a gold-and-ivory toothpick from an inside pocket and examined it thoughtfully. Deftly, he unscrewed the pick from its case and began mining fragments of his meal.

"We have completed your additional stock purchases of Petrol/Malaverde securities," he told Mercado. "My personal loan has secured this, because the price has gone very high. Fortunately, there was some rather active selling in the past few days so our overall price, while high, was not deplorably so."

"Selling? Why selling? Why would bankers sell the goose which lays the golden eggs?"

DePrundis smiled. "Don't worry. The sellers do not know what we know. The markets have their own standard practices. One of them, called profit-taking, is used by a speculator when he has made a handsome gain. His instinct is to seize his profit and to invest it somewhere else equally well. This practice is particularly evident in the case of stocks that have advanced rapidly, like Petrol/Malaverde."

Mercado nodded rapidly. "Why don't I . . . we . . . do that?"

"Because, my friend, the stock will continue to go higher. If you sell now, you will miss the future profits and since you control both the country and its oil, it is unlikely that anything will happen to them."

"I am rather shrewd, after all," Mercado said smugly.

"Yes, but we must step up production."

"In due course I will employ some of my riches for much needed travel abroad."

DePrundis sighed. "If we are to maximize profitability on our investment here, we must pump more effectively."

"I have never been to Spain."

"We are bringing in new equipment."

"Perhaps I will make the tour within the year. A grand state visit to the mother country."

DePrundis smiled faintly. "By sheerest coincidence

our . . . ah . . . predecessor organization ordered a pipeline survey. I saw copies of some of the papers the other day. Some equipment, in fact, will be delivered aboard one of my ships here tomorrow."

"Do your ships carry passengers?"

"This ship is carrying equipment. I understand it is some kind of mobile construction equipment. I'm not sure what the predecessor's problem was on the pipeline, but we might as well let them pay the bill."

Mercado was lost in his own vision. "We will show the world the Malaverdian revolution."

"For some bizarre reasons our predecessor company apparently ordered a shipload of fertilizer. All paid for. All we have to do is accept delivery, and we have more than 40,000 tons of fertilizer."

"There will be parades," Mercado continued. "And special masses for the heroes of the revolution. For me."

"Fertilizer of this type apparently sells for more than thirty dollars a ton on the world markets."

Mercado's face clouded. "I wonder if I must do something dramatic, like Castro. Grow a special beard, perhaps, or wear workers' clothes." He immediately regretted the idea. "I will not! It does not suit the dignity of the Peoples Republic of Malaverde!"

DePrundis was faintly surprised. "I believe I shall have the *baba au rhum* for dessert. They do it passably here." He wondered why the Bradford interests would order and pay for a shipload of fertilizer. Perhaps there was an agricultural enterprise somewhere inland that had not yet come to light.

DePrundis motioned for the maître d' and ordered dessert.

In the harbor workmen disconnected tubing from one great illuminated ship and moved it to the next ship in line.

Execution

27

I

BEHIND THEM THE AIRCRAFT'S turbines continued to whine. As they disembarked, Kinsey surveyed the beige, parched field. The atmosphere of jet fuel and scorched rubber was smothering. Kinsey associated the pervasive odor of charred insulation, acrid and penetrating, with crashed aircraft and fragmented, broiled bodies.

As they moved toward the customs shed, the craft that had brought them swung sharply away and prepared for takeoff. Kinsey was reminded of the fast in-out landings at scooped-out strips under mortar fire in Southeast Asia. He could almost see the dusty puffs of mortar bursts and feel the compressive thuds.

"There's the helicopter hangar," Wolfram said.

"They've painted it a different color," Kinsey replied. "It was white on your slides."

"Blue must be the national color. There's the chopper."

The helicopter rested on the asphalt in the middle of a white circle. Like the hangar, it was painted pale blue.

Behind it was a one-story building with a flagpole. The row of Korean War vintage F-85s lined up near the building—and the flag on the pole—bore the forest-green cross-fitché edged in white of the Malaverde Flying Corps.

They picked up their bags from a cart just outside the customs building, a triangular structure of precast concrete and tinted glass. It was much newer than the shabby uniform of the porcine customs official inside. He wore a hat several sizes too large, embellished with a tarnished sun-burst ornament. He poked at their belongings and glanced at their passports. "You are tourists in Malaverde?"

Wolfram produced an official-looking envelope. "We are here on important business. From the Cosmo Construction Company, you see." He pulled a set of onionskin papers from the envelope.

The customs official was confused. "Should I make a report?"

"Absolutely!" Wolfram was totally in control. "I was told to give this copy," he pulled out another flimsy, "to the entry official. That's you, I believe."

"Of course." The official was instantly solicitous. This Wolfram was apparently a man with high connections. He looked at the form. "You are inspecting our pipeline?"

"Inspecting *and* servicing."

"I see."

"We have been instructed to pick up a helicopter at your Air Force hangar."

"Oh?"

"Yes." Wolfram nodded toward Kinsey. "Our pilot. He has authorization."

"Oh?"

As Kinsey started to produce his own fake papers, the official shook his head. "No need, señor. Show them to the appropriate Air Force officer."

Wolfram looked at his watch. "There is still a lot of time left in the day, Harrison." This was Kinsey's cover name. "I suggest we slip into our coveralls and get right out on location."

Kinsey agreed. "We cannot afford to waste time."

The customs man shrugged. These Canadians were like the Yankees—always pushing. "I have no further requirements of you, señors. Please proceed."

"Would it be possible for you to call a government car? Since we are here on official business it might . . ." Wolfram's voice trailed off significantly.

"Of course, señors. I will arrange for this vehicle and you may, as you said, put on your special garb."

"Excellent."

Carrying their bags, Wolfram and Kinsey strolled through

the chilled lobby of the airport toward the door marked "*Hombres.*" Someone entered just ahead of them.

Inside, they placed their bags across two wash basins and began to undress. The third man ran water full blast into a basin. "Good to see you again. How does it go?"

"It goes, but it goes quickly." Wolfram spoke into the mirror to Harada's reflected image. "The helicopter is on line. We think it might be on call for some functionary, and we want to get to it before he does."

"My report shall be quick, then. First, Esposito and his lady friend have made contact. Right now they are at my fishing establishment by the telephones." He handed calling cards to Wolfram and Kinsey that bore the name of José Martinez and identified him as the Director, Oil Pipeline Inspection and Repair. "The critical thing about these cards is that they have my telephone number on them. Everything else corresponds to your papers, Hugo. However, it might be useful to have the guard place a call to my number. I have instructed Miss Juanita and Mr. Esposito to stand by as secretary and director."

"A good touch." Wolfram appreciated Harada's sense of small theatrical details.

"In this bag are the tools you requested," Harada continued.

Wolfram and Kinsey zipped up their coveralls. Harada stuffed their traveling suits into their bags. "Also, as directed, I smuggled the appropriate correspondence into the government files."

"Are Esposito and Juanita prepared for tonight's expedition?"

"Yes. They will take my small panel truck."

"Any word from Magraw?"

"He has requested a pilot. The port has given him preliminary clearance, and he will arrive at approximately 8:00 P.M."

"Will it be dark?"

"Not quite. But within the half-hour it will be pitch-black. I was out on the water myself last night. There is virtually no moon and anything in the channel itself is just about invisible."

"And the other ship? Will it make port?" Wolfram asked.

"You mean the *Queen DePrundis?* It has already docked," said Harada. "As instructed, I have spoken to the authorities about off-loading the mobile equipment." He rubbed his thumb and forefinger together. "It took special arrangements, but the vehicles will be on the dock tomorrow morning. You and I can pick them up then."

"You have the papers I gave you?"

"Of course."

"Kinsey and I will start this afternoon at the far end of the pipeline and work our way toward the coast. Do you have your map?"

Harada produced a wrinkled Bradford Petroleum Company road map.

"Tomorrow morning, Harada, meet me here." Wolfram indicated the intersection of the coast highway and the pipeline. "Kinsey can drop me off early, before anyone is up."

"I will drive the truck," said Harada. "But suppose there is trouble in the channel tonight with our friends? Or suppose the truck is seized or otherwise lost?"

"We'll make our appointment early, say, 6:00 A.M." He looked at Kinsey. "Is it light enough then to see?"

Kinsey nodded.

"Six o'clock then," Wolfram continued. "If you have not arrived by seven, I will presume something has gone wrong, at least as far as the truck is concerned. I will walk along the pipeline toward the harbor."

"The refinery area is fenced off," Harada said.

"Then I will follow the fence around toward the harbor. You can meet me anywhere along the way."

"And if the news is very, very bad?"

"I will make my way to your fishing station."

"For emergency I will leave keys to my place in the large potted plant near the main doorway."

"With them, also leave the keys to your boat, please. Any questions?"

Harada shook his head.

"Tomorrow, then."

Harada left the lavatory ahead of them.

II

As the customs functionary had promised, an aging Dodge sedan,

186

painted government blue, awaited them at the curb in front of the building. Wolfram ignored the sallow young man slouching insolently beside the car. He snapped open the door arrogantly and climbed into the car. Over his shoulder he mumbled important-sounding phrases at Kinsey. Nonplussed, the young man hurried around the front of the vehicle and got behind the wheel. Wolfram barked instructions in Spanish, and they were on their way.

The helicopter pad was within walking distance of the main airport building, but Wolfram wanted the official blue car to help him past the gate guard post. The guard, however, did not stop them.

"You have the key handy?" Wolfram whispered to Kinsey as they climbed out of the blue sedan next to the helicopter. "Then get aboard and check the fuel. Start the machine when I give you a thumbs-up signal." He seemed disappointed at the lack of security. "There's no one here to check papers."

"How about that noncom?" Kinsey pointed across the way to a soldier who was apparently giving a guided tour.

"We may have to draft the bastard. I have to ram these documents down somebody's throat."

"Why don't we just climb aboard and fly?"

"This is a covert operation, which means we have to smother them with official paper and confusion to give us time."

Shrugging, Kinsey turned to open the door of the craft. A wave of hot air buffeted him as he climbed aboard and began checking the instrument panel.

Wolfram walked a few steps away from the craft and, with a drillmaster's shout, attracted the attention of the noncom. He beckoned emphatically. The sergeant looked at his group, back to Wolfram, at the group again, then came jogging.

"Yessir?"

"I have been assigned to take this helicopter on an inspection tour of the pipeline," Wolfram declared in Spanish.

"I don't know anything about it."

"*You* would not be told in any event. I must leave this receipt with someone in authority, who must then make a confirming telephone call to the appropriate ministry."

The sergeant was a monument of concern and indecision.

"You will take care of this for me?"

"I am not in authority, sir."

"Who is?"

"The Officer of the Day, sir."

"Where is he?"

"At siesta, sir."

"I have no time to waste on this! *El Libertador* wants this work completed!" Wolfram brandished his papers. "This has been contracted and paid for by your government."

"But, sir, I am not in charge."

"Look, my friend," Wolfram said softly, "all you have to do is accept these papers. When your officer returns, give them to him. Tell him when he has these receipts to call the number on this card and confirm that all is in order and that the Cosmo Construction Company is satisfied. Is that understood?"

The sergeant reluctantly accepted the sheaf of papers and the card. "I will tell him."

"Good, good." Wolfram smiled. "You are a good sergeant. If your lieutenant were at his post, as he should be, you would not have to deal with this affair."

"I will see that he gets the material."

"Tell him to make sure that he calls the bureau on the card or he might be in serious trouble. Sometimes there are confusions over who is to have access to the craft. We don't want that."

The sergeant nodded emphatically.

Wolfram turned and gave the thumbs-up signal to Kinsey. The helicopter's turbines went to work.

Wolfram walked over and climbed in beside Kinsey.

"How did it go?"

"Sometimes I believe we overplan," Wolfram snorted. "I could have driven up a truck convoy and made away with the entire Malaverde Air Force and not one person would have stopped me."

Kinsey laughed. After a moment of warm-up, he took the chopper up. As the airport receded below them, Kinsey was struck once again by how two-dimensional things looked from the air. Miles to the north he could see the old castle by the sea channel. The harbor waters were murky brown and the deeper

188

ship channel was an alligator color. Two miles to the east he could easily make out the sprawling refinery complex. Huge ships studded the harbor rim, each squarely in the channel, like freight cars on a track.

"Fly across the refinery to the pipeline," Wolfram shouted above the sound of the helicopter. He had a small tablet, on which he seemed to be tallying the ships in the harbor. "Take her lower, I want to see the names."

Kinsey maneuvered the helicopter down to a hundred feet above the water. All five ships looked newly painted and bore a Greek Delta on their stacks. The four tankers—the *DePrundis Lady*, the *DePrundis Beacon*, the *Standard*, and the *Flyer*—were lined up in the channel. The fifth, the *Queen DePrundis*, was the only one moored at a dock. Half a dozen lines of rubber piping snaked over the side of the *Lady*, loading oil from the refinery.

"Let's go on out the pipeline!" Wolfram shouted.

Kinsey could see the pipeline streak away from the refinery, up a shallow ridge, under a highway, out of sight on the other side of the ridge. It reappeared at a viaduct across the Rio Paraná, then ran over the horizon into the arid wastelands.

III

The lieutenant glared at the flimsy papers.

"So," he snapped at the sergeant. "In return for a handful of papers, which you cannot even read, you turn over a craft of the Malaverde Air Force to a stranger!" He tossed the papers on the desk.

"The pilot had the appropriate keys, sir," the soldier mumbled.

"Keys can easily be forged—or stolen!"

"But where, Señor Lieutenant? Who would have them?"

"Get out!" the officer barked. "I will handle this myself!"

The sergeant saluted, turned on his heel, and made his getaway.

The lieutenant sighed as he picked up the papers and glanced through them. They were quite official, even bearing the seal of Malaverde. One appeared to be a receipt for the helicopter. It bore someone's illegible signature, along with some instructions:

The authorizing officer should confirm this receipt immediately, write in the time of departure of the aircraft, and affix his signature.

The lieutenant rubbed his chin. He had been on a long siesta and the plane had been taken more than an hour before. He found the card left by the sergeant and dialed the number. After two rings an operator's voice came on.

"The director, please."

There was momentary static while the connection was made. "Director's office."

"The director, please."

"Who is calling?"

"Lieutenant Sanchero of the Air Force. I call from the aerodrome."

"One moment, please."

Sanchero waited impatiently. A minute later a brusque voice came on the line. "Yes, what is it?"

"Lieutenant Sanchero of the Air Force. A short time ago two men from the Cosmo Construction Company came here and left with our helicopter."

"They were to have been there more than an hour ago."

"Yes, sir. They were, but as we are very busy here, this is the first opportunity that I have had to call you to confirm the receipt."

"What do you require?"

Sanchero was puzzled. "Only that they are authorized personnel, señor."

"Authorized? Of course they are. *El Libertador* himself."

"Thank you, señor." He paused. "Señor . . ."

"Yes, yes, what is it?"

"Would it be permitted if I entered the earlier time confirming this call? My superiors often are not so understanding about the difficulties of catching up with paper work at the appointed time."

"Of course, my dear lieutenant," the voice chuckled. "I will coordinate my records. Shall we say 12:45 P.M.?"

"Most excellent."

"Very well. Good day."

Sanchero smiled as he filled in the time and signed the paper with a flourish. Then he stapled all of the papers together and put them into his file tray. No need to retain the personal card of the director. He would be reachable again. He tore up the card and threw it into his wastebasket.

28

I

EVEN AT A THOUSAND feet the heated air from the inland plateau occasionally buffeted the helicopter. They followed the pipeline across the bleak, parched landscape below. The whup-whup of the helicopter rotor and the high-pitched whine of the turbine precluded conversation.

Wolfram crouched over in his bucket seat, a case of tools between his knees, concentrating on the pipeline stretching out ahead of them.

Far ahead of them they could see drilling-rig towers, squares of buildings, a lacework of trails, faint tinges of dust rising in the air. Wolfram pointed at the horizon, then motioned to Kinsey with his hands, palms down. As the craft descended, he could see stubbles of large cactus. The pilot picked a flat area and set the helicopter down, then looked at Wolfram, who nodded assent. Kinsey shut the turbine down.

Sweat showed on Kinsey's face. They opened the doors of the craft and climbed out. Wolfram reached into his bag of tools and produced two cotton baseball caps. "Wear this. The sun here can fry your brain in ten minutes."

Kinsey pulled the cap on. "What next?"

Wolfram looked around. There was no breeze, no sound. "You and I are going to make sure that this pipeline cannot be turned off." He stared at his companion for a moment. "We want the oil to continue flowing even if someone should want to stop it."

"We could have picked a cooler day."

Wolfram pointed at a huge cast-iron fixture on the pipeline. "That is known as a gate valve. There is one gate valve every five miles along the pipeline. Each one has a wheel that can be turned like a faucet to shut off the flow."

"Plumbing," Kinsey muttered.

"In most cases the wheel is held on by a heavy nut. We remove the nut with our wrench. If the nut happens to be rusted in place, we use this." He took a battery-driven hacksaw from his bag. "If the nut won't budge, we slice off the wheel."

"What do we do with the wheels, once we've removed them?"

"One of us will remove the wheel while the other digs a hole and buries it."

"Frankly, Hugo, the removal of obvious parts won't appear to be an accident."

"In that pile of phony memoranda are several references to the fact that gate-valve wheels were removed, for some unaccountable reason, prior to the new government. They must be replaced. Cosmo Construction Company is looking into that."

"Do you think anyone will ever read that junk?"

Wolfram selected an entrenching tool from the bag. "Plausibility is the key, Kinsey. Entire governments will accept the plausible fraud. 'That junk,' as you call it, is part of the game."

II

Wolfram's concern that rust might have joined the retaining nuts to the shaft threads was unfounded. The dry desert air had inhibited corrosion.

Quickly, they used the helicopter to get as close as possible to the next gate valve down the line. They moved as swiftly as they could to unbolt the iron wheels and bury them. They alternated jobs, one digging, the other wrenching, as they proceeded down the pipeline. During the short flights from one gate valve to the next, Kinsey kept his door open, allowing the air to cool them off before their next descent.

At one juncture, laboriously lugging one of the heavy iron wheels toward the shallow pit Wolfram had dug for its burial,

Kinsey panted, "What the hell's the point of all this? What if they can't stop the oil flow for a day or so? They'll have a wheel of some kind in a couple of days and shut it all down."

Wolfram raked powdery soil back over the buried wheel. "The unimpeded flow will jam up their refinery," he said finally. "It will force it to close down . . . at least for a time."

Kinsey mopped at his face with a bandanna. The explanation seemed plausible. That it did not satisfy him entirely was, after all, secondary.

III

Late in the afternoon Wolfram and Kinsey reached a point on the pipeline where there were shacks near the now-familiar gate valve.

"This is the radio relay point." Wolfram said as he climbed out of the aircraft and, with Kinsey trailing him, walked toward the building. Kinsey strolled twenty or thirty feet to his right, kicking up dust.

"Hey!" Kinsey shouted. "Look here!"

Wolfram trotted over to him.

The ground was littered with bones and shredded rags, among them three skulls, dusty and yellow in the late afternoon light. A fourth skull was half buried face down in the sand.

Wolfram stooped down and fingered some of the cloth fragments. "Bradford Petroleum insignia," he said. "Probably employees patrolling the pipeline." He pointed to a clean small hole in one skull. "Bullets."

"Who the hell would kill some poor workmen?"

Wolfram stood up. "It happens every day. My guess is that these fellows happened to be in the way when Mercado took over. Mercado gunned down a whole work crew at those oil rigs we saw." He squinted at the sky. "We'd better get done while we have time."

They retrieved their tools.

"This setup is a bit different, Kinsey."

"I can see," said Kinsey. He wrenched the nut loose, twirled it off the end of the shaft with his fingers, and hurled it out into the desert. He rapped the wrench sharply against the wheel, loosening it, then lifted the heavy part quickly. "These things must weigh thirty pounds," he grunted. Twenty-five feet away Wolfram had scraped a shallow hole for the wheel and Kinsey dumped it gratefully.

"Next valve, here we come," Kinsey panted.

"We're not going to the next gate valve. At least not yet."

"The sun will be down shortly. I don't want to fly this thing at night."

"We'll spend the night here. Besides, you have an assignment here Sunday morning."

"Here? Sunday?"

"The radio."

"What radio?"

Wolfram looked around. "Why don't we make ourselves comfortable. I'll tell you all about the radio while we eat."

Kinsey took the tools back to the helicopter and returned with tins of corned beef, canteens, and Wolfram's flask. They walked over to one of the sheds and sat down, then opened the cans of rations and Wolfram's brandy.

They ate in silence, then lit up the Havana cigars Wolfram produced from a pocket in his coveralls.

"All right," said Kinsey, exhaling a cloud of smoke. "Tell me about the radio."

Wolfram stood. "Let's tour the place and get an overview."

As they walked around the buildings, Wolfram pointed to utility poles that were ranged parallel to the pipeline, following it toward Malaneuva.

"Follow the telephone poles. The wire lines carry their traffic into this shack where the modulated telephone signal is translated into a radio signal and transmitted, via this radio tower, to the oil fields."

"Why didn't they just string telephone cable out to the field?"

"Who knows? Perhaps to save money. More likely it was a temporary expedient, pending the construction of a regular telephone line."

Wolfram picked the padlock on the door of the radio transmitter shack and went in. He shined his flashlight around the dark room until he found what he was looking for. Kinsey followed him over to a small table in one corner. "Type L470 radio link equipment," Wolfram said, pulling a wiring diagram out of an inside pocket of his coveralls. "Remove that front panel, will you?"

"There," said Wolfram, pointing at the diagram. He glanced at the exposed circuit, then put his finger on a plug-in solid-state component. In a small plastic bag stapled to the wiring diagram, there was an identical component. "On Sunday morning at precisely 11:30 A.M., you will remove the component that is in the equipment and replace it with this one attached to the wiring diagram."

"Which, of course, does not work."

"It isn't easy to find solid-state components that have failed," said Wolfram. "This one will appear to have been hit by lightning."

"Plausible," Kinsey conceded, "except they don't have thunderstorms here in the desert."

"But they do have lightning, Kinsey." He seemed impatient. "I've worked this out."

Wolfram tucked the diagram into the circuit panel. "Don't forget to bring the replaced part and the diagram with you when you leave. Also, lock the door."

By the time they left the shack, the sun had set. Wolfram glanced at the illuminated dial of his watch. "I suggest we get what sleep we can now. Remember, you are going to drop me off early to meet Harada."

"We're only about twenty miles from Malanueva now. That means I'll have to do four or five gate valves by myself tomorrow."

"Shouldn't be difficult."

"Does the Malaverde Army patrol the line?"

"I noticed no tire tracks today, did you?"

"They would sand over in twenty-four hours. Sooner if there is a breeze."

"Then keep your eye peeled tomorrow. After all, you have a perfectly plausible reason to be out here and the papers to prove it."

"I'll avoid a meeting, if you don't mind." He pointed at the skulls. "Maybe they had plausible reasons, too."

29

I

TWENTY-FIVE MILES NORTH of the radio shack Esposito reclined against a hummock of dune grass and watched the sun sink. He wore only swimming trunks and a heavy layer of repellent to ward off mosquitoes. He puffed contentedly at a cigar, rolling the rich smoke around in his mouth and blowing it out with satisfaction. Beside him, Juanita lounged in the sand, tracing designs with her fingers.

Across a narrow, steep strand of beach, the tide ripped on the ebb, making the lighted buoys bob. Just as well that they were jostled by the tide, he mused. Their natural motion would help camouflage his and Juanita's movements.

He glanced at his watch. Darkness had turned the castle walls nearby from white-washed broken stone to ebony shadows. Only the far-off spotlights illuminating the great tankers reflected from the water.

For some time he had been watching the pale lights of a ship approach. It should be the *Charon*. His cigar finished, Esposito carefully pushed it deep into the sand, then piled grains on it with his cupped hand.

"It's time, *muchacha*."

Slowly they got up and made their way to the old panel truck. There they began buckling on the familiar apparatus. Juanita looked up as she zipped herself into a black rubber scuba suit with its luminous yellow side stripes.

"You're not wearing your suit, Espo?"

"Too much trouble."

"You might scrape your skin on barnacles."

"So I scrape," he said impatiently.

"You ought to wear your suit."

That decided it for him. "Nonsense! Let's get on with this! The sooner this is over, the sooner we retire." He rummaged in the truck for the canvas bags that contained the inflatable buoys. Methodically, he unzipped the case. Each of them would take three cover bags and three buoys. He had bundled two sets into easily transported plastic bags.

Some distance from them toward the sea, they heard a boat motor throbbing.

"It's the pilot boat," said Esposito. "They are going to pick up the *Charon*."

He noticed Juanita shivering slightly. "Just do the job," he said. "Concentrate on your tasks. You won't have time to think of fear. Remember you will be swimming against the ebb tide part of the way."

"I'm ready."

"You have your buoys?"

"Yes, *muchacho*, I have my buoys."

"Then we go."

She was nearly invisible in her black diving gear, but she could faintly make out his lighter skin as he made his way into the channel.

II

The *Charon* was aligned directly with the narrow channel of Malanueva. Beneath Magraw's feet the ship throbbed asthmatically. It was incredible, he thought, that it had held together this long. A five-knot breeze could have troubled the voyage.

"Take the wheel," Magraw said brusquely to the mate, who had already done some celebrating in anticipation of their arrival. He took the helm, hugging it like an old friend, and squinted into the night.

Magraw took his binoculars from the locker and scanned the harbor.

"Five big ships in the channel, Number One."

"Oil for the lamps of China," the mate replied.

Magraw's glasses picked up a white wake against the sea and some dim running lights. Behind him the radio man poked his head into the bridge. "Cutter radios. They want to put the pilot on board."

Magraw studied the cutter through his glasses for a few more moments, then said quietly, "Heave to, Number One." On the intercom he ordered a ladder put over the side.

It would not be long now, he thought. He hoped the mate could swim. They might not have time to put a boat over.

A searchlight blinked on, illuminating the side of the ship and the ladder. The crew stood around, waiting for them.

Five minutes later the Malaverdian cutter pulled up beside the boat. A rotund man wearing khaki fatigues and a black moustache scrambled up the ladder with an agility that contradicted his shape. A moment later he was on the bridge. He and Magraw exchanged salutes.

"I'm Captain Abdullah," Magraw said in Spanish.

"Ah, you speak the Malaverdian language," said the pilot. "I am Punta. May I see your papers, please?"

Magraw handed him a package of documents. The pilot skimmed them quickly. "We must, as the Yankees say, double in brass here. I must make the manifest inspection, too." It didn't seem to bother him.

"May I offer you some hospitality, Captain Punta?"

"I am on duty."

"A little something to ward off the chill of the night." They both laughed.

"Well, all right. Something for the chill."

"Number One, will you fetch a bottle and some glasses." Magraw chuckled. "I'm sure you'll be able to find the liquor locker."

The pilot was studying the manifest. "A cargo of *gravel,* Captain? What on earth for?"

Magraw had expected the question. "The cargo is consigned, as you can see, to the Cosmo Construction Company, which has been retained to do some work involved with the pipeline." He smiled knowledgeably. "The gravel, plus cement, to be delivered soon, will be used for the construction of some concrete facilities. A pier, I believe."

"Yes, of course." It made sense. He folded the papers carefully and handed them back to Magraw. "All seems to be in order."

The mate returned with a bottle of rum and three glasses. Magraw poured a generous portion for the pilot, then one for himself. He handed a glass to Punta, then raised his own. "*Salud!*"

The pilot murmured a response and drank. "Very good rum. American?"

Magraw chuckled. "They do not know how to make rum in America. It is from Jamaica. Would you like a bottle?"

"I could not accept."

"Nonsense, my friend. I insist." He turned to the mate. "Number One, bring up a bottle, one of the *good* bottles, for our friend." He turned back to the pilot. "Is there difficulty taking a ship into this harbor, Captain Punta?"

The pilot shrugged. "It depends largely on the kind of ship. The truly big ones—such as the tankers that are in port now —require some very careful maneuvering. We take them in only on the flood tide and, of course, they depart the same way."

"The channel is narrow?"

"It is deep enough for those ships that call, but barely wide enough. It takes management."

"I am impressed," said Magraw, lighting his pipe. "Do you conduct these ships under their own power to their mooring?"

"Not the giants." The pilot smiled. "A ship such as this, yes. It will be done quickly. But the large ships require tugboats to pull them into position. It is a tricky business."

"What tide will we have going in tonight?"

"Very nearly dead low. But it will be no problem with your ship, Captain. There will be more than enough water all around." He emptied his glass. "Tomorrow morning at flood tide, you will see some tricks done. We have two ships loaded with refined fuel oil. The *DePrundis Flyer* is 78,000 deadweight tons and the *DePrundis Beacon* is 100,000 deadweight tons."

"Incredible."

"Already they are in the channel, pointed seaward. As the tide floods, we will haul them straight out to sea and they will be on their way to Brussels."

"Brussels?"

"Yes. DePrundis—that is to say Petrol/Malverde—has additional refineries and storage there for its European operations."

"The refinery here makes only fuel oil?"

"Oh, no. They make many petroleum products. Diesel oil, fuel oil, some petrol, and so on. Very modern."

"I am anxious to see it."

"You have not been to Malanueva before?"

"Not for many years."

"We must be on our way," the pilot said. He put his glass down and moved to the helm. "We will take her in like a sailboat."

The ship moved full ahead for a time, then the pilot took the speed down sharply. "Five knots in the channel," he said to Magraw. "The giants can only do it in two or three."

III

Esposito's fingers moved deftly and his body worked well as he pursued his watery tasks—swim; remove black bag; cover lighted buoy; swim; drop anchor; inflate false buoy; switch it on; swim.

He could feel the throb of engines, the characteristic grinding pulse of gears and propellers, as the *Charon* approached. If the ship caught up with him, he could be minced by the propellers. He was shivering, his teeth were chattering, yet the water was not cold.

What if my muscles cramp? he thought. Why didn't I put on my scuba suit? The swim against the tide was more difficult than he had anticipated. He could feel his heart pounding.

He reached the last buoy and embraced it gratefully, panting heavily from his exertions. The ship was some distance away. There was still time—ten minutes, at least. Catching his breath, he pulled his equipment to him and removed the black bag. The red beacon cast more than enough light to see. He covered its beam with the bag.

He pushed off toward the position of his final anchor and false buoy. All his years of swimming told him how many strokes he had to make to cover a fixed distance.

"Sixty meters," he panted. Treading water, he removed from the net bag the last of the five-pound anchors, a mushroom of cast iron with thin nylon line threaded through a hole in its stem. He dropped the anchor, paying out line until he felt it thud on the bottom eight or nine feet below. Juanita was dropping hers in water over seventy feet deep.

Carefully Esposito bunched up the extra line and hitched it snugly to the bottom of the false buoy. Then he pressed the carbon-dioxide cartridge and with a snap the red-and-white striped plastic ballooned into shape. He switched on its lamp and let it go.

Across the channel, he could see red lights on buoys. Juanita had done her work well. Looking back toward the sea, the parallel lines of false buoys seemed true. Far inshore, of course, there were other channel markers that might be visible to the pilot if he made a point of looking for them. But why should he? He had no reason to expect anything out of the ordinary.

The *Charon* loomed at the channel mouth. Esposito could see three heads silhouetted on the bridge.

It was going to work.

His fear disappeared, for a moment at least.

The *Charon* entered the outer channel.

30

I

MAGRAW HAD CHOSEN TO stand on the starboard side of the bridge. When the ship foundered, it would lurch to port. He would fall, grabbing the wheel and twisting it hard a'port, hoping the crippled ship's momentum would bring it back into the true channel before it went down.

The pilot was relaxed at the helm, perhaps a little too casual. For this exercise, Magraw thought, that was desirable. The first mate stood slightly behind them.

As they entered the channel, Magraw could see that the markers were slightly off the true course. The pilot suspected nothing, but Magraw maintained a running dialogue that together with a glass of rum should dull his alertness.

"You must have been a pilot for many, many years," he said. "I can tell by the sensitive manner in which you handle the con. It is apparent that you can . . . feel the soul of this vessel."

The pilot nodded. "I have piloted my share of the world's vessels into Malanueva." He looked at Magraw. "Captain, it would not be a lie if I told you that I have held the wheel in this very channel on more than one thousand vessels."

"Incredible!" Magraw sounded genuinely impressed. "It must give one an enormous sense of being part of history to know that he has handled such a great proportion of the world's merchant fleet."

"Naval vessels also. Since we are friends, I can tell you. One of my greatest pleasures has been the piloting of warships, particularly the American warships, into this port."

"It must provide a sense of great power."

"Indeed!" The pilot shook his head sadly. "For those few moments I am part of the long line of great naval commanders." He shrugged. "But now we no longer have visits from the gringos."

"Because of your revolution?"

"Yes." He sniffed contemptuously. "The gringo is bitter that our *Libertador* has seized the property that they stole from us." He frowned. "It is true, Captain. The gringo is a terrible imperialist."

Magraw nodded emphatically. "I have seen it everywhere. But I am sure that everything has gotten infinitely better."

The pilot shrugged. "We still have a great distance to go, of course. But I am most confident. *El Libertador* can work wonders!"

As the pilot spoke, Magraw felt the first vibration of impact, then the jarring lurch. Even at five knots, the jolt and yaw of the ship hurled the pilot and the first mate off their feet in exactly the direction Magraw had intended. Magraw himself was too busy with his own calculated sprawl at the helm to watch them. Frantically he spun the wheel to port.

The ship continued to move slowly, its props still churning. Magraw could feel the vessel answering the helm ever so slightly.

"What happened?" The pilot struggled to his feet, dazed. "We were right in the channel! Squarely in mid-channel!"

Magraw, sensing that the *Charon* now was coasting into the channel, grabbed the intercom. "Engine room! Engine room! Report!"

Static and a voice choking with hysteria squealed back at him. "We hit something, Cap'n. She tore up the whole bilge. We're flooding fast and the boilers are gonna go!"

"Any casualties? You hurt? You need help?"

"Bumps and bruises. Firemen are already topside. I'm coming up."

"Don't waste time! Get the hell out! Abandon ship!"

"I cannot believe it! I cannot believe it!"

"Not your fault, Captain," Magraw said, taking his arm. "We must get off this ship. She's going down fast." Below the bridge there was scuffling as the crew put the decrepit raft and lifeboats over the port side. Magraw made a quick head count. Everybody was up. Only fifteen to contend with, and there were more than enough boats and rafts.

As he assisted the pilot down the ladder from the bridge, Magraw held a large handkerchief over the cut on the wounded man's head, making sure it veiled his eyes as much as possible. Fortunately, the pilot considered himself mortally wounded, and was not about to make observations. Magraw helped him down into a lifeboat. Straightening up, he noticed a buoy light suddenly appear where there had not seemed to be one before.

Another light disappeared.

He hoped he was the only one to observe this phenomenon.

Water was rushing along the scuppers now as the ship continued to settle. Magraw noted with some satisfaction that the *Charon* was settling evenly.

After checking to be sure that all crew members were accounted for, Magraw stepped into the nearest lifeboat, now nearly even with the ship's rail. "Cast off, gentlemen!" The crew pulled at oars. "Say good-bye to a proud ship, gentlemen!"

When they were twenty meters off the port side of the ship, the *Charon* gurgled and went under. The generators winked off at last, the spotlights faded. But even in the darkness, Magraw could see that, after the ship had hit bottom, the upper fraction of her bridge, the stack, and the masts were exposed.

No ship would be able to pass this channel.

II

After inflating and switching on his last false marker, Esposito had swum to the nearest covered buoy to await the *Charon's* demise. Shrouded in its cloth bag, the real buoy was now squarely in the middle of the fake channel.

He clung to the pitching shape with his arms wrapped around it. Below the water line its bark of sharp-edged barnacles and mussels scraped at his bare skin like glass. He wished he had worn his scuba suit.

The *Charon* loomed large now; it seemed to be almost upon

him. Its bow was pointed straight at him. Still, he knew it was at least two hundred meters away. He would have some time to get away from it if something went wrong.

He checked the knife strapped to his ankle. When the ship foundered he would have to move quickly to unbag the real buoy, swim to the fake, slash it, and sink it. The stink of the marsh and the channel—or the renewed smell of fear—filled his nostrils. His teeth chattered.

The rush of water sluicing from the bow of the *Charon* was audible now, a steady slap, slap, heading directly toward him. God, these chattering teeth! He muttered curses.

On the bridge he could see the pilot speaking emphatically to Magraw, who seemed to be nodding assent.

Suddenly, there was a grating sound.

The old ship shuddered and seemed to rise from the water. The fantail swung toward him, the bow pointed obliquely toward mid-channel. Esposito gasped with relief. The ship still moved, more slowly to be sure, but in the direction of the channel, not him.

The yawing of the hull thrust a shallow wall of water that hit the buoy sharply, twisting and bouncing it against him. He felt the barnacles rip his flesh like a hundred razors. To hell with it! He was exhilarated now. This crazy scheme had worked!

Quickly he tore the shroud off the buoy and pushed off toward the false buoy. There he slashed its plastic balloon. With a great hiss, it collapsed. Deftly, he sliced the nylon cords that held the red lantern in place, letting it sink separately. His lacerated legs stung, but the pain seemed to spur him, rather than slow him down.

Shortly he made it to the second shrouded buoy. This was trickier, for it was closer to the rapidly sinking vessel. He would have to move very quickly—help for the *Charon*'s crew might already be on the way. Fortunately, they were not making their escape on his side.

Once the shroud was off, he stroked to the second false buoy and sank it. Behind him, the *Charon* went under with a huge flatulent sound. Its lights went out and now the danger of illumination was gone.

I must be bleeding in a thousand places, he thought. He

could feel the burning stings across his thighs and calves, on his chest and stomach, his arms—all the places that had touched as he embraced the buoy.

Esposito reached the last false buoy and sank it, then swam to the real marker and removed the shroud. Its ruby light winked and gleamed against the water as if it had never been gone.

Now to shore. It occurred to him that the lifeboats might row ashore where he and Juanita had parked their truck. But somehow the idea of confronting a derelict crew or even an army patrol on land did not disconcert him much.

He stroked slowly into mid-channel, perhaps fifty yards from the boats. The tide was dead slack now. Soon it would begin to flood.

The crewmen had spotted the lights of the castle's pilot-boat wharf, which were a great deal closer than the lights of the harbor wharves. The lifeboats came down the channel, pulling within twenty feet of him. He ducked under water until they were past. Then he began the slow swim to shore.

I feel good, he told himself. Top form. Not fatigued. Pulse as it should be, considering the exertion, the excitement. The job, after all, was a piece of cake. Fifty thousand dollars!

Unexpectedly, something brushed his leg.

Shark!

Again the shape brushed him. It had a hide like sandpaper.

Frantically, Esposito threw all of his remaining strength into swimming the rest of the distance across the channel.

I must not flail! I cannot seem to be a wounded fish! He stroked powerfully, smoothly.

Ahead he could hear Juanita calling him softly through the darkness.

Then, abruptly, his hands hit the mucky bottom. He was in shallow water. Safe at last.

He stood in the waist-deep black water, gasping.

"Juanita! Over here!"

At that moment, there was a jarring thud against his thigh and a searing, stabbing pain like a thousand skewers goring his leg. "Juanita! Shark!"

Even in the darkness he could see its blunt snout clamped to his thigh just below the hip. The torpedo-shaped body swung from side to side as the shark tried to saw away his flesh. Incredibly, it was only a small shark, perhaps five feet long.

Juanita ran toward him through the gloom. He lurched toward her with the creature hanging on.

"Get that damned thing off my leg!"

Sobbing desperately, she stabbed at the conical head and gills with her knife, but the blade would not penetrate the tough hide.

"Nose!" Esposito choked. "Hit end of nose!"

She hammered with the metal butt of her knife at the point of the shark's snout. Reluctantly, the serrated jaws unclamped his leg and the creature slid back into the inky water.

Almost fainting with agony, Esposito hauled himself to the beach, Juanita struggling to help. He lay there groaning.

"Espo, Espo, you need help quickly."

"We did it, baby! We did it!" He was numb with shock.

She laughed through tears. "We did. I saw."

"Get me to the truck. I must need a hundred stitches. I must stop the bleeding." He struggled to his feet.

"Lean on me," she said.

He put his arm around her. She had already removed her diving outfit and had slipped into slacks and a shirt.

Limping, hopping, they got to the truck.

"Give me your shirt."

She stripped it off and handed it to him. He knotted the material tightly around his thigh at the groin. "That will stop it temporarily," he said.

"We must get you to a hospital immediately where they can stitch you up."

"No!" he snapped. "Take me to Harada. He is prepared for these emergencies. He has some medical supplies and light." He felt terribly faint. "I must lie down."

"Is the pain very severe?"

"Yes, but not like the pain when that monster was chewing on me."

"We must leave immediately. Are you ready?"

"Yes," he said. "I will crawl inside the sleeping bag. It will help warm me against shock. I can lie down to take some of the pressure off the leg. If the patrol stops you again, tell them I drank too much and fell asleep."

"What if they know of the ship?"

"Tell them you heard sounds, but know nothing else. Make it plausible, *muchacha*." He felt increasingly light-headed. Turning, almost crawling, he worked his way into the back of the truck.

Juanita found a flashlight and switched it on.

"Don't look at the leg! Just open the sleeping bag so I can get inside!"

She unzipped the puffy quilting. Cursing with pain, Esposito rolled over into it. "Zip it up."

The flashlight showed a trail of gore leading out the back of the truck. Her hands were covered with blood. She shined the light in his face. He was sickly pale. "Are you sure you will be all right this way?"

"Get going, *muchacha*. Our money is waiting."

She scrambled out the back of the truck and slammed its double doors, then ran to the surf and washed off the blood.

"We're on our way, *muchacho!*" she called, climbing into the driver's seat.

He didn't answer.

31

I

THE CREAK OF OARLOCKS and the slap of the oars against the water accented the sound of heavy breathing. The survivors rowed across the slack water toward the illuminated wharf of the pilots' and customs station nestled against the castle wall.

"What happened, Klausen?" Magraw shouted in the direction of another lifeboat.

"Cap'n?" It was Klausen, the chief engineer.

"Yes?" Magraw wanted them to remember first impressions, but not think too much about the apparent contradiction of sinking in a safe, calm channel.

"We was operating at low revs, like the telegraph orders, Cap'n, and suddenly there's this grinding sound."

"Right," said another voice. "Like we was running up on a coral reef."

"Shut up, Goetz. I'll tell it. There's this grinding sound, then suddenly the whole bilge splits right across the beam. The deck busts right up at us and water is spouting into her. I order the boys out, then call you." There was a pause. "We was going down fast."

"Okay, Klausen." Magraw felt suddenly weary to the bone. The bizarre voyage had taken more out of him than he thought.

Beside him the pilot spoke up. "I tell you, Captain, we were squarely in the middle of the channel. I have made that run a thousand times."

"And I will so testify, Captain, at the hearing," said Magraw.

The word "hearing" closed like a fog over further conversation.

Moments later they shipped oars by the customs wharf. There seemed to be no one around. The pilot's cutter rocked quietly at its mooring, untended.

"Is it possible that no one knows our ship went down?" Magraw asked the pilot, assisting him from the lifeboat.

"You had no time for a radio message, did you?" The pilot still held the handkerchief to his head, but the bleeding had long since stopped.

"Sparks!" Magraw shouted. "Could you get off an SOS?"

"No time, Cap'n."

Magraw turned to the pilot. "Well, Captain, I think we had better go up and tell the authorities."

The pilot picked his way toward the customs building. "In the main channel of the Harbor of Malanueva," he muttered softly, almost to himself.

"She can be refloated," Magraw said, knowing full well that there was no chance the splintered ship could be brought up intact. "In a week or so she'll be sailing good as new."

"Captain, I fear your ship is there for good."

The pilot turned the knob of the customs building door and they entered.

II

DePrundis examined his platter as if it were a contract with a treacherous clause. Mercado looked about the veranda suspiciously.

"Our young honeymooners are not with us tonight." A waiter poured champagne into Mercado's stemmed crystal. He frowned slightly. "Too bad, too bad."

"There is not enough spice in the picadillo," DePrundis complained. Without looking up from his plate he raised an arm, and a squad of servants responded.

"The harbor is so peaceful tonight," Mercado murmured.

DePrundis explained the spice problem patiently to the waiters. They scurried to comply. "A foreign tramp freighter was cleared for passage tonight."

"So?"

"A construction company."

"Construction?"

"Your predecessors bought and paid for a shipload of gravel."

"What on earth for?"

"Apparently, the idea was for some kind of new pier. For tankers. Not a bad idea, really," he said through a mouthful of food.

"Of course," Mercado said absently. His mind was already on something else. "It is not many harbors, you know, that can feed great tankers around the clock, day-in, day-out, as we do here. It is a miracle of the revolution."

"It is a miracle of the elder Bradford," DePrundis asserted, chewing vigorously.

"Do not mention that name!" snapped Mercado.

DePrundis belched. "I only meant to remind you, *Libertador*, that technology, whatever its origin, is as important to the revolution as . . . élan. And" he raised a sausage like finger "technology is motivated by money."

The head waiter interrupted. "Excuse me, *Libertador*, there is a telephone call for you."

"I cannot be bothered."

"It sounded most urgent, *Libertador*. A ship has sunk."

DePrundis looked up sharply. "What ship?"

"I do not know, sir."

"Bring the telephone to the table," Mercado ordered.

Moments later Mercado was talking to a nearly hysterical voice.

"Calm down, damn you! *This* is your *Libertador*."

The voice stopped a moment, then began again. "*Libertador*, this is the Commandante of the Pilots' and Customs Base at Castel Mala."

"Yes, yes."

"A freighter named the *Charon*, registered in Liberia, has unaccountably sunk in the main sea channel."

"What do you mean 'unaccountably'? Ships do not just fill up with water!"

"What's happened?" DePrundis demanded.

Mercado held up a cautioning hand. The voice said, "The pilot and the crew have landed in lifeboats here. The pilot says . . ."

"Put him on the line."

There was excited chatter at the other end. Another voice came on. "This is Pilot Punta."

"What the hell happened?"

"This freighter, the *Charon*, Liberian registry with a cargo of gravel consigned to the Cosmo Construc tion Company in Malanueva, was proceeding at five knots down the channel . . ."

"You were piloting?"

"Yessir."

"At the wheel yourself?"

"Yessir."

"Go on."

"We were proceeding normally when suddenly there is . . . there is . . ." He broke into tears.

"For Jesus' sake! Get a grip on yourself!"

". . . this great grinding sound. It tore a hole in the bottom of the boat and it started to go down. Immediately. We had to flee for our lives."

"Put the Customs Chief on."

The other voice, more self-assured now, came on. "Yessir?"

"Have the pilot and the captain of the ship put under arrest by the army. Bring them to the prison. Also, any other ships' officers. There will be a hearing at the prison tomorrow morning. Notify all of the appropriate officials. I will attend personally. Nine A.M. Not an instant later."

"Yessir."

Mercado slammed the telephone down.

DePrundis sat immobile. "The ship is sunk in the channel?" he asked.

"Apparently."

"The gravel ship?"

"That's right."

"Sabotage?"

"Why do you ask that?"

"I have enemies. Blocking this port would be one way to get at me."

Mercado's eyes narrowed. "We will find out tomorrow morning."

"If that ship cannot be refloated immediately, it must be dynamited." DePrundis' voice rose. "Dynamited!"

"We will proceed with all speed, DePrundis, but first we must find out what happened."

DePrundis thumped the table with the butt of his fork. "Every day, *Libertador*, that my ships are blocked in port, *you*—and Malaverde—lose hundreds of thousands of dollars. Every single day. There is no other way to get cargoes out, nor ships in, except through that channel." His tone softened slightly. "After all, *Libertador*, we are weighing the value of one freighter, an old freighter, and a cargo of stone, against the prestige and power of this whole nation." He smiled. "It seems most absurd."

Mercado nodded. "You are right, DePrundis. Hard decisions must be made."

He enjoyed making hard decisions. Someone would suffer.

III

It was a mile and a half down a bumpy road from the Castel Mala to the low wooden trestle bridge between the City of Malanueva and the island. A sentry waved a lantern at the bridge. A black-and-white striped guard rail was down.

"Your papers, señorita."

"It is señora." She handed him her papers and Esposito's. "My husband has had too much wine. He sleeps in the back."

The sentry walked around to the passenger side of the truck, climbed in and flashed a light into Esposito's face. She did not turn around.

"He sleeps like a baby."

"Sometimes I think he *is* a baby."

The guard smirked. "Perhaps you married the wrong man, señora."

She winked at him. "Perhaps I did at that."

The guard grinned and raised the guard rail. "Come back and visit us, señora."

She smiled and put the truck in gear. "Thank you, Sergeant."

The wooden trestle rattled under the weight of the truck. A moment later she was on the waterfront of Malanueva. Expertly, she drove onto one of the main thoroughfares leading to the great central plaza. The streets were virtually empty.

214

From the plaza she drove down another wide street to a modern drawbridge. The sentry there was for show: he merely stood in a full-dress uniform with crossed white-duck belts and a patent-leather cartridge box.

The bridge led across the main channel of the Rio Paraná onto a broad macadam road. After a quarter of a mile, past the Navy Yard and barracks, Juanita drove onto a paved turnoff that led to the refinery and its associated harbor facilities. The complex of pipes and rows of huge round storage tanks reflected the light from thousands of incandescent bulbs.

A quarter of a mile down the turnoff, she turned again onto a narrow dirt track leading to the harbor's edge, and pulled up in front of Harada's fishing establishment. A potted palm stood in a huge redwood container at the entry to his living quarters. No lights were on, but she sensed that he had her under observation. She tapped lightly on the door. "Harada!"

He opened the door but did not show a light. "How went your mission?"

"The mission is accomplished." She fought to restrain a sob. "Esposito is hurt—badly. He's in the truck."

"I'll get my equipment." He disappeared into his quarters and reappeared a moment later. "Let's look at him."

"Have you stitched wounds before?"

"Many times. What happened?"

"He was coming from the water, and a small shark bit his leg."

"Sharks usually pay no attention to people in diving equipment." Harada fussed with the door of the truck. "The rubber suits are not like their food."

"The fool didn't wear his suit." She began to sob.

"Please," Harada said softly, "don't cry. I'll need your help, you know."

He clambered into the truck. "Esposito, old man. What have you been up to?"

There was no response.

Harada shined his flashlight into the silent face. He felt for a pulse, then peeled back an eyelid and shined the light directly into it.

"How is he, Harada?"

"He's dead." Harada opened up the sleeping bag. Pools of blood lay in the folds of the material. Carefully, he closed the bag again, this time over Esposito's head, and pulled the zipper around, sealing the dead swimmer inside. Following Japanese custom, he bowed three times to honor the dead man's spirit and climbed out of the truck.

Juanita was weeping uncontrollably. "He was my brother, my father, my mother," she sobbed.

"He was very brave."

"For what?" she said bitterly. "He died of Wolfram, not shark bites!"

"Don't say that!" Harada's voice was low, but commanding. "Wolfram was only the medium. Wolfram is the hand that uses us to draw these missions, but we have leapt into his hand like eager brushes."

Harada glanced thoughtfully at the truck. "We don't know whether all of this has meaning or not. We may never know."

They stood quietly for several moments.

"The mission goes on," Harada said at last.

"I will continue, too, then."

"It may not be necessary." He glanced at his watch. "After all, your main assignment is over."

"Better to have something to do than to dwell on this." She paused. "What will become of him?"

"Best to leave him where he is for now. When I meet Wolfram in the morning, he will know what to do."

"I will report myself to Wolfram that the mission was accomplished."

"You saw the ship go down?"

"Very quickly."

"And Magraw?"

"I saw him get into a lifeboat before the ship's spotlights burned out."

"Good." He took her arm. "We must rest now."

She followed him into the small house.

32

I

THE SUN WAS JUST BEGINNING to emerge above the horizon when they set out to follow the pipeline north.

Directly ahead Kinsey could make out the Rio Paraná snaking toward Malanueva, still sleeping. The huge tankers in the harbor floated on the morning mist.

Kinsey nudged Wolfram and pointed. Wolfram nodded and leaned over, shouting in his ear, "Just past river! Pipe intersects highway! Sit down there!"

Kinsey reduced altitude to four hundred feet as they crossed the Rio Paraná. Dead ahead he spotted the intersection of the highway and the pipeline. Close by the crossing Kinsey saw an old panel truck. He could make out no people.

Kinsey picked a spot fifty yards past the highway, just over a small rise that would partially shield the craft from the eyes of passing traffic, though it seemed unlikely that traffic ever passed here. He brought the helicopter down gently and they waited without speaking while the rotors slowed and the clouds of dust receded.

They climbed out to find Harada standing just over the rise, awaiting them. His expression was blank. Juanita sat alone in the truck some yards away.

Kinsey sensed trouble.

"Did the *Charon* go down?" Wolfram asked.

"Like a sieve filled with gravel," Harada said quietly.

"In the channel?"

"Squarely in the channel, we believe. We will see for ourselves when the sun is higher."

"What's wrong?"

"Esposito is dead."

"How did it happen?" There was no emotion in Wolfram's voice.

"The improbable accident." He told them about Esposito's silly refusal to wear his scuba suit, the cuts and lacerations he received from barnacles on the buoy, the last-minute appearance of the small shark. "Esposito was very badly cut. Juanita helped him to get free of the shark and out of the water. He bled to death before they could get to me."

"Absolutely useless." Wolfram squinted at Harada, then at Kinsey. "We put luck into our equations, but somehow we cannot put in the stupid human factor."

"Let it alone, Hugo," said Kinsey. "He lost his life on this mission."

Ignoring Kinsey's remark, Wolfram motioned toward the truck. "How did she handle it?"

"Mechanically, she did very well. But I think that for her the mission is over."

Wolfram cursed softly. "I needed two divers to complete this mission. Now I have none—except me."

"What about Juanita?" Kinsey asked. "She will go with you. Keep her busy."

Harada reminded Wolfram, "Esposito's body is in a sleeping bag in the truck."

"We'll put him on the chopper. Kinsey, you and Juanita must bury him in the desert."

Kinsey walked to the truck. "I'm very sorry," he said to her.

"He was a foolish man. He knew better." Her face reflected fatigue and grief. "What happens now?"

"We will put him to rest, you and I, Juanita, in the desert."

She laughed bitterly. "It will be a good place."

Wolfram approached the truck. "There is nothing I can say, Juanita, that would make any sense of this. We will proceed with the mission. You will travel with Kinsey."

218

They backed the truck across the parched ground to the helicopter, and wrestled the corpse of Esposito, now stiff inside its quilted bag, into the helicopter.

Wolfram took Kinsey by the arm. "Tomorrow—first, the radio. Then, follow the pipeline. Cross the refinery. Follow the axis of the *Queen DePrundis,* the big bulk carrier that's docked. Magraw, Harada, and myself will be in Harada's motorboat out in the harbor."

"A pickup from water?"

"Is it a problem?"

Kinsey shrugged. "No, but it's easier on land where I can put the chopper on the ground."

"That will be impossible." Wolfram signaled to Harada, who climbed into the driver's seat of the old truck. Wolfram hauled himself into the truck and they left.

Kinsey and Juanita did not move for a long time, until the truck had disappeared down the highway. Then she ran to him, flinging her arms around him, sobbing uncontrollably.

Tenderly he helped her into the front of the helicopter, then got in himself, and took the craft up.

Behind them only ruts in the dust indicated that anyone had been there.

II

An hour later, Wolfram and Harada sat at a bare wooden table, a teapot and Japanese cups between them. Wolfram had penciled a list and now he read it to the actor.

"One: Locate and retrieve Magraw.

"Two: Retrieve the pyrotechnic devices from the bridge of the *Charon.*

"Three: Put pyrotechnic devices in place.

"Four: Claim heavy motorized equipment at the main pier and put it in place for tomorrow."

He glanced quickly at Harada. "Questions?"

"You plan to put the pyrotechnic devices in place in daylight?"

"This order of priorities is desirable but not absolute." He ran a hand through his hair. "In short, Harada, we'll play it by ear. And, the word 'ear' reminds me . . ." He reached for the telephone. "What time is it?"

"Eight-five."

"What government agency would know about the *Charon*?"

"Start with the Customs and Pilots' Bureau at Castel Mala."

Wolfram nodded. Speaking rapid Spanish, he began working his way patiently through the sclerotic arteries of Malanueva communications. Finally a far-off metallic voice answered at the customs Building.

"This is the Director of the Cosmo Construction Company. A ship of ours, the *Charon*, was to have made port last night, but we cannot locate her. Have you any word?"

"It did indeed enter our outer channel, but there has been a mishap."

Wolfram smiled at the understatement. "A collision?"

"Not exactly, señor. Unfortunately, your ship has sunk in our channel."

"Sunk?"

"No lives were lost, señor. We were able to rescue all."

"But what has become of our crew? Why have we heard nothing?"

"The crew itself has dispersed to the city. The ship's officers and our pilot have been detained in custody."

"Where? Are our men under arrest?"

"It is only a routine investigation, señor. The hearing is in the principal detention center facing the main square of the city."

"When is the hearing?"

"Nine o'clock this morning."

"We must speak with them."

"I am sure, if you go there, you will be able to speak with your people."

"May I go to the site of the accident this morning?" Wolfram asked.

"We have a patrol boat posted there. We will tell them you are coming out. However, you may remove nothing from the wreck nor disturb it."

"I will send an expert scuba diver we have on our staff who will go down to look at the damage. He will neither disturb nor remove anything by my direct order."

"I see no harm in that."

"Thank you, Captain."

"A pleasure to be of service, señor."

Wolfram hung up and looked at Harada. "We can do it!"

"How will we get the flare case from under their noses onto my boat in broad daylight?"

"First of all, *we* don't do it. *I* do it. You are going to put on a necktie and go to the hearing as representative of the Cosmo Construction Company. Try to talk to Magraw."

Harada frowned. "I should have no difficulty talking to him. But how do we rescue him, if they choose to detain him for more hearings?"

Wolfram touched his forefinger to the side of his nose. "I have a plan."

"And the flares?"

"I have another plan."

Harada shook his head sadly. "You always have a plan. A man dies and you plan around him as if he never existed, as if you were some cosmic poet. You rewrite your lines to fit the meter, not the emotion."

"The important thing, Harada, is that my poems scan. Now, then, here is what we do . . ."

III

Juanita and Kinsey sipped canned orange juice in the shade of the radio-telephone shack. The helicopter rested a short distance away.

"I must do the digging before the sun rises too high. The heat out here gets brutal." He scooped a hole in the desert and buried the juice can.

"This whole mission is brutal," she whispered. "I will help you dig."

"There's only one shovel."

"I want to participate. I owe this to him."

"Then gather rocks and stones," he said, standing. "We must cover the grave with them. There are wild animals out here though God knows where they hide in the daytime."

It took him less than an hour to scour out a deep trench

for Esposito directly beside the helicopter. He dragged the body, still shrouded in its orange sleeping bag, to the grave, and gently rolled it in. Carefully, they placed stones over him and Kinsey raked the powdery soil over the hole. He tossed the shovel into the back of the helicopter. "There is still work to be done."

Without looking back at the grave, she climbed aboard the aircraft.

IV

Wolfram cut the engines on Harada's boat and let its forward momentum carry it toward the sunken *Charon*. The tide was rising now, but the upper portions of the bridge, the stack, and the forward and rear masts and booms projected above water.

Wolfram scrambled to the bow of the fishing boat to drop anchor precisely beside the sunken ship. It was important to position the boat not too far from the bridge and not to let too much anchor and line down into the channel. The anchor line hissed like an angry wasp through its bracket. With a solid thud the anchor hit the mud bottom of the channel. He tugged at the line until convinced his anchor flukes had a firm purchase below.

A customs cutter was anchored cross-channel off the stern of the sunken ship. Wolfram could see them putting a small launch over the side to come investigate. He moved back to the cockpit of the boat and checked his oilskin pouch of faked documents—a plastic-shielded card, complete with fingerprint and photograph, identifying him as a project manager for the Cosmo Construction Company; a wad of obscure but totally believable technical trivia; a clip board with a written notation "Damage Report" at the top.

While the launch putted slowly his way, he checked Esposito's scuba gear. He hated diving but, unlike Esposito, he had no morbid fear of the sea. He felt only that it was a medium that made simple tasks more difficult; that it complicated missions; that it was in his way.

The customs launch pulled up beside him. A seaman held the launch against Harada's boat with a boat hook.

222

"Did your Commandante tell you I would come?" Wolfram inquired genially.

"Yes, señor, but we must check papers in any event. A formality."

"Certainly." Wolfram handed him the oilskin pouch. "Will you come aboard for a drink?"

"Your generosity is appreciated, señor, but alas, mine was a long and lonely vigil with the bottle last night."

Wolfram laughed. "Too bad."

The officer took a perfunctory look at the papers, then stuffed them back into the pouch, and handed it back. "Will you be here long, señor?"

"Less than an hour."

"Very well. Please do not remove anything from the ship or disturb it."

"Thank you, Captain."

"My pleasure, señor."

The launch putted back to its mother ship, while Wolfram hooked himself into the scuba gear. He did not like the idea of diving alone, but it was necessary that Harada be at the hearing to contact Magraw.

Gear ready, Wolfram lunged backward over the side of the boat, plunging down into the green, sun-streaked world below. It was only a few feet to the port bulkhead of the bridge. Its door wafted slowly to and fro in the incoming tide. Some papers, Magraw's pipe, a cap, floated inside the bridge.

There was the chest marked "Flares." Wolfram tugged at it. The chest moved easily. Its net weight was only a little greater than the water around it. He pulled the chest out the bridge door to the top of the down ladder. Then he swam over to the anchor rope of his boat and tied a butterfly knot in it. Swimming back to the chest, he removed a length of nylon rope from his belt and ran it through the handle brackets at both ends of the chest. Then, gauging the distance he would have to swim hauling the weight of the chest, he unhooked his lead belt and let it drop. Kicking hard, tugging the bulky chest behind him, he edged his way to the anchor rope and tied the chest's rope through the loop of the butterfly knot.

He had spent ten minutes at the task—not long enough to

make a damage estimate. Implausible. He floated into the bridge and looked around. From his vantage point, it seemed as if the bow were plunging down a slope into a bottomless abyss. The hull was studded with tiny bubbles of air. From the hatches streams of bubbles continued to race upward. It gave him the feeling of being on a craft plunging straight down.

Enough of this, he thought. Time to go topside.

He checked the arrangement of the chest on the anchor rope, then surfaced, and clambered over the side. After starting the engines, he went to the bow to free the anchor. The chest was easily visible about eight feet down in the water. The trick would be to get the anchor and its rope up and over the side, leaving the eight-foot loop trailing.

Wolfram tugged the anchor around the chest with a gaff, glancing at the customs cutter to see if he was being watched. Apparently not. He got the anchor up. The loop trailed down tautly. He hitched the dangling end of the anchor rope to a cleat. Now the problem would be to keep the chest from planing up when the boat moved forward.

He put the craft into gear and moved it forward at very low speed. The chest rose but did not surface.

There was a toot from the customs boat. Wolfram looked around to see the young officer waving good-bye. He waved back.

An hour later he was at Harada's dock.

33

I

THE COURTROOM HAD ONCE been a chapel. Gothic timber arches curved into a dingy ceiling far above him. Now a series of fans with ponderous leaf-shaped blades pushed sullenly against the atmosphere, but did little to alleviate the hot, festering dankness.

Magraw sat in a row of pews perpendicular to the main tiers. Where an altar once had been, there now was a jurist's bench badly in need of varnish. Behind it perched a tribunal, divided two and one on either side of a thronelike chair.

"I have heard that *El Libertador* himself plans to attend," said Punta in an anxious whisper.

Behind Magraw, in another tier of pale oak pews, sat his ship's officers, red-eyed and grizzled. Smartly uniformed guards lurked near the walls. The audience seemed listless. At the rear Magraw picked out Harada wearing a well-tailored cord business suit.

"They want us to be the scapegoats," Punta was saying. "They will say we are counterrevolutionaries and make examples of us."

"Nonsense," said Magraw cheerfully. "I am sure this is merely routine. We will explain that it was an unfortunate mishap. Probably something floating in the channel."

"I hope *El Libertador* will accept that."

"All rise," shouted a stentorian voice from the apse. A heavy

225

door at the side of the dais banged open and *El Libertador* strode in. He stumped up the three steps to the bench and jostled his way into the big chair.

"Commence," he growled.

One of the tribunal seemed to have some kind of agenda in front of him. "This tribunal has been called into session to consider the evidence in the sinking of a freighter, the *Charon* by name, in the main channel of the Port of Malanueva last night. After hearing the evidence, the tribunal will decide what charges should be brought against those responsible."

Magraw didn't like the bland assumption that someone was guilty. Captain Punta sighed noisily.

"We are most honored and pleased today to have *El Libertador* sitting, *ex officio,* as a member of this panel. His participation today is one more symbol of his abiding interest in the well-being of our country." He nodded at *El Libertador,* who nodded back curtly.

"First witness." The jurist looked at his papers. "Señor Garcia Punta, a pilot of the Customs Department."

Punta seemed paralyzed. "Señor, I . . . I . . ."

"Stand up!" shouted Mercado.

Grabbing the edge of the railing in front of him, Punta pulled himself to his feet. Sweat poured from his face. Magraw felt sorry for him.

"You are the one who sank this ship?" the jurist attacked.

"No, sir. The ship . . ."

"You were the pilot, were you not?"

"Yes, sir, but . . ."

"Were you at the wheel, Punta?"

"Yes, sir, I . . ."

"And you ran the ship aground?"

"Oh, no, sir. I . . ."

Mercado slammed his fist on the bench. "You sniveling freak! You are being evasive!"

Punta choked.

Mercado pointed his finger at Punta. "Admit it now and save some semblance of your dignity! You are a member of the counter-revolution, aren't you? You deliberately sank that ship in the channel to destroy the economy of Malaverde!"

Magraw suppressed a smile.

226

"I am a loyal citizen, *Libertador,*" Punta protested feebly. "I have performed this pilot's task a thousand times."

"Then how do you explain that just this one time suddenly the ship goes to the bottom?"

"I cannot explain it at all, *Libertador*. It . . . just happened."

Mercado waved his hand. "Enough. Let us hear from the others."

The jurist consulted his papers. "Captain Abdullah?"

Magraw stood. "Here, sir."

"You were master of the *Charon?*"

"That is correct."

Mercado interrupted. "What kind of a name is Abdullah?"

"I am from Trinidad, *Libertador*." He smiled ingratiatingly. "The name, however, comes from Africa."

The jurist went on, "Your ship was registered in Monrovia, Liberia?"

"That is correct."

"And what of the owners?"

"The charter, sir, is the Cosmo Construction Company, of Montreal, Canada. I have not yet had a chance to notify them of this accident. However, I know they have a representative here in Malanueva, whom I have not met, who should vouch for me."

"Where is he?"

"I don't know, sir. He was to contact me when the ship made port."

Mercado was impatient. "I want to know what happened to make this ship sink, Captain."

Magraw frowned. "By my honor as the ship's master, sir, the *Charon* was squarely in the middle of the channel. While I was not at the wheel myself, I was watching along with Captain Punta, who seemed most alert. The channel lights were well to both port and starboard sides. Suddenly, there was a sharp thump, just as if we had hit something. At that moment my engineer called from the engine room to report heavy flooding. I ordered the ship abandoned." He paused. "And a good thing, too. For the ship sank like a stone. We were most fortunate no lives were lost."

"Don't count your blessings, Captain!" Mercado snapped. "Let us hear from the engineer."

Magraw sat down and motioned the engineer to stand. "It's like the Captain says, you know. The water was coming fast into her and we had to get out in a hurry."

"What happened before that?" the spokesman jurist asked.

"We was proceeding at very low RPMs . . ."

"What's that?"

"At slow speed, sir."

"How slow?"

The engineer glanced at Magraw. "About five knots, if that."

"And . . . ?"

"The whole deck comes right up, as if she'd some kind of big spear poking up through the bilge. She busts the deck right across the beam."

"You heard no explosion?"

"No, sir Just a grinding sound and this, whoopf . . ."

"Can you account for this at all?"

"Never saw nor heard about anything like it. It was like a great big thing on the bottom of the ship, ripping her right open."

"What would you speculate would do that?"

The engineer shrugged. "I'd have to say some kind of obstruction in the channel, sir."

"You may sit down."

There was a pause while the jurist and Mercado consulted. Then Mercado, glaring at the culprits, declared, "I am not satisfied."

The proceedings went on.

II

When Mercado demanded coffee, the spokesman jurist suggested an intermission. The jurists and Mercado retreated into the apse.

Magraw stood, stretching his legs, and edged slowly toward the audience. From the back Harada slipped through the crowd without attracting attention. When he was within earshot of Magraw, he spoke in the Tonkin dialect of Vietnamese they both knew.

"Tomorrow. At noon."

Magraw nodded and smiled, as if acknowledging a pleasantry. Harada bowed slightly, smiling also. "If you are detained . . . tomorrow. Noon. Fantail. *Queen DePrundis.*"

"I have it," said Magraw. "What do I do?"

"Commit suicide."

Magraw laughed. "That's a sick joke, of course."

Harada explained Wolfram's plan.

A guard moved toward them.

"Most important," Harada muttered, "do not under any circumstances be late!"

Magraw nodded. His smile faded. "I think Wolfram has cracked."

"No conversation!" the guard ordered. "You! Back to the benches!" he growled at Magraw. Bowing obsequiously, Harada backed away.

Magraw moved back to his place in the front pews.

III

Coffee did not mellow Mercado.

"Captain! You of the ship."

"Yes, sir," Magraw responded, standing.

"What is this Cosmo Construction Company?"

"Forgive me, *Libertador,* I am not aware of the details of the company's business. In my own case, they retain me to master a ship."

"You are regularly employed by them?"

Magraw pursed his lips. "Alas, I am not regularly employed by them. However, I have worked for them before."

"As a ship's officer?"

"That is correct."

"And your crew?"

"The same, *Libertador.*"

"What port did you visit before . . ." he referred to the papers in front of him, ". . . your ship docked at Freeport, Texas?"

"I picked up the *Charon* at Freeport." Magraw tried to recall the image of pages in his bogus passport. Undoubtedly it was

229

in the file before Mercado. "Prior to becoming master of the *Charon*, I had visited several ports along the coast to get a berth." He smiled. "Looking for work, you see. I was in Galveston . . ."

Mercado slammed his fist against the bench. "You are evasive!" There was a murmur of excitement in the audience.

Mercado was suddenly calm. "Now then, Captain, let us begin this all over again."

Magraw began to retell the story, then stopped. "*Libertador*, why don't we all make an inspection of the sunken ship in order to determine what happened?"

"My men are already there," Mercado said curtly. "Do you think we are slow-witted?"

"Yes, sir, but perhaps if we . . ."

"I do not take orders from prisoners!"

"My apology." Magraw bowed stiffly. "I did not realize I was a prisoner. I was under the impression . . ."

Mercado was on his feet. "You are herewith charged with deliberate sabotage by sinking of a ship in our harbor! You will be tried! The pilot too! It is a conspiracy!"

The audience grew noisy. A voice shouted, "*Viva El Libertador!*"

Guards surrounded Magraw. Mercado stood, arms uplifted, both fists clenched, and greeted his audience. They cheered wildly.

"My friends!" he shouted. The audience quieted down. "Because this ship is clogging our channel, we must get rid of it." He paused and scanned the audience slowly. "Immediately!"

There was applause.

"Therefore, starting right now, barges will be filled with explosives. These will be placed in the hulk and then exploded. You will see one magnificent salute to the revolution; a gigantic blast of triumph for our cause!"

34

I

WAVES OF HEAT FLOWED from the vast concrete surface of the pier where the *Queen DePrundis* was docked. A paunchy guard in faded khaki edged toward them from the other side of the chain-link fence.

"What do you want?"

Wolfram and Harada wore Cosmo Construction Company overalls. Wolfram hid behind aviator's green glasses and wore a frayed panama hat.

Harada tugged at the visor of his baseball cap. He, too, wore dark glasses.

"Yesterday, I arranged with José Carlo to pick up some heavy machinery," Harada told the guard. "Two tractors."

The guard referred to a crumpled note that he retrieved from a breast pocket. "You are from the construction company?"

Harada nodded and indicated with his thumb the embroidered Cosmo insignia over his pocket.

The guard fumbled with his keys and fiddled with the padlock holding the chain on the gate of the fence.

"José said you were very, very generous to him."

"We are always generous with our good friends," Harada murmured, removing a larger Malanuevan bill from his wallet. "I find myself unable to hand you my calling card, Captain. The gate bars the way. Perhaps, if you open . . . ?"

The padlock snapped. The gate chain rattled abruptly and

the gate swung inward. Harada stuffed the bill into the unbuttoned breast pocket. "Please be good enough to stand by with the gate open. A few minutes only. We will drive our equipment right out."

The guard pointed at a large shed with overhead doors. "In that building, señors."

"Was José kind enough to put diesel fuel into the tractors, as I requested?"

"Sí."

"Very good."

"About tomorrow," said Harada as they walked toward the shed. "How will we employ two tractors without Magraw on hand?"

"I've been pondering that ever since you told me we are going to have to go through with our rescue plan. I hadn't counted on this problem with Magraw."

"You say it yourself—we must factor random circumstance into our plan."

"Indeed, I do say that, Harada. But, statistically, the random happening occurred with Esposito. Now we must deal with the statistically improbable."

"Meaning what?"

"Meaning we shoot from the hip."

They reached the wide overhead doors and rolled them up. Two large tractorlike machines stood before them, gleaming with new paint. There was the tang of diesel fuel in the air.

"I chose this type because it has power steering," said Wolfram. "They're as easy to operate as the family car."

Harada examined one of the vehicles' huge iron wheels. It had triangular lugs studding it all the way around, like a medieval mace. "What kind of tractors are they?"

"They aren't tractors, as a matter of fact. These are Model CS-70 Trash-Pak vehicles manufactured by the Clark Equipment Company. Each weighs 26,000 pounds. It rides on oscillating wheels." He tapped one of the wheels' metal protrusions. "These lugged wheels exert a pressure of more than 1,000 pounds per linear inch."

Harada climbed up to study the controls of one of the vehicles. "Looks simple enough. The keys are here, Hugo."

232

"Actually they're designed to smash and compact refuse in landfill operations. They're crushers, Harada. And that's what we want them for."

"How fast?"

"They each have 130-horsepower diesels. They'll do at least twenty-five miles per hour."

"This weight, the wheels, the speed, should crack the pipeline easily."

"Easily." Wolfram moved quickly to the other vehicle and climbed aboard. "Gentlemen, start your engines!" The diesels roared to life with thick clouds of fumes and smoke. They rolled out of the shed in tandem and, chewing great gouges in the surface of the pier, drove through the gate.

II

They manuevered the huge machines along the shoulder of the road parallel to the harbor until they came to a chained gate without a guard post. The fenced-in area was part of the vast tank farm. They halted their machines and inspected the chain.

"Can you pick this lock?" Harada asked.

"I don't have tools with me—except for that big 26,000-pound tool behind me. We will lean on the gate, ever so lightly.

"When we get through," he went on, "we'll drive straight to the pipeline terminus at the refinery. It's about a half-mile from here. We must make sure we are on the city side of the pipeline, because you may use the second Trash-Pak as your getaway vehicle."

"I'll be alone on the job of crushing the pipeline, then?"

"For the moment, yes. The vehicle you crash into the line in all probability will be incapacitated. Especially if you go in at top speed. After you have hit the line, get aboard the other vehicle, and cut straight back cross-country to the highway. I'll be in the truck."

Wolfram inched his huge diesel machine carefully into the break in the gate. Against the weight of the vehicle, the links of the chain offered no resistance. Wolfram backed off, got down, and flung the gate wide. They both drove their machines through.

Methodically, he halted inside the fence and closed the gate, rewrapping the chain around the closure.

He climbed back on board his machine and, with a roar, they rolled away around the gigantic silver tanks.

III

A sharp, dry wind blew from the desert to the south. Their progress through the silver canyons of tubing and storage tanks was unimpeded.

They didn't see another human being. Oil circulated through these iron arteries, passed through cracking towers, and flowed into huge bladders of steel to await transfer into the tankers in the harbor.

Wolfram, leading the way, drove down a shallow slope to the northern abutment of the pipeline, where it divided into smaller arteries of piping leading to refining facilities or to storage. The pipeline extended up the slope for about a quarter of a mile, to a point where the land leveled out. Wolfram drove to the top and shut his engine off. Harada followed.

The plateau was just high enough to look over the refinery into the harbor, where the giant tankers, filled with oil, rode deep in the water. In the other direction, a quarter of a mile away, the pipeline intersected the highway where they had met early that morning. It seemed days ago. Three-quarters of a mile beyond the highway, the pipeline bridged the Rio Paraná.

"Look!" Harada pointed toward the desert.

Wolfram squinted at a tiny sparkle in the sky lifting away from the pipeline. "Kinsey. He's completing the pipeline chores."

"What's our plan now?"

"We park the machines here, just below the crest, so we don't attract sightseers from the city." He pointed to a place on the pipeline about a hundred meters below them. "I suggest you hit the line about there. The oil will flood down the slope into the refinery complex."

Harada seemed faintly puzzled. "It seems very obtuse. Won't they deduce that the pipeline was struck deliberately?"

"Perhaps, Harada, but I think not."

234

"What makes you so sure?"

"First, they will have the fire to worry about."

"What fire?"

Wolfram took from his pocket two small canisters like aerosol spray devices. He held them up for Harada to see.

"Thermite bombs?"

"Exactly. We'll leave these here. After the oil has flowed for a while, Harada, drop these into the current. They have time fuses."

"Isn't it still rather overt, Hugo?"

"Not to worry, Harada. Before they can begin to make deductions, we will have created a diversion that will make it all academic anyway."

They hiked to the highway, then followed its shoulder two miles to Harada's pier.

35

I

THEY HAD SETTLED THE helicopter just before sunset near the litter of bones by the pipeline. Now Kinsey and Juanita leaned against the still-hot side of the radio-telephone shack, making a simple supper of canned hash, dried fruit, and water. Kinsey had a flask of Wolfram's brandy to toast the end of the day.

"Night before last I dined on the veranda of the finest hotel in Malaverde," Juanita said softly. "The breeze was soft, the wines excellent. A little band played. It was true elegance." She seemed to be recalling events long past. "Years later—last night—I swam in dark water and fear. My only dinner was bread and tea. And tonight I dine in the middle of a desert, beside the grave of my brother."

He took her hand. "And tomorrow night you will dine with me by candlelight in Caracas. We can toast our success."

"Success?"

He squeezed her hand. "We will have the mission behind us."

II

Harada's boat slipped smoothly across the oily scum of the harbor toward the illuminated bulk of the giant tanker, *DePrundis Lady*. Behind him Wolfram checked the scuba tanks and masks, fins, and lead belts. He peered thoughtfully into the trunk marked "Flares." Satisfied that everything was ready, he came forward to stand beside Harada. "Will we have low tide when we get there?"

Harada glanced at his watch. "Dead low tide in twenty minutes. That's when we arrive."

"Perhaps the best thing will be to take the boat straight under the pier from the dark side opposite the *Queen DePrundis* mooring. Will there be enough head space?"

"Head space is not so much a problem as clearance between the pilings. I think we will not have trouble. However, I suggest you rig up the fishing gear. There are patrol boats out every night. We might encounter them."

Wolfram picked up some rods, already rigged with hooks and sinkers. Then he sat down in the fishing chair at the stern and scanned the harbor.

Away to the starboard of the boat the *DePrundis Lady* still drank in hundreds of tons of oil an hour. Perhaps a hundred yards ahead of her the *DePrundis Standard* rested fat and silent, illuminated only by red lights at the tips of her masts and one dim white bulb over a gangway. A half-mile away, their mooring lights barely visible, were the *DePrundis Flyer* and the *DePrundis Beacon.*

"Patrol boat approaching!" Harada called back to him.

Wolfram leaned the fishing rods against the gunwales, as if ready for use as soon as an anchor dropped. He pulled a tarpaulin over the scuba gear.

Harada was waving vigorously at the patrol boat and smiling. "They see me come this way almost every night."

The patrol boat slid past them on their starboard side. A sailor hailed them through a speaker. "What do you fish for tonight, Chinaman?"

"Dorado! Very fine eating!"

"Be careful of the wreck in the sea channel!"

Harada nodded and waved. The patrol boat cruised on past, making its way toward the darkened ships farther up the channel.

"We're coming up on the *Queen DePrundis*, Hugo."

Wolfram swung around in the fishing chair as they passed close behind the ship's fantail. The heavily cargoed vessel rested close to the limit of her red-lead Plimsoll line. Her huge propellers were fully immersed. Wolfram estimated the distance from the deck of the fantail to the water to be thirty feet—not enough to injure a jumping man, especially one who knew how to get over the side of a ship swiftly.

Above them a crew of workmen circulated busily.

"What are they doing, Harada?"

"Clearing the decks to unload bulk cargo."

"Surely not tomorrow!"

"This is a work party to get everything prepared so that the ship can be off-loaded in one long day Monday."

"Then they *won't* be working tomorrow?"

"It's not on the schedule, so I assume they will not. Sunday is serious business in Malaverde."

Ingots of magnesium, bound together by straps of thin steel, towered in bales above the railings of the ship's deck. Wolfram knew the straps would snap in a millisecond under unusual stress. Crewmen maneuvered a boom and crane, shifting the bales of the light metal to clear space around the hatches.

They were past the *Queen DePrundis;* two minutes later they swung past the end of the pier, moving slowly into the shadow cast by illumination from the ship. Harada cut the engine. With boathooks they worked the craft under the pier. It fit with clearance of about six inches to a side. The concrete pilings were covered with weeds and mussels.

Harada switched on a red lantern. "I'll help you put on your suit," he said. "We want no more scratches from mollusks."

They set to work.

III

The wine was not as chilled as it should have been. The Crab Louis had no flavor. The vichyssoise had been bland. The nondescript room was plastic and it smelled of jet fuel.

He sighed. To dine at an airport was insufferable.

"We will be sorry to see you depart so soon, DePrundis," Mercado remarked.

DePrundis threw his fork aside and wheezed. "It is not enough that my principal source of revenue finds itself constipated by the wreck of some scow, but the food is poor also."

He gulped wine, while Mercado sipped a cup of coffee. DePrundis watched him with deep suspicion. A man who did not eat was up to something. "I am troubled by several things. Foremost is that wreck blocking the channel of Malanueva."

"Don't worry about that, my friend. A barge is being loaded with high explosives from my naval reserves. It will be taken forth tomorrow morning and the explosives will be put aboard this sunken ship. Tomorrow, a magnificent fireworks for my people."

"*Libertador*, do you have any idea how much explosive it will take to demolish such a ship?"

"It is not very large."

"But it carried a cargo of gravel, *Libertador*. Do you comprehend?"

Mercado's voice rose. "Nonsense. Gravel is loose stuff. It will roll to the side. It will wash out with the current. Your ships will sail with the high tide on Monday."

"I wish it were so, *Libertador*," DePrundis sighed. "Perhaps with luck, it will be possible to get one of the smaller ships over the hulk, but I doubt it." He poked his fork at the shreds of his crab. "Meanwhile, I must attend to other worries."

"What?"

"I have contracts for delivery of fuel oil on certain dates."

"They will understand the delay when you explain it to them."

"They will understand, but it will cost me money nevertheless. It is not a question of whether I pay, but how much."

"You can't tell them to go to hell?"

"*Libertador*, this is not revolutionary action we are talking about, this is international trade. Already I am committed for the equivalent of more than thirty million dollars in future deliveries."

"How is that?"

DePrundis stared at him ruefully. It was useless to speak of finance to this belligerent man. "I sold thirty million dollars' worth of French and Swiss francs for delivery in four weeks," he sighed. "The shiploads of oil trapped here would have covered my debt and then some."

"Future delivery?"

"To simplify, I guaranteed, for a price, to deliver these monies to certain parties at the time I said I would. When I made the contract, I believed I would have many shiploads of oil to cover the requirement several times over." He sighed. "Now I can deliver neither the monies nor the oil."

"It sounds serious."

"Not insurmountable. Fortunately, I have ample collateral. Some of my ships are not encumbered by debt."

"Then everything is all right."

"Everything is *not* all right!" De Prundis' voice exploded, then immediately decrescendoed. "What is *not* all right is that all of this is going to cost me . . . *us* . . . unnecessary expense. After all, *Libertador,* you . . . that is, Malaverde . . . will profit more than anyone from our transactions."

He gestured for more wine. "There is one other thing that nags at me."

"What is that?"

"There have been unusual transactions in the stock of Petrol/Malaverde." ˙

Mercado scowled. "The price—it is all right?"

"Oh yes, yes. The price is fine. Going up, in fact. It is the short sales. There has been an unusual volume of short sales. Yet, the price goes up. The prospects of the company advance. It is puzzling."

"What is this short sale?"

"One borrows one hundred shares of stock, at, say X francs per share for the sole purpose of selling the borrowed stock at the X level, hoping that the price will go down to, say, one-half X. At that point one buys the hundred shares back and repays the debt."

Mercado was losing interest. He snapped his fingers, summoning an aide. "José, I want you to order the helicopter prepared for tomorrow morning. After I have attended Mass, we will fly over for an inspection of the ship in the harbor. Perhaps a way will suggest itself for removal of the wreckage."

"Perhaps it will," DePrundis observed. "But I think it will not be so easy." He glanced at his pocket watch. "It is time for me to be on my way." He hated flying. It would be a long night, working against the dawn in Europe. "Perhaps, if I took a bottle of the white with me . . ."

"But of course." Mercado issued the order.

They arose and made their way out of the airport building. A squad of uniformed men armed with M-3 submachine guns fell in behind them.

At the exit, DePrundis braced his bulk against the assault of the outside heat, then plunged through like a diver. Fortunately, his personal jet was only a few yards away and he climbed aboard. Within minutes, the plane was taxiing away down the airstrip, while Mercado remained behind on the apron watching. A moment later his aide approached.

"*Libertador?*"

"What is it?"

"The helicopter is in use."

"What!" Mercado wheeled around. "No one takes priority over *El Libertador!*"

"Yes, sir," the aide stammered. "But the craft is *gone.*"

"Gone where?"

"It was requisitioned on Friday afternoon. Some men from the Cosmo Construction Company, who have not yet returned."

"Requisitioned?"

"They had the correct papers, *Libertador.* They required the craft to make an inspection of the pipeline."

"I want that helicopter on the landing field here tomorrow morning at 10:00 A.M. or there will be some more counter-revolutionaries for the hangman by 10:15! You understand?"

"I understand."

Mercado spun on his heel and headed for his limousine. His guards sprinted ahead of him.

IV

Far above them a jet plane roared toward the eastern horizon. Wolfram and Harada might have been interested if someone had told them that DePrundis was aboard the plane, but it would not have changed their plans.

"Give me just one of the cones from the trunk," Wolfram said. He was already in the water, sleek and black against the bark of the pilings. He carried a red lamp, designed for underwater work, but he hoped there would be enough reflected light from the ship's spotlights to let him see what he was about. There was always the outside chance that someone would spot a red light bouncing below in the water and investigate.

Harada struggled to the edge of the boat with one of the cone-shaped objects. "Heavy," he grunted.

"Sixty-four pounds each." Wolfram slipped a nylon rope through the ring in the tip of the cone and made a noose that he draped over his shoulder like a large sling. "I'll put this one in place, then I'll come back for another."

The water under the pier was only eight feet deep at low tide. He rested the cone on the bottom and, tugging and bouncing it, moved it to the edge of the pier nearest the ship. Here the bottom dropped suddenly into the dredged area. The ship seemed to fill almost the entire basin. There was perhaps four feet clearance at the sides.

Leaving the heavy cone on the bottom, Wolfram crawled up the side of a piling. The ship's reflected spotlights brightened the water next to where he surfaced, but he was in shadow. Just above him the feet of crewmen moving back and forth to the pier thudded on the gangway. The crane's engine alternately roared and purred as it did its work. The clank of magnesium bales echoed through the ship.

Wolfram found himself just about midships, slightly aft. Good, he thought. It was just about right. Using the piling as a guide, he pulled himself back down into the water. Having retrieved the rope noose, he rolled his burden to the edge of the abyss under the great ship and let its weight pull him down.

The descent seemed interminable. Except for a faded olive rim at the edges above, the narrow clearance of the ship in its basin shut out most of the light in the chasm, walled on one side by viscous mud and on the other by sheer steel. Some thirty feet down he switched on the red light. The vast steel bottom of the ship curved away from him beyond the pale beam.

Wolfram kicked hard to overcome the momentum of his descent. He did not want to drift into the neck-deep ooze at the bottom of the basin and perhaps lose the cone—or himself —there. At last he reached a point some ten feet to starboard of the keelson.

Struggling to hold his light and the cone noose at the same time, he worked off a pair of wing nuts at the flat end of the cone. They retained a thick plastic cap, which he let drop off into the murk below. The exposed base was now a circle of thick steel, a specially crafted alnickel magnet that could hold as much as a hundred pounds snug against steel. With a heave, Wolfram pushed it up toward the bottom of the *Queen DePrundis*, where it jumped against the iron plate with a loud *clonk*.

For a moment Wolfram rested. Then he carefully removed another set of wing nuts and removed a smaller plastic cap from the cone, exposing a mechanism. After inspecting it carefully, Wolfram switched the light off and, brushing his way past the steel bottom and sides of the ship, floated toward the sliver of pale green above.

For the next trip, Wolfram employed an inflatable life jacket, which offset most of the cone's weight. This one he placed a hundred feet closer to the bow and about ten feet further away from the keelson. The last device he placed still further forward and close to the point where the curved bottom straightened out into the side of the ship.

On his last trip under the giant ship, he brought a reel of detonating cord with a special explosive core of one hundred grains of cyclomite per foot of length. He threaded the mechanisms of the three cones together with triple circuits. Then he swam to each cone and triggered a timing mechanism.

V

At that same moment Bradford watched a shooting star streak across the smudged night sky of Houston. Behind him in the office he could hear the soft chink of Simon's glass.

There was no more to talk about. They had hammered each other on the possibilities, the probabilities, of what would happen. They had asked each other "why" a hundred times, and in the end they no more knew the answer than in the beginning.

The telephone signal hummed. Simon switched on a light and answered.

"Who is it, please?" Simon cupped the mouthpiece. "He says you know who it is. He does have the private number."

"I *do* know who it is." He took the receiver. "Bradford here."

"One moment." Another voice came on. "Bradford?"

"Chairman."

"Any word?"

"Nothing. I must assume that all is according to plan."

"And tomorrow? What is our deadline?"

"Half-past noon."

"We'll count on that, then."

"Count nothing before it hatches." Bradford paused. "You will hear before me. You have the contacts."

"I will inform you immediately."

"Thank you."

"Good night."

The line clicked.

36

THE SOUND OF THE cathedral's bells jarred Magraw awake.
For a moment the reverberations seemed part of his half-dream,
a torpedo striking amidships. He thought he heard the shouts
of trapped men. But it was nothing.

He remembered it all now. An instant of fear dissolved in
humor. That insane hearing could have been conducted only in
a place like Malaverde. He smiled. Even if suspicions were truth,
the rules of the game would have freed him elsewhere. There
seemed to be no rules here. He remembered Mercado, and
Harada, and the plan.

He glanced at his watch. Plenty of time.

An hour went by.

Finally, a guard brought him breakfast on an iron-wheeled
cart: papaya, bananas, oranges, a pitcher of warm chocolate, and
a thick slice of dry bread. At least he wouldn't starve, he mused.
He took his time. There was an old rule: when you can eat,
eat.

He stood and stretched. Prison wasn't all bad. He glanced
at his watch again. Ten o'clock. Time to act. It was getting hot
again.

"Guard!"

"You finished your breakfast?"

"Finished! I want to talk to the head guard."

Keys rattled in his door. "The chief will be at home. It is
Sunday, after all."

"I want to talk to the head man. It is very important."

"It will have to wait until tomorrow."

"That will be too late."

"What will be too late?"

"My information."

"You can trust me with it."

"It is most important and of interest to *El Libertador* himself! After all, my friend, who do you think personally ordered me held here?"

The guard hesitated. "It will take time," he said finally.

Magraw handed the guard a wad of bills. "Perhaps these will hurry your feet."

"You are serious."

"*Most* serious, my friend. It is important."

A half-hour later the guard was back with the chief of guards.

"Good morning," Magraw said genially.

"You have disrupted my Sunday!" the chief snapped.

"You will be grateful that I have called you out."

"What is it?"

"You will recall that yesterday there was a lengthy hearing."

"Yes, I was there in the afternoon."

"You will recall that *El Libertador* expressed concern lest the sinking of my ship was a conspiracy."

"Yes, yes, I remember that."

"Of course, I denied this at the time, as did the members of my crew."

"You brought me here to tell me this?"

"Patience, my friend. At that time I truly *believed* there was no conspiracy."

"You believe differently now?"

"I now believe, very definitely, that there *is* a conspiracy, but I must be taken to the ship *Queen DePrundis,* which is docked in your harbor, to demonstrate how it is being effected."

"I cannot take you there until I consult higher officials."

"By all means, consult. But if I am to demonstrate my case, which is dependent on the tide, then I must be there soon." Magraw consulted his watch. "Please hurry. Before long the tide will be wrong again."

The chief stood and moved quickly out of the cell. Magraw heard the clack of boots receding down the corridor.

Time was now critical.

II

From the window of his suite in the palace, Mercado could see the harbor clearly all the way to the tower of Castel Mala. Slowly he swung his binoculars to the left across the harbor. The white ship tied at the dock was partially hidden behind the giant gray tankers moored in the main channel. He could see a crew of riggers on the *DePrundis Lady* working to unfasten the lines of tubing.

His stomach ached. Those ships had no place to go until the sunken hulk was obliterated. Only that morning his radio had intercepted the signals of a tanker diverting its course from Malanueva to another port down the coast.

His glasses swung further left. At the Navy Yard a crew of sailors was working to load the last of the cases of explosives aboard a giant barge. What a fireworks it would be! Thousands of people would line the Castel Mala road to watch.

Behind him, his telephone buzzed. "What is it?"

"*Libertador,* the chief of the prison guards is on the telephone. He insists that the black man, the one from the hearings yesterday, has confessed that there is a conspiracy."

"Put him on!"

"*Libertador?*"

"Speak up!"

"This man—the black man—says there is a conspiracy. He says it has something to do with the tide and he wants to show me what it is. He says he must go to the white ship moored in the harbor . . ."

"The *Queen DePrundis.*"

"To expose the conspiracy he must go there *now.* To show something."

"Yes. I think you should take him there."

"Right away, *Libertador* . . ."

"Wait, you idiot! Take the black man to the ship, but he is to tell you nothing until I get there."

"What time will that be, *Libertador?*"

Mercado looked at his watch. "Eleven forty-five. Perhaps a few minutes later. Do nothing until I arrive."

"Yes, *Libertador.*"

"One other thing."

"What is that, *Libertador?*"

"Have this man in chains and under a heavy guard. The conspirators might make an attempt to rescue or kill him. There might be gunplay!"

"It shall be done, *Libertador.*"

Mercado slammed the receiver down.

Picking up his binoculars, he focused once again on the white *Queen DePrundis.*

37

I

JUANITA AND KINSEY STOOD in the shadowed doorway of the radio shack and looked out at the desert. There were no sounds but the faint hissing of the overhead wires. Only the heat seemed alive.

"Can we go soon?" Juanita asked.

He checked his watch. "Well, it would be a little bit early, but I believe I will change the circuits now."

He went to the radio equipment and removed the front panel. Then he took the small bag with the damaged circuit and peeled the plastic away.

"It's a strange kind of killing," he said over his shoulder. "I pull the plug and the system dies." He put in the damaged circuit, then replaced the front panel. Next he blew a bit of dust over the equipment to obliterate signs that it had been tampered with. "The operation is a success," he said, putting the wiring chart and the good circuit in the pocket of his coveralls.

"What does that mean?"

"The oil-producing wells seventy-five miles south of here will keep on pumping oil through the pipeline. No one will be able to tell them to stop." He looked quickly around the shack, then grabbed her hand. "Let's go!"

They made for the helicopter.

"Wait!" she said. "We must lock the door."

Five minutes later the sound of the helicopter's rotors receded toward Malanueva. The incoming wires hummed with messages going nowhere.

II

They spent the hours after sun-up checking and rechecking the diving equipment and the running gear of the craft itself. Harada reset the carburetor in the boat's engine to give them more speed.

Later, they drank tea and ate rice biscuits in the coolness of Harada's shack.

"There is nothing here that could identify you or us, is there?" Wolfram asked as they prepared to leave.

"Nothing."

"Good. Let's go, then."

Wolfram drove. "Time the trip, Harada," he said. "It might be useful to know." He maintained a slow, steady pace. The few miles took them seven minutes.

Wolfram pulled the truck well up on the shoulder just past the point where the pipeline crossed the highway. They walked the rest of the way across the plateau and down the long, shallow slope toward the harbor. The huge iron-wheeled machines were just as they had left them the day before.

Wolfram checked his watch. "Let's make this short. Then we'll have an ample time cushion all around.

"Drive one of the machines up the slope at a forty-five degree angle," he went on. "Then, turn around, head it in the correct direction, throw the throttle to 'full,' and get the hell off fast. Jump as hard as you can toward the rear, Harada. It will soak up some of the impact of your fall."

Harada climbed aboard and gestured toward the other Trash-Pak. "What about this machine? What is its function?"

"A spare, if the first machine overturns or breaks down or fails to shatter the pipe. Shall we get to it? I'll ride up the hill with you."

The diesel engine thudded into life in a cloud of pale-blue exhaust. In a minute they were at the top of the slope and Harada had idled the engine down.

Wolfram clambered down from the machine. "Don't forget.

250

As soon as you hit full throttle, jump backwards. No time to waste."

"One thing, Hugo."

"Yes?"

"The thermite bombs."

Wolfram removed them from the tool box where he had put them the day before. "If there is a substantial break in the line, a strong current of oil, drop them in. The fuses will give us thirty minutes, so waste no time coming back uphill."

Harada motioned Wolfram to stand aside. The big iron wheels churned back down the hill again, slowly at first. Wolfram watched Harada carefully maneuvering his way out of the driver's seat, keeping one hand on the wheel to steer. He saw him reach forward with his free hand, give a thrust to the throttle, and then suddenly jump free of the big machine. Harada hit the ground, rolled, and, remarkably, came up on his feet, running.

The sharply accelerating iron wheels of the Trash-Pak threw up clods of baked earth. As if with a mind of its own, the machine went lurching forward, accelerating as it lumbered down the slope like some antic rhinoceros.

Wolfram smiled. The angle was just right.

The diesel engine thudded and banged. Faster, faster. Closer, closer to the pipeline.

Impact!

There was a clanging shower of sparks. The iron wheels of the machine rolled ahead for an instant and then seemed to leap, as if trying to claw their way over the pipeline. The reddish steel instantly showed a black stripe around its girth and then a ragged black strip longitudinally. The Trash-Pak keeled over and rolled on its side, then over on its back, wheels spinning angrily. Diesel fuel spilled out of its tanks and ran in streams down the side of the engine. With a clanking, sputtering sound, the engine suddenly died. The wheels kept spinning, but more slowly each second.

Jet-black, gleaming fluid spurted fanlike from the broken pipeline. It gathered rapidly in thick pools and puddles that merged and began to run down the slope.

The break in the pipeline followed a weld where two sections abutted. The lengthwise split probably followed a fault in the steel. The heavy machine had crushed in the end of the section of pipe on the harbor side, allowing the heavy flow of oil to rush virtually unimpeded down the slope like lava. Wolfram knew the pipeline pumped at a rate of more than 500 barrels a minute, upward of a million gallons an hour.

Harada waved to get his attention. Wolfram mimed pulling the pin on a grenade.

Harada nodded vigorously and trotted down the slope again. There he removed the pin from one fuse and hurled the bomb downhill into the torrent of oil. Quickly, he did the same with the other. The canisters bobbed along in the ebony flood in the direction of the refinery.

With a last look over his shoulder, the Japanese jogged up the slope to the truck. There, both men paused a moment, gasping for breath; then they climbed in.

They drove back to Harada's pier in silence, drained by the heat and tension. Wolfram made the return trip in less than five minutes. Time was critical now.

"Did you see the barge-load of explosives?" Harada asked as they got out of the truck.

"I saw the barge." Wolfram smiled. "Mercado couldn't be more helpful."

They walked quickly to the moored fishing boat. Harada took the helm and started the engine. Wolfram peeled off his coveralls and donned a scuba suit.

"Cast off aft," Harada called.

Wolfram unhitched the line and dropped it, pushing the boat away from the pilings. Harada immediately edged the boat's throttle ahead.

It was 11:17 A.M. by Wolfram's watch.

252

38

MINUTES LATER, A BLACK limousine shepherded by armed personnel carriers made its way down the Camino Real toward the drawbridge.

Magraw's hands were manacled; the manacles, in turn, were linked to a heavy belt around his waist. At least I'm not chained to some other poor devil, he thought.

There were few automobiles on the wide boulevard. Sunday strollers dotted the esplanade. It was a day for promenading, despite the heat.

Behind the screen of palms the empty government buildings stood like sepulchers. All of the structures, as well as the few private office buildings along the route, seemed to have been built in the spring of 1923. But now, the elements had eaten away their marble exteriors. No doubt, Magraw mused, the atmospheric acids from the refinery accelerated the process.

At the drawbridge the procession stopped momentarily, then proceeded toward the harbor area. Through the window of the limousine Magraw could see activity on the waterfront by the Navy Yard. Tugboats gingerly nudged a long wooden barge away from a pier toward the channel. Magraw decided it was the barge full of explosives alluded to by Mercado the day before.

They followed the main coast highway for a quarter of a mile or so then veered right onto the refinery highway. To his right Magraw saw a rutted dirt lane that he believed led down to

Harada's fishing shack. He could see plain wooden buildings and the pier at the water's edge.

The fishing boat was gone—a good sign. So far, at least, plans were proceeding.

Chain-link fencing, eight feet high and topped with triple strands of barbed wire, lined both sides of the highway. Behind the fencing, dwarfing everything, were the silvered ranks of huge storage tanks. Soon the tank area gave way to the refinery itself, simmering under the sun. He knew it was working at capacity, refilling its tanks in anticipation of a new fleet of ships once the outer channel was cleared.

The whole refinery and its associated tank farm covered an enormous area. They drove more than two miles through its middle before a turnoff appeared leading to the harbor. At a gate in the fence a guard unfastened a chain and swung the barrier away. They were expected. A hundred yards or so further on, they were at the pier.

The *Queen DePrundis* extended the length of two football fields along its mooring. Magraw studied the fantail section, jutting out toward the main channel. The ship rested quite low in the water. The deck was piled high with some kind of shiny light-colored metal. Aluminum, probably. Or magnesium. He didn't know. Wolfram had not told him.

At the gangway of the ship they disembarked from the limousine. The guard vehicles swung into flanking positions. One carbine-armed trooper from each dismounted and took a position near the prisoner.

"We must go aboard," Magraw said. He tried to gesture, but his manacles restricted him. "It is essential that we go to the rear of the ship if I am to explain the conspiracy."

The chief remembered his orders. "Silence!"

Magraw started to move toward the gangway.

"Stop!"

"You idiot!" Magraw snapped angrily. "Do you want to know about this conspiracy, or are we waiting for a photographer?"

"We must wait. I have no choice."

"How long?"

"Not long."

"Why can't we go aboard the ship and wait there?"

The chief shrugged. His orders had not covered that.

"At least we could go to the position at the stern where I must make my explanation."

For a moment the chief weighed his curiosity against his anxiety. Curiosity won out. "We go aboard," he snapped. He shouted instructions at the guards. To Magraw he said, "I warn you. Try no tricks. These men are crack shots and they are well armed."

"Try tricks? With these?" He shook his chains.

They walked to the gangway and went aboard the ship. "This way," Magraw said. Now that he had exerted some influence over the chief, he would have to keep it up or lose it.

They had to climb a ladder to get to the poop deck. Like the tankers, the bulk cargo carrier's superstructure and engine area were aft of the cargo area. Mercifully, the fantail was partially shadowed from the sun.

"Not too close there!" snapped the chief as Magraw moved near the railing. Magraw glanced quickly over the side. He judged the water to be perhaps thirty feet below the fantail. A hard sock on the feet, the belly, or whatever hit first. The tide was coming in briskly.

Magraw had been mentally rehearsing his story. It would have to be plausible, one that would require time to check. "Now, then," Magraw said briskly to the chief, "as I see it . . ."

"No talk!"

It was incredible. The chief was terrorized. Magraw squinted. They all stood silently, the soldier guards standing back ten or twelve feet. They seemed to be waiting for someone, which made it simpler for him. There would be less time to check his story, less time for suspicions to emerge.

From the elevation of the ship he had a clear view of the whole harbor. In the middle of the ship channel, about a quarter-mile aft of the *Queen DePrundis*, a fishing boat droned at top speed. It was the only thing moving on the mirror-slick olive surface of the harbor. He stared hard at the fishing boat. Two men aboard. Even at this distance, he could make out the white hair of one of them. Calm began to replace his mounting anxiety.

He was careful not to make too much of staring at the boat. He turned, casually, face away from the chief. He watched the boat humming across the water from the corner of his eye. It seemed to be turning now, in a wide, almost imperceptible arc toward the shoreline. He turned full away from the scene and looked back toward the pier. The fishing boat would eventually make its way to the other side of this very pier.

The plan would work.

From a distance the sound of approaching sirens echoed off the refinery structures and the pier warehouses. The chief became visibly agitated, the guards appeared nervous. Obviously, this was what they had been waiting for. Inshore, the fence guard unfastened his chain and swung the gate open.

A minute later a caravan of black sedans and an armored car turned down the road to the pier.

Without slowing, the vehicles roared down the pier and skidded to an abrupt halt. One limousine stopped directly in front of the gangway.

An Air Force officer leapt out of the front of the long black automobile and snapped open a rear door, saluting at the same time with his free right hand.

It was 11:35 A.M.

II

"The authorities are bringing Magraw to our rendezvous," Harada said.

"Perhaps," said Wolfram. He hoped that was the case, but if it were not, the machinery was going to go by itself. "We will tie up only by the stern." He went to the back of the boat while Harada maneuvered it into the bulkheading. "Get it a bit closer to the end of the pier, Harada." He shrugged into his air tanks and checked equipment.

As Harada backed the craft gently into the bulkheading. Wolfram threw a hitch around a piling and tugged it firm. "That will hold it long enough. We'll want to cast off in a hurry."

He fixed his face mask, checked his breathing, and with a thumbs-up sign, fell backwards over the side. He scarcely made a splash. Harada went to the stern and handed the extra scuba gear over the side to him. Wolfram hooked it carefully in his arms and sank slowly into the murky waters. For a moment,

Harada could trace his path by a wake of silvery bubbles, but soon even they disappeared.

He glanced at his watch: 11:38. In an hour it would be over.

III

Sweat soaked Magraw's khaki shirt and trickled down his back.

The sweat was not only from the heat. The approach of Mercado and his entourage created a clamminess of their own.

Magraw edged closer to the ship's rail. The attention of the guards and their chief was focused on *El Libertador,* now banging up the metal ladder leading to the poop deck. His hat appeared first. The face beneath it was a poor, mean thundercloud. But the eyes were bright with malice and the mouth was a rigid line.

Magraw glanced at the rail, then at his watch. Five minutes. Goddamn all this, he thought. It wasn't in the plan!

Mercado clumped forward and planted himself in front of Magraw, arms akimbo. "So the black pig is ready to grunt," he snarled.

Magraw's jaw muscles tightened. Don't cave in, he told himself. Hold off. This bastard will have his problems soon enough. Play your role, conspirator, play.

"I have recognized the error of my attitude, *Libertador,*" he confessed. "You are correct. The revolution is too valuable to be subverted by greedy men."

"Then you confess that you deliberately sank your ship in the channel?"

"That is most assuredly *not* what I confess, *Libertador.*" He smiled. "My motive is cooperation. I believe that I, too, have been ill used." He drew himself up.

"Used?" Mercado's eyes narrowed. "How?"

"I am an innocent victim, *Libertador.* Just as are the people of Malaverde whose oil is confined to the harbor."

"Explain."

"I picked up my ship and cargo in Freeport, Texas, consigned to Malanueva." He smiled again. "It was my first command of the vessel."

"Who owns this ship?"

"My papers said the Cosmo Construction Company."

"I know what the papers *say*," snapped Mercado. "But what do *you* say? Who owns this Cosmo Construction Company?" He raised an arm as if to strike. "Speak, you black fool, or I'll split your lips!"

Magraw hunched down as if to ward off the blow, glancing at his watch surreptitiously. One minute. Time to tell a lie, then go mad.

"*Libertador:*" he shrieked. "I confess! The owner of the Cosmo Construction Company is a Greek. I am not sure of his name. A fat man, very rich." —

Mercado blanched. "A Greek? A fat Greek?"

"That is so."

"Speak up!" This time he did strike Magraw on the temple.

"The Greek! Now I remember his name!" He rolled his eyes wildly. "I am going mad! The heat! The fear! The name of the Greek is . . ."

"The name, man! The *name!*"

"The name is . . ." Magraw staggered the backward toward the rail. "I can't stand this! I can't . . ."

"Stop him!" shouted Mercado. "Jesus, he *knows* something!"

The guards rushed forward. One managed to grab Magraw's shirt, but it tore away in his hands as the black man's body plummeted down toward the murky waters beneath the fantail.

"Goddamn all of you! Get a boat! Swimmers! We *must* have him!"

In the distance a column of black smoke curled into the clear sky.

39

THE GIANT PROPELLER HUNG motionless in the turgid water. Wolfram checked his watch. A few minutes to go. Other clocks were clicking away their seconds and minutes, too.

Utter silence. He checked his watch again. This should be the time.

He looked toward the surface. It gleamed and rippled, nothing more.

Silence. Nothing.

Now he felt the beat of his own pulse, anxiety. He did not want to swim back alone—it would be an admission of failure. Worse, he did not like this untidy end left undone.

Silence.

Movement!

A heavy shape struck and plunged in an explosion of luminescent bubbles.

Wolfram plunged after it, hauling the extra underwater gear.

Now the shape was rising again, slow motion, the black face of Magraw bulging at its top, eyes wild, cheeks puffed out.

Wolfram grabbed him by the belt and struggled to keep the two of them from rising. Fortunately, he had enough spare weight. Quickly, he thrust the mouthpiece of the extra equipment between Magraw's lips.

Wolfram twirled the knobs of the scuba tanks, opening up the air supply, then slipped the extra mask over Magraw's face.

Goddamn them! There was no way to get the tanks strapped over Magraw's shoulders.

Wolfram pulled Magraw over on his back and tucked the scuba tanks under the manacled hands. Then he hooked one arm through Magraw's and signaled the black man. They must get under the pier quickly. Would the guards see the bubbles? Would they be looking?

Wolfram began dragging Magraw in a powerful sidestroke. Magraw assisted with a scissor kick. Slowly, they rose up toward the edge of the ship's trench. There was a gap there, perhaps ten feet between ship and pier, that had to be traversed before they would be out of sight under the bulkhead.

Wolfram stepped up his pace. God, why did he slice his time so thin?

Struggling together they made it to the top of the trench, then, virtually crawling over the muck bottom, edged their way well into the darkness under the pier.

Less than two minutes had passed.

Wolfram used pilings as handholds for his free arm, propelling him and his burden along fairly quickly. Brighter water ahead told Wolfram they were getting close to the other side of the pier.

Now he could feel the throb of the boat engine.

He redoubled his efforts. Time to rest later. Magraw, too, kicked harder. But the nightmare quality of water, the frustrating sensation of swimming against the tide, gripped Wolfram.

He stopped at the next piling. Don't grab and jerk. The barnacles are cutting your hands. The spasmodic yank is not as effective as the long, slow pull.

Feel, carefully. Get a good purchase. Then pull. He was in control again.

Wolfram broke surface first and flung his mask aside.

"The boat hook, Harada! Magraw's arms are bound!"

Quickly Wolfram unstrapped his own equipment and let it sink, then removed Magraw's.

"Jesus!" the black man exhaled mightily.

Wolfram held Magraw above water until Harada put the boat hook over the side. Wolfram carefully put it through Magraw's chains. "Hold him above water, Harada. I'll come aboard and help you get him up."

Aboard the boat, he and Harada swiftly hauled Magraw up and over the side. Wolfram unlooped the mooring, while Harada went to the helm.

"Go!" Wolfram shouted.

Harada accelerated the engines. Wolfram, thrown off balance by the sudden forward motion, sat down heavily on the deck. Magraw began to laugh. For an instant Wolfram cursed; then he, too, began to laugh.

Harada hugged the shoreline for a distance, keeping the pier buildings between his boat and the view of the guards aboard the *Queen DePrundis.* At a safe distance, he turned the craft to starboard and gunned for the open harbor.

Wolfram came forward. "Take her well out into the channel, then get dead astern of the *Queen DePrundis.*"

"From what direction will Kinsey arrive?"

"He's going to vector on the ship, on a line from bow to stern, so we should be as much on that line as we can be."

"No problem."

Magraw got to his feet and joined them. "When do I get unchained?"

"Damn, I'm sorry, Magraw. We should have thought of that first. Where's your tool kit, Harada?"

The Japanese pointed toward a locker. "There is a small bolt cutter at the bottom of the locker. I use it for trimming fuel line."

Wolfram opened the locker and fumbled among the tools until he found the bolt cutter. "Now we will test the steel of Malaverde." He hooked the blunt snout of the bolt cutters to the belt chain and pressed the handles together. It cut easily.

Magraw raised his arms. "Now the bracelets."

Wolfram snipped the chain connecting the bracelets, then the bracelets themselves. "Cheap alloy."

"Enough to hold me." Magraw rubbed his wrists gratefully. "You can't imagine what a helpless feeling that is. Trapped, absolutely trapped."

"It took guts to make that dive," Wolfram said. "You had no real way of knowing whether I'd be there."

"But you were there, Hugo. It's a hell of a way to make a living."

Wolfram nodded. "It was a good plan. It worked."

"I had a kind of push, you might say."

"Push?"

"I was being interrogated by that lousy grub Mercado, himself."

"Mercado? On the *Queen DePrundis?*"

"I was only a few feet from him. The bastard was screaming in my face. It was a strong incentive to do my Steel Pier diving horse act."

"I hope he stays aboard."

Wolfram went to the helm and retrieved the binoculars. He focused on the fantail of the *Queen DePrundis.* "He's still there!"

"What's he doing?"

"Leaning over the rail, waving his arms." He moved the glasses. "There are people in the water."

"Looking for my ebony cadaver, I suppose."

"Probably." Wolfram swung the glasses back up to Mercado. The large head slowly pivoted upward. The face looked at the channel, then toward their boat. An expression of exasperation gave way to one of incredulity, and then, comprehension.

"He's seen our boat!" Wolfram blurted.

"What's he doing?"

"Moved away from the railing. Waving his arms again. Men running."

"He'll call a patrol boat." Magraw pointed downchannel toward the wreck of the *Charon,* where a gray cutter rested at anchor. "That boat can be within gun range in five minutes."

Wolfram checked his watch. "We'll be just about on our way by then."

"They took me and my crew into Malanueva on that cutter," said Magraw. "It's armed with twin fifties."

"Maybe we should turn upchannel, away from that patrol boat," Harada suggested. "Might give us an extra three or four minutes."

Wolfram studied the cutter through the binoculars. "It hasn't hauled anchor yet. They may not have gotten the message." He swung the glasses toward the channel. "There's a big tug coming, hauling a barge."

"Let me see." Magraw took the glasses. "That's the explosives barge that Mercado ordered. He plans to blow up the *Charon* where she lies."

"I know. Harada told me about it."

"Maybe if we keep our craft between the patrol boat and the barge, they'll hold off firing for fear of setting off the explosives."

"If we were dealing with reliable, commonsense sailors, I'd say yes. Therefore, I must say no. A barge load of TNT wouldn't hold them up thirty seconds."

Magraw scanned toward the *Charon*. "They're weighing anchor."

"Let me see." Wolfram took the glasses. "They mean business. They're bringing out their extra ammunition."

"We can almost match speed with the patrol boat, even if we can't outrun it. If it comes to a showdown, we'll head straight into the shallows. At high tide, there is enough water for the patrol boat to follow us, but they'll have to slow down considerably."

Wolfram turned to scan the horizon.

"Any sign of Kinsey?" Magraw asked.

"We won't see him until he flies in over the *Queen DePrundis*. He'll be flying low." He brought the glasses down and pointed. "Look!"

A thickening smudge of black smoke darkened the sky. "Your work?"

"Harada, mostly."

At that moment, Wolfram heard the distant whup-whup of a helicopter.

"It's Kinsey!" Magraw shouted.

Wolfram glanced at his watch. "Only three minutes late." He called to Harada. "Shut her down and drop anchor!"

"The patrol boat is coming fast!"

"We'll have to risk it. We need to be reasonably stationary for the pickup."

The boat motor died with a cough. Harada clambered to the bow and hurled the anchor overboard.

"Pull down the radio mast."

With a pocket wrench, Harada unfastened the retaining bolts.

"Timber!" Magraw shouted as the radio mast toppled into the water.

The big Bell helicopter came upon them fast and seemed to skid to an aerial stop, hovering fifteen feet overhead. The

263

48-foot rotor's downdraft beat the water to a frenzy and set the boat to swaying. A metal link ladder unrolled down at them, thudding on the cabin roof.

The three men scrambled to the top of the small housing. Wolfram pushed Magraw to the ladder first. The black man hesitated, then grabbed the jumping ladder and began to scramble up while Wolfram held the bottom of the ladder steady.

Harada was next. Wolfram looked back over his shoulder as he held the ladder. The patrol cutter was within a thousand yards, still coming at top speed. There was a man on the bow guns and an ammunition man kneeling beside him.

Tiny, silent flames studded the ends of the weapons and, almost instantly, a dozen geysers of water leaped into the air a hundred meters short of the boat and fifty meters to the right.

Wolfram looked up. Harada was scrambling aboard assisted by Magraw.

My turn.

He started up the lurching, swinging ladder, his eyes riveted on the helicopter above. Harada and Magraw hauled in the ladder, even as he climbed.

Snap! Snap! They're shooting at the chopper!

He heard the angry zing as a bullet nicked the ladder below him. A rung twirled end over end into the harbor.

Now he was at the door. Hands and arms hauled him into the craft on his stomach.

At the same instant he felt the sudden pressure of ascent. For a moment he lay there on the floor of the craft, not moving, as Kinsey maneuvered it up and out of range of the patrol boat.

Slowly, Wolfram pulled himself into a sitting position and looked around. His eyes asked: Everyone all right?

There were nods.

Wolfram made the thumbs-up sign and grinned.

It was quarter past noon by Wolfram's watch. He pulled himself to his feet and worked his way past the others to Kinsey. "Fly on a bearing of 220 toward Caracas," he shouted. He pointed at his watch. "When you have 12:25 set the chopper down. There's something we will want to see."

40

KINSEY BROUGHT THE 204B down on an acre of flat sepia rock.

"What's the matter?" Magraw wanted to know. "Why have we landed?"

"Don't worry," Kinsey called above the dying whine of the turbine. "This was Hugo's idea."

Wolfram looked at his watch. "We will be here for no more than five minutes." He opened the door and climbed out into the oven heat, carrying the same soft bag that he had brought into Malaverde forty-eight hours before.

He unzipped the bag and took out a pair of khaki slacks and put them on over his trunks. Then he shrugged on a flowered short-sleeve cotton shirt. From the bottom of the bag he produced a pair of rubber-soled canvas slippers and put them on.

The others watched silently from the door of the helicopter.

"Come on out," Wolfram said. "Magraw, your clothes will dry in an instant."

"You look like a tourist," Magraw told him as he got out of the helicopter. "Do you mean you put us down in this borax barrel for you to . . . ?"

The others got out.

"This is part of the plan, isn't it, Hugo?" Juanita asked.

"It's true, children," Wolfram said, buttoning his shirt. "As a matter of fact this *is* part of the plan." He glanced at his watch.

"To be more precise, in exactly . . . seventy seconds this mission will have been accomplished. Let's watch." He gestured in the direction of Malanueva. The city was concealed from them, well over the horizon. Only a low smudge of black smoke marked the place.

"Any instant now," Wolfram whispered hoarsely.

There was no sound in the noontime desert. The sky was like translucent blue quartz. The sepia and ocher rocks seemed suspended.

It happened!

It was brighter than the desert noon, a burst of silent brilliance that momentarily blinded them and was gone, a titanic spark jumping at the sky. Then, within milliseconds, from the edge of the earth rose a perfectly round orange ball.

They all gasped. Wolfram chuckled—a barely audible sound.

Higher and higher the fireball rolled, pushed, it seemed, by a column of coiling flame streaked with brown and tangerine and magenta shades. The column twisted like a tornado, sucking up the land itself.

"Brace yourselves!" shouted Wolfram. "Shock wave coming."

They stood transfixed. The swelling glob of flame rolled, turned, changed color. It seemed, now, to be flattening out against the sky, perhaps six thousand feet in the air.

Seconds later the shock wave hit them. It struck their ears first, shattering sound like a prolonged crack of lightning. It squeezed them in fists of air. Then the shock hit their feet, tugging their rock this way and that way, almost jarring them off balance.

"This is hell," Harada said matter-of-factly.

There seemed to be smaller flashes of light now. From the fire cloud itself, pinpoints of brilliance fell like snow.

"Look!" Magraw exclaimed. "Are they fragments of the dynamite barge? Or the ship, maybe?"

The sounds of secondary explosions reached them, a series of far-off crumps that one felt more than heard.

"Were they your explosive devices, Hugo?" Harada seemed stunned.

None of them knew for sure what had exploded, Wolfram thought—even Harada hadn't put it together. He told a plausible story. "My charges would have made a big bang, indeed. But

266

there was the TNT barge. It must have gone up." He wouldn't lie to them. He wouldn't tell them the truth. They didn't need to know. Not now. "Let's go. It's over."

Wolfram was first aboard the helicopter. Magraw was the last to board. "Those sparks are weird," he said. "Like hundreds of flares coming down. Weird."

Wolfram sat in silence. It had worked.

Kinsey fiddled with the controls, and then the turbine began its windup. Soon they were aloft and soon after that the dry terrain of Malaverde began to give way to the deep green of Venezuela.

41

I

DAWN TINGED THE HOUSTON airfield with red, giving the oily haze a luminescent beauty it didn't deserve.

The Viasa flight from Caracas touched down on time, wheeled sedately into the foreign-arrivals area. Simon watched from the chilly interior of the arrivals building. The place reeked of jet fuel. Wandering airport personnel had the burned-out look of those who have been up all night. The morning shift had not yet arrived.

Shortly a flock of passengers came through the doorway into the customs area. Among them Simon spotted a tall figure wearing a red-flowered shirt, a baseball cap, and dark glasses. The person carried no bags. The customs people waved him through respectfully.

Simon signaled the page girl.

"Will Mr. Winkle please report to the TWA ticket counter?"

The message was repeated. The toneless amplified voice seemed to underline the name Winkle. Simon wondered whether that name had any significance.

The TWA counter was an unlikely spot for a covert rendezvous. But Wolfram had said, when he telephoned yesterday, that the more crowded the better. No one would recall them.

A hand took his arm from behind, startling him. "Jesus! How did you get there?"

"Easily. Let's move on."

268

Quickly, they strode toward the exit.

"Your car nearby?"

"Right in front. I have a man watching it."

"You go first. Pay him off. Then I'll come out."

At the long dark sedan Simon gave the car watcher a five and sent him back toward the building. Simon signaled. Wolfram came out and slid into the right front seat, while Simon climbed in the other side.

"Why do you wear a flowered shirt if you're trying to avoid attention?"

"There's attention and attention." Wolfram looked drawn with fatigue.

Simon nodded. "How was your flight?"

"I napped."

"After your call, we tried to get radio reports."

"And?"

"It was several hours." He laughed shortly. "I thought maybe you'd given us a bum steer. I almost hoped you had. I should have known better."

"What were the reports?"

"Fragmentary, confused at first. They got horribly clearer as the night went on."

"Why horrible?"

"At least eighteen missing."

"That was less than we contracted for. What about Mercado?"

"Nothing. Why?"

"We should have gotten him."

"I hope you did. I hope the son-of-a-bitch was fried."

"What did the radio say?"

"The first reports merely said that some catastrophe had struck. It didn't indicate what. It could have been a volcano."

"It could have been."

"The reports continued sketchy for some time. Then new information came in. A dynamite barge. That ring a bell?"

"A coincidence." Wolfram laughed quietly. "The most plausible part of my plausible accident."

"I don't remember dynamite being part of your . . ."

"Skip it for now. You'll hear the whole thing when I report to Bradford."

"I'm worried about him."

"It cost a hell of a lot of money."

"I mean his *son*. His *company*. He talks about ending it all."

"You mean his corporations?"

"I mean himself."

Wolfram said nothing.

"I tried to dissuade him from the . . . mission . . . at the beginning," Simon continued.

"I know."

Wolfram seemed remarkably unresponsive, so Simon changed the subject. "Were there any complications?"

"None that I'll tell you about." He made an effort to remember Esposito's face.

"Any difficulties getting away?"

Wolfram decided to ramble about that. "My . . . team used the old Bradford Petroleum helicopter."

"You flew direct to Caracas?"

"More or less. We landed at the airport and then abandoned the chopper. We went to the main terminal building and, just like tourists, hired taxis to carry us downtown to a hotel."

"Were others of them on your Viasa flight?"

"No, they'll be coming up in the next few days, I suppose." The conversation was getting tedious. "We have a meeting arranged later. To complete the payments." He stared out at the streets of Houston, not yet filled with morning commuter traffic. "I hope Bradford has that little item prepared. I'd prefer this to be my last visit for some time."

II

As they entered the office, Bradford's back was to them. He sat in his swivel chair facing the view of Houston. "Come in, gentlemen," he said, swinging the chair around.

Wolfram thought, my God, he's aged. "How are you, G.B.?"

Bradford stared at Wolfram walking toward him across the deep carpeting. "You look none the worse for wear." It sounded like an accusation.

270

They didn't shake hands.

Wolfram sat down in a green leather chair.

"We've had only sketchy reports."

"The objective was attained according to specifications." Wolfram shrugged. "I can't say it went exactly according to plan. Such things never do."

A desk buzzer sounded.

"A messenger is delivering a late edition of the newspaper, Simon," Bradford said. "Would you get it from him, please?"

Bradford and Wolfram sat in silence until Simon returned. A page-wide headline exclaimed:

BLASTS, FIRES WRECK S.A. OIL PORT
MANY MISSING, HURT; DAMAGE IN MILLIONS

TNT BOAT STARTS HAVOC
MALAVERDE LEADER MISSING

Raging Fires Continue;
Fed By Out-of-Control
Tank & Pipeline Supply

Bradford stared at the newspaper without seeming to see it, then handed it back to Simon. "Would you be good enough to read it aloud, please? My eyes . . ."

Simon read the headline, then the subheads, aloud.

Bradford glanced quickly at Wolfram. "What's that about Malaverde leader missing?"

"The probability is quite high that we got him."

"How?"

"Let's hear the news account first. Then, I'll fill in the blanks."

The younger man began to read:

Malanueva—This oil port capital of Malaverde was devastated at 12:30 P.M., EDT, today when a TNT barge blew up, triggering massive secondary explosions and fires that left scores missing or dead.

The port's entire oil refinery complex and harbor facilities were leveled. At least a half-dozen major oceangoing vessels were sunk or set ablaze. The business and residential areas of the city, some four

271

miles from the blast site, suffered structural damage and virtual total destruction of windows and other glass features. The known dead numbered 14.

Believed to be among the missing is Jaime Mercado y Suarez, Malaverde Premier . . .

III

"I can't say you did a *good* job, Hugo. I am not even sure it was a *correct* one. However, I am sure that it was a well-executed one. That's why I retained you."

Slowly, almost painfully, Bradford opened the large bottom drawer of his desk. He brought out a thick accordion file bound by a webbing strap and placed it on the desk.

"Here's the other half of our bargain, per arrangement. Plus a bonus."

Wolfram stood and picked up the file. "Perhaps our paths will cross on some other business enterprise. An oil-well fire, a mountain in your path . . ."

"I will never see you again, Hugo," Bradford said. "For whatever it means to a man like you, good luck."

Wolfram tucked the heavy file under his arm and turned to go.

"Hugo?"

"Yes?"

"What happened to us?"

"Happened?"

"Back then. The old years."

Wolfram shook his head uncomprehendingly.

Bradford stared at him a moment. "Never mind, then. Thank you."

Wolfram closed the door behind him.

Slowly, Bradford got up and went to the sideboard. "Can I fix you one?" he asked Simon as he poured himself a glass of whiskey.

Bradford poured a heavy Scotch over ice and handed it to Simon. "Help yourself if you want more."

"It's been a long day," Simon said, "and productive, if one

accepts the standards of Wolfram." He paused, awaiting a reply. There was none.

"You've known Wolfram a long time, haven't you?"

"There was the war," Bradford said, looking into his glass. "We had to find and train personnel to carry our programs out . . ."

"And you found Wolfram?"

"You could say we created aspects of him."

"How do you *create* a Wolfram?"

"You amputate his conscience."

The two men sat in silence for some time.

"Well, Simon," Bradford said finally, "as you say, it's been a long day. Why don't you go home and get some rest?"

"You'll be all right?"

"I'll be fine."

"Shall I tell your chauffeur a time to pick you up?"

"No thanks." He sighed. "I may just sleep in at the apartment here. If I change my mind, I'll get a cab."

Bradford moved toward the door to show him out. As Simon left, he hoped the old man would now find some peace.

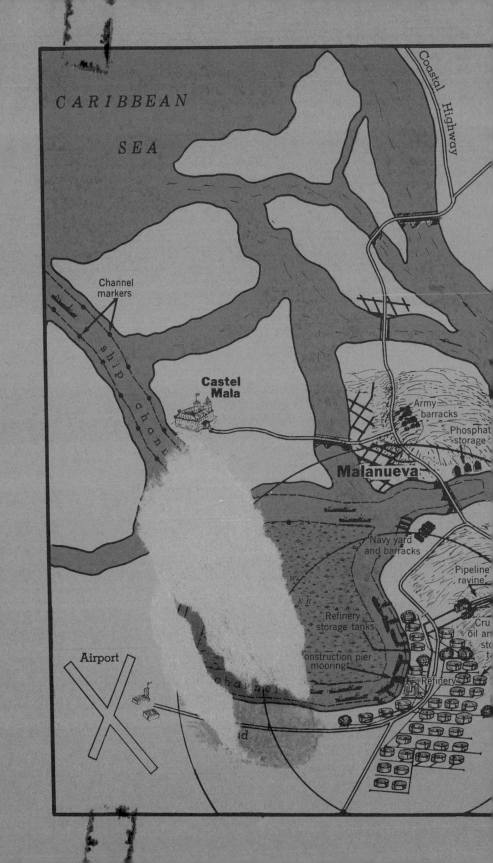